Chapter 1
HALLIE

I rush down the sidewalk, clutching my bag and tucking away a few loose strands of hair that won't stay in place. I'm late, mostly because I spent the last hour deciding whether I would even be able to leave the hotel room. Somehow, I managed to convince myself that this meeting wouldn't be as bad as I knew it was going to be, so I put on my shoes and walked out the door. I'm definitely reconsidering that particular life decision right now.

I check the address again on my phone, and sighing, I glance up at the cool gray façade and the unmistakable gold-plated sign that reads FFG Studios. I need to fortify myself, so I look down to see the flash of a diamond catch the light. This is for him. It's what he wanted. I have to keep reminding myself of that fact over and over again, because what I really want to do is jump in a cab, hop a plane home, and leave New York in my rearview mirror forever.

After taking a deep breath, I open the door and find myself in the midst of a movie set version of an office. People bustle back and forth, carrying large envelopes and shiny mobile devices. I hurry over to the desk, where an impossibly beautiful girl with black hair greets me with a slightly imperious look.

"Can I help you?"

"I have a meeting at noon with Mr. Rivers."

"Name, please."

"It's probably under Hallie Caldwell."

She checks her computer before giving me a friendly smile. "Right away, Miss Caldwell. I'll tell him that you're here, and he should be down shortly. Is there anything that I can get for you while you're waiting? A latte, perhaps?"

"No, I'm fine. Thank you very much."

I take a seat on one of the black leather sofas in the corner of the lobby. The sick feeling of dread that has weighed on me ever since I got off the plane is heavy now, weaving my stomach into a thousand little butterfly knots. I twist the ring around my finger in endless circles until my skin starts to feel raw.

"The elusive Miss Caldwell," a booming voice announces.

I look up to see a bear of a man hulking into the lobby, clearly making a beeline for me. I stand up, too quickly, so much so that I stumble over my own feet. Stupid heels.

"Mr. Rivers, I presume. Hello. I'm Hallie Caldwell."

I'm trying to sound professional, but my voice and hands and body are all trembling uncontrollably. He doesn't seem to notice and instead takes both of my hands into one of his enormous ones.

"Please. It's Jeff. I'm head of production for FFG Studios. It's nice to meet you in the flesh." He chuckles to himself, his tongue running over his lips as he eyes me with appreciation. "And what a piece of flesh it is, if I may say so."

So. Gross.

I think I manage to give him my best attempt at a cordial smile.

As we make our way across the lobby, his other hand curls into the small of my back. Our bodies are so close together that the warmth of his skin is radiating heat against mine. I consider using some of my best self-defense moves, but I ultimately decide against it. That would only prolong the meeting. Besides, filing a police report would be a huge hassle.

"Come this way, Hallie. I can call you Hallie, right?"

That doesn't even elicit a response from me. Shaking his head, he ushers me into an elevator and presses 4. His hand stays firmly placed on my back, even though I try to twist away.

"How's your trip to New York? The hotel treating you all right? If there's anything you need, just let me know and I'll put someone on it. How long are you here for?"

His questions all run together, like he's used to doing the talking and not so much used to asking. He continues, undaunted by my lack of response, whispering conspiratorially into my ear, "I'm not supposed to tell you this, but we love the script. We're willing to sell our souls to get it."

My lips curl involuntarily into a smile. "You were definitely not supposed to tell me that."

"She speaks! You should keep doing that, honey. It looks good on you."

I try to smile, but I'm pretty sure my face betrays my total disgust. He shakes his head and clucks his tongue as the elevator doors open.

Thank god. Ben's agent (my agent—I correct myself) is sitting in a chair outside of a glossy conference room that's decked out in rich mahogany. I manage to extract myself from Jeff's grip and I rush towards her. Her face lights up when she sees me; she knew my trepidations about this silly meeting and probably figured I wouldn't show up.

Jeff gives her a long, lecherous look up and down before turning his attention back to me. "You two probably need a minute to talk. But don't take too long. I'm not used to being kept waiting." The flash of his smile reveals even rows of too-white teeth.

Again. So gross.

I shake it off and turn to Eva, who wraps me in a tight embrace.

"Hallie."

"You clean up well," I say, eyeing the red suit and elegant chignon.

She means business, then. She looks nothing like the woman in blue jeans and a ratty sweatshirt who sat for long hours with us on our porch, talking about characterization and prose and the need for more action and less talking.

That was three years ago, I realize suddenly. It feels like yesterday and a lifetime ago at the same time.

"How are you holding up?" she whispers, putting a strong arm around my shoulders.

"I'll be fine." It's true. I will be fine, just as soon as I can get out of this hellhole.

"Look, I'm going to play hardball a bit in there. FFG wants this screenplay so badly that they're practically salivating for it. This, my dear, is because they know it's going to be the next blockbuster. They would be fools to let us walk out of the door without locking you down for the whole enchilada."

She's looking at me like she expects some kind of reaction, but I give her my best stony stare instead, which makes her laugh.

"Hallie. Do you even care about any of this?"

I don't think she actually wants to hear my answer to that question.

Undeterred, she continues, punctuating her words with a little smirk. "Just to recap, in case you forgot the details or neglected to read any of the thousand memos that I sent you, FFG wants the rights to the first book and they want to take the screenplay as is, although they'll probably add another writer. They'll want to make it more commercial, to add the taglines that will be printed on the merchandise. That's how these things are done."

I nod, but I don't think I'm doing a very good job of pretending to care, because Eva's checking my face carefully, as if she wants to make sure I'm not going to crumble right in front of her. I stand up straighter and try to focus on her words.

"They want the rights to the rest of the trilogy, too, but they've been fuzzy on the details so far. Lightgate is offering a guarantee that they'll make all three movies. We can meet with them tomorrow, if we're not getting what we want here. And you know that there are other offers on the table, too."

My eyes glaze over. "This has to be over today. No more meetings."

She gives me a wicked little grin. "Well, maybe if my favorite client even tried to look at any of the contracts I send over, she would have some idea of which deal she actually wanted. Maybe then, we wouldn't have to schedule so many meetings."

I frown. She raises her eyebrows. This is an old dance between the two of us. And probably a good illustration of why you shouldn't do business with friends.

"I do read the contracts," I say, a little too defensively. Kind of. I definitely took a good look at the cover of the last one. Right before I threw it into the trash can.

"Sure." She's still skeptical, so I give her my best innocent face, which elicits a small grin. "We're talking millions and millions of dollars, Hal. Maybe more than that, if we play our cards right. It's wise to make sure that we've considered all of the options."

"I know, Eva. And I'm grateful for your help. I really am. I just hate New York and I'm being a giant baby about this whole thing."

"You won't get any argument about that from me." Still, her face softens slightly. "Did you at least manage to get a decent meal last night? We do have some of the best restaurants in the world, you know."

I had ordered room service and stayed in my room with only bad reality TV for company, but I don't tell her that. "I had some pasta with organic vegetables made on an antibiotic-free farm-raised co-op. Yum."

Eva laughs, for real this time. "Just remember, if anyone in there asks you about hormone-free, antibiotic food, you just say you love it. It's your favorite. Cage-free eggs, too."

I make a face, and she sighs and loops her arm through mine as we join the stream of people piling into the room.

"Hang in there. It's going to be a bumpy ride."

As it turns out, Eva's right. Almost an hour later, my head is spinning with the talk of international rights and back-end profits and three film guarantees. Rapid-fire speech is coming from all of the faces around the long table, and I can't keep any of them straight. They're talking about the dazzling dialogue and the potential for merchandising and action figures and all of that nonsense, but what they're really talking about is money. I haven't said a word.

"It's this generation's epic tale," one of the suits offers finally. "The timeless story of man fighting against evil, of one poor guy just trying to make it in a world torn apart. And we're going to make sure that millions of eyes all around the planet can't look away."

Eva isn't impressed by his flattery. She holds firm. "We need three things from you to make this deal happen today. You know that we can walk out that door right now and go straight to the next meeting and get everything that we want—a three film guarantee, a piece of the back-end, and a check. A very, very large check. Lots of zeroes. We're only here because you promised that you would make the best offer, one that involves creative control. If you can't make that happen, this deal is over before it started."

Eva starts to gather her things, but Jeff holds up his hand to stop her. She smirks back at him as he bends his head to converse with another man in hushed tones. Finally, he pushes a scrap of paper at Eva, who tucks it under her tablet with a smile.

"We'll give you a minute to speak with your client. Clear the room, guys," Jeff says.

He eyes me again before shooting me an exaggerated wink. I roll my eyes in response, but that only seems to encourage him, because he does a little stage bow before exiting the room with the rest of the suits.

Eva glances at the paper, stretches her arms contentedly, and shoves it across the table at me. I take it into my hand, but I don't look at the numbers, because

I'm not ready to look and frankly, I'm not here for the money.

"The deal is actually better than I hoped for. They're willing to guarantee that all three of the movies will get made, and there's a lot of money for you if any one of them falls through. Since you're the cowriter, they're going to give you the first stab at revising the screenplay for the first one. If that goes well, they'll make an offer for the next two. It's smart for them to realize that they need a feminine touch. Women drive the box office, which is something that men in Hollywood finally seem to be realizing."

I only heard one word. "Cowriter? I never agreed to that. This was his baby, not mine."

"The book is his, I'll give you that much. The story is his. But this screenplay is yours, Hallie, and we both know that. And honestly, the reason that all of the studios are clamoring for this piece is the screenplay. Your voice is all over it, and you deserve credit for that."

"I told you that I didn't want my name on it. When, exactly, did that happen?"

"I added your name to the last revision. I didn't tell you, because I knew you were going to get all high and mighty about it and say no. But it's done, so there's no use arguing about it now."

I stand up. "I don't want any of this." We've fought about this before, and she knows how I feel. "This is for him. Not for me. It's not mine."

"This is for you, too," she says in a low voice. I'm walking out the door when her next words stop me in my tracks.

"It's got box-office gold all over it. You can go hide wherever you want, but if we don't do this deal now, they'll still be beating down your door—next month, next year, in ten years. It's a great story, Hallie. A Hollywood story. All of it—not just the screenplay. And you're stuck with it, whether you want to be or not. At least if we get it settled now, there will be some peace for you. You can finish all of this business and start to move on with your life. I know you do want that."

She's right, even though I don't want to admit it. I'm exhausted and I need some measure of normalcy and that will never happen with the screenplay hanging over my head. I sit back down and open my mouth to respond, but she's not finished.

"They also want a guarantee that you'll do the press junket when they start filming and when it comes out in theaters."

The thought of sitting on someone's couch and revealing all of my dirty little secrets makes me want to throw up. But I nod. That one was always a given. I'll deal with it later. Avoidance. It's a good strategy.

"There's up-front money for the production rights and there's a nice little piece of the back-end profits on the films, increasing with each one. Here's the number."

She slides the piece of paper even further across the table and when I give it a cursory glance, I can't do anything but laugh. It's a ridiculous sum.

"This is the budget for the movie?"

"No, Hallie. That's the amount of money that they're going to give you for the rights to the trilogy and the first script. It doesn't include what they'll pay for the next scripts or the back-end, which will be significantly more than that. Lightgate's willing to give us more up-front, but they're not budging on the rest of your requirements, so I think we should just take this offer and be done with it."

Hearing her tell me that this is about to be over is music to my ears, at least until I look back down again. There are so many zeroes that I can't even begin to fathom what I could ever do with a tiny fraction of the sum.

Millions and millions of dollars. For some pieces of paper.

"Take it. I just want to get out of here."

She jumps up and does a little victory dance, pulling me to my feet and practically lifting me from the ground with her final spin.

"Fabulous! You won't regret this. I promise."

I can't quite match her enthusiasm, but the relief that all of this is about to be over has calmed my initial fears and the slight rumbling in my stomach reminds me that I haven't eaten since the hormone-free room service fiasco. As she leaves the room to rally the troops, I glance around to see if someone had the foresight to leave some food out. I scramble hastily from my chair when I see elaborate baskets with pastries and fruit, complete with tiny jars of expensive jellies, sitting untouched along the back counter. There's even a fancy silver urn that I'm praying contains coffee.

As Eva reaches the cluster of people standing just outside the door, I hear clapping and cheering all around. Great. My fleeting moment of solitude is about to be interrupted again.

I busy myself with the condiment packages as loud chatter about casting and location scouting fills the room as people begin to take their seats. I figure that I can spend at least five minutes figuring out which creamer I want to use. I've been in enough Starbucks lines to know that people are generally very indecisive with their coffee selections. At least the little packages of hazelnut and vanilla and mocha chocolate peppermint rosemary blueberry pineapple cinnamon are a good excuse to ignore the celebrations, because there's no way in hell I'm putting that crap in my coffee. I'm pouring in a few drops of plain old cream and cursing the fact that there are no jelly-filled donut options when the air fills with an unmistakable presence that makes my spine tingle.

I grab the table for support as all of the celebrations stop precipitously.

I know what's happened, deep in my bones.

I'm just praying that I'm wrong.

"So, where's this Benjamin Ellison III? I need to meet the man who's going to make me a fortune."

Nope. Not wrong.

A drop of the creamer spills over the side of my cup. I'm frozen.

I know that voice, musical and low and laughing and teasing, better than I know my own. Hell, half of America probably knows that voice better than they know their own. Of course he was here. Of course, he had to be here.

The voices are scrambling for an explanation.

"He's not…"

"He…"

"The cowriter…"

"She's…"

Everyone tries to speak at once, but his voice again silences them.

"Cowriter?"

"She's his…his…"

Eva's searching for something to say and she's going to pick the wrong word, the one I don't want to hear.

"His wife," I say. I stir the coffee again and again, watching the milky white substance instead of his face as I turn around. "Benjamin Ellison III's wife."

Chapter 2
CHRIS

Jesus goddamn motherfucking Christ.

She's stirring a cup of coffee over and over, and I can't see her face. Eventually, after what feels like a lifetime of waiting, she looks up just for a moment. Muscle memory takes over and before I even know what I'm doing, I'm crossing the room. Instinctively, I need to be closer to her, to drink in her presence, so long absent. Only her blue eyes, seemingly made of ice, and the memory of her voice saying the word "wife" stop me in mid-stride.

Of course. I should have made the connection. How many times did I listen to her tell stories about the amazing Ben Ellison, who came off as a combination of Jesus Christ and the Dalai Lama and Mother Teresa? Apparently, her amazing Ben Ellison was the same person who had taken the literary world by storm with his book series the year before.

I had blown through all three books in a week while I had a short break from shooting my latest movie in Thailand.

I was less than three pages in to the first book when, unable to wait a moment longer, I tore myself away to call Jeff. I wanted the script more than I'd wanted anything in a very, very long time.

It had been five years since I wanted anything that much. Five long, lonely years.

Damn it.

"*I don't care what it costs,*" I told Jeff. "*Get it for me. I want all of them. All three books. I'm going to make a fortune.*"

"*I wouldn't be so sure about that. It's not coming fucking cheap,*" he retorted. "*Those fucking books are everywhere.*"

Jeff wasn't cheap either, so I had full confidence in the fact that the trilogy was going to be mine. I expected a rant or a rave about the asshole agent or a competing studio, but he had merely called back the next day at the exact same moment as a brown envelope was delivered to the door of my hotel suite.

"*There's a screenplay and it's fucking good.*"

He didn't say anything else. And he was right. It was fucking good. Usually, scripts made from books were crap, filled with rambling speeches and all of the lame parts and none of the good ones. This one was pitch-perfect and even more nuanced, layered, than the book had been. I was only ten pages in before I picked up the phone again.

"*If it's not locked down tomorrow, I'm ditching this set and coming to New York and I'm not leaving until we have it.*"

Jeff had hemmed and hawed about impossible literati, but he got the meeting. Since that call, I had thought of nothing but how I was going to convince Mr. Ellison that I was the right person to make his movie. During the whole last week of shooting the stupid buddy comedy, another piece of trash in a long line of pieces of trash, I ran through my arguments in my head. This script? It was going to be my Mona Lisa. I wanted to see the writer in the flesh, to look into his eyes to tell him that I could make this movie, that I understood this character down to his very bones.

Of course, I hadn't realized that I had already met Ben Ellison, and that there was little I could say that would convince him that I was the right person to make his movie. I look around for him, but he isn't here. No, he did me one better, sending his wife instead. That label catches my tongue and twists it, causing me to cough a few times. A blond intern rushes over with a glass of water and I take a long gulp. Damn it. I wish the glass contained something stronger.

The other people in the room, half of whom I've never met before, are looking back and forth between Hallie and me, but thankfully, Jeff makes an asinine comment and everyone's attention is at least temporarily diverted. As I settle back into one of the plush leather seats, I glance at her again. She's twirling the little stick in her coffee back and forth, but her hands are shaking and her brow is furrowed when she glances back up. It takes a minute before I see that the ice in her eyes has melted into a desperate plea, meant for me. She doesn't want me to say that we know each other, I realize suddenly. Part of me wants nothing more than to cross the room in two steps to demand answers to a thousand questions, but that wouldn't help either of us now.

Fine, Hallie. We'll play it your way.

"Chris Jensen," I say, not taking my eyes from her. The effort of trying to make myself sound detached almost kills me.

She relaxes visibly and nods. "Hallie Caldwell Ellison."

The sound of the last name cuts deeper than a blade.

The tension in the room is palpable, and Jeff hurries to cut through it. He's never been a fan of silence. But then again, Hallie isn't normally, either.

"Chris is planning to play the lead."

Hallie chuckles, but it sounds nothing like her laughter. Her cadence is all wrong, clipped and serious and harsh.

"Of course he is."

I need to get out of here.

"I, um, I…" Now, I'm the one who sounds nothing like myself. I look at her, the way I used to, for strength. But even though she's looking at me dead in the eye, there's nothing for me in her face. "I just came in case we needed a closer, you know to deal the deal, but I just heard the news, so I guess that's it…"

People are saying things to me, but I don't hear any of it. I need to look at her, to stare, to inspect her face for any sign that she's still the person I couldn't imagine life without. The person who still occupies the first and last thought in my head every single morning and night. As people break into smaller conversations and lawyers start shuffling papers, I lean back in my seat and sneak a glance in her direction. She's seemingly absorbed in a conversation with the woman in the red dress, but I do notice that the woman is doing most of the talking.

I had imagined her at 25, at 40, at 60, at 100, but in all of those musings, she had been laughing and happy in my arms. This Hallie is neither laughing nor happy.

Technically, she's gotten more beautiful, I suppose. As she moves to speak with Jeff, I realize that the years have given her a kind of unconscious grace that's normally associated with ballet dancers. There's no chance that she's going to fall off the edges of any balconies now. The flip flops are gone, replaced by a pair of black stilettos that make her legs look impossibly long. Her hair still defies any description of color, chestnut reds and autumn browns all mixed up together, but it's pulled back from her face and highlights the fact that her cheekbones are standing out in sharp relief against the flawless, too pale skin. She's lost weight that she couldn't afford to lose in the first place, and it gives her an ethereal appearance, like she could just disappear into thin air. There's no trace of the girl next door that I once met on a balcony overlooking Central Park. Even the most seasoned account reps, who deal with famous and impossibly beautiful actresses on a regular basis, are taking an extra moment to stare.

Despite all of that, looking at her fills me with an incredible sense of loss. Everything that made her Hallie, her laughing eyes and animation and warmth and joy, is gone. Even her eyes, ostensibly unchanged by the passage of time, are still the same shocking shade of blue, but they're impenetrable, frosted over with a thick layer of ice.

I had been able to pretend, for all of these years, that she hadn't grown up, that she was still out there somewhere. I even managed to make myself believe that maybe when I'd gotten my shit together, I could find her. But even though she's sitting right in front of me, I haven't found her at all. This woman bears only a slight resemblance to the girl I remember.

My Hallie.

She doesn't belong to you, I remind myself.

And the fault for that was entirely mine.

Before I can make a move to steal her away from the table, she shoots the woman in the red suit a murderous look and the pair of them stand up and start shaking hands with various people around the table.

"Thank you, boys," red suit says, giving Jeff a wicked little grin. "I think we got everything that we came for. I look forward to this. Certainly. I'm sure you'll be in touch?"

Jeff looks gleeful. "Now that the preliminary is signed, we'll work on the full contract. Chris generally rules over these things with an iron fist, so we'll probably have to go another couple of rounds before we lock down the details. But the deal's done. Finito."

"We're very happy to hear that." She crosses the room to shake my hand briskly, pulling Hallie behind her. "Mr. Jensen. A pleasure."

Hallie's arms are firmly glued to her sides.

"Mrs. Ellison."

"Mr. Jensen."

I reach for her hand and she hesitates for a moment before offering it to me.

My fingers brush against hers, and the shock runs through me.

Lightning. Still. After all of these years.

I glance at her face to see whether she feels it, but she's already out the door.

Jesus goddamn motherfucking Christ.

Chapter 3
HALLIE

I'm still shaking my hand free from the feel of him as I step into the brisk air. The tingle is traveling up my skin, filling my entire body with little currents of electricity. Eva calls out a final goodbye and some last-minute instructions as we part ways on the sidewalk outside of the building, but I don't hear any of it. She's probably already sent an e-mail with copious notes and endless rows of figures that I'll never look at. She'll take pity on me and take care of the details, as she always does. I'm sure of that, if nothing else.

My hotel is only a few blocks from FFG's offices, but it's an eternity before I reach my room. Even the elevator ride was interminable. There was a family, man and wife and a pair of perfectly matched little boys with enormous Statue of Liberty hats who were chattering away as I got on. I saw the look in the woman's face as they shied away from me, probably scared that my twitching was a sign of some deadly disease. Or an impending zombie apocalypse. I'm scaring total strangers now. Awesome.

I mindlessly pace back and forth across the carpet. I've been trying desperately for a year to put the broken pieces of myself into something that resembled the person I had been, and one look at Chris Jensen was all it took for me to fall completely apart. What's worse, I must have known that he would be there. Subconsciously, maybe I even wanted him to be.

I managed to stare at him for long enough to satisfy my sick curiosity. Of course, it wasn't like I could escape Chris Jensen's face entirely. In the five years since I had last seen him, he had become a bona fide movie star, his every move documented by the paparazzi. There was even a weekly column in one of the movie magazines solely dedicated to the trials and tribulations of whatever two-week relationship he was having with an up-and-coming starlet or supermodel or actress. I usually comforted myself with the delusional notion that the magazine pictures I surreptitiously looked at in the check-out aisle had been Photoshopped. It was practically my patriotic duty to examine him in the flesh, to make sure that the publishers weren't perpetrating some sort of photo alteration scam.

If I had to guess, not a single one of those pictures had been Photoshopped. It should be a capital crime to be that handsome.

But if I was really being honest with myself (something I have tried desperately to avoid for a number of years now), the reasons that I stared far too long were much more personal. I wanted to find some trace of our old connection. Part of me had even hoped that he would start singing that line about pina coladas from the Jimmy Buffett song I loved, the one that always made me laugh when I was angry with him.

It had hurt unbearably to look at him. His face had honed into sharper planes and some of the youthful innocence had hardened into masculine strength, but he looked basically the same as the day that I met him, standing on that balcony and asking me for a light. Hah. I had wanted to find a social recluse, someone to help me escape from the loneliness of crowds. But Chris Jensen, in all of his glory, had appeared instead.

That memory begins playing a reel of a dozen other memories of him and me over the years we had been together. He's flicking his fingertips over my hands and face and laughing with me in cafés and falling down on the ice and dancing on rooftops and brushing his lips against my temples and we're making love on a beach in Spain while he whispers "I love you" into my hair.

It kills me that he looks almost exactly the same as he did at eighteen. I don't even recognize myself when I look into the mirror now. But even if Chris Jensen had never become a movie star, even if his face wasn't on billboards and television shows and grocery stores, I still would have known him in the middle of any crowded street. Of course I would. His face is imprinted on my brain.

Shoot. I ram my head against my hands over and over again, as if that could make the memories disappear. He shouldn't have the power to affect me like this. I should have been prepared.

But neither the glossy photographs nor the memory reel in my head had prepared me for the way he dominated a room with his presence, the way the air changed when he stepped inside it, the way everyone around him became more alive. Time and distance had eaten away at the edges of my memories, and I had let his physical presence take me by surprise.

I hadn't been the only one who was taken aback. He hadn't known I was going to be there. I would bet my life on it, even if I make some minor adjustments for his prodigious acting skills.

I shouldn't have been there.

When Eva had first mentioned the name of his company, I had thrown a fit.

"No," I told her. "Not that one. Any one but that one."

After days of pleading with me, she had finally said the only two words that would have gotten me to change my mind—creative control.

Ben would have wanted that.

Judging from the look on Chris's face when I said the word *wife*, he didn't know about Ben and me, either. It meant that he either didn't know about *it* or he hadn't made the connection. I wasn't going to do it for him.

I'm about to give up my pacing and throw the heels out the window when I hear a relentless knock at the door. I would know that knock anywhere. When he had given in to the plea of my eyes at the meeting, I had the faintest glimmer of hope that he wouldn't try to hunt me down. Maybe he had forgotten what we had been, once.

Enough time had certainly passed. He hadn't tried to contact me in five years, not even after…

The pounding is loud and insistent. I have two choices, really. I can curl up into my bed and pretend that none of it ever happened. Or I can go to the door and face him and do what I hadn't done five years before.

The first choice is infinitely more appealing. However, he's a man with unlimited resources and he's always had a penchant for dramatic scenes, so the chances that I'm able to escape without ever having to see him again are slim to none. Just like the stupid meeting, it's probably better to get it over with.

Maybe if I had looked away, if I had marched out the door the second I saw his face, Eva and millions of dollars and Ben's wishes be damned, he wouldn't be knocking at my door right now.

The little voice inside my head whispers an alternate truth: All of this was inevitable.

Him. Me.

Like ripping a bandage from a still-fresh wound, I open the door hastily. He nearly falls into my arms, but I take a giant step backwards and narrowly avoid disaster.

"Mr. Jensen."

I try to echo Eva's brusque tone from earlier. Maybe it's possible that we can both pretend that this is nothing more than a business meeting.

"Hallie."

Nope.

It's been five years since I've heard him say my name and the sound of it on his tongue conjures a thousand memories that burn and tear at me.

His mouth curls into a tiny smile, and he looks up at me. There's danger there, and something else that I can't quite read.

"If you want to pretend like we don't know each other, Hals, that's fine."

He leans an arm against the door and gives me a long look up and down. I have no words, but he has plenty of them. And even if he didn't, the look in his eyes is crystal clear.

"I can be the stranger at the door and you can be the damsel in distress. It works for me, even though I seem to remember that you're more of a tiger and not the girl in need of rescue. But people change. Sometimes, they even change their names. I get that."

"Chris." My voice is filled with censure, but my body betrays me. Unconsciously, I've been inching closer to him, so that we're practically touching. I take another step back, putting as much space as I possibly can between the two of us.

There's one major difference between the Chris Jensen I once knew and the Chris Jensen standing in front of me right now and I don't know how I could have overlooked it earlier. The Chris I was hopelessly in love with was completely unaware of his power over women. Over me. It was an oddly endearing trait, especially given the thousands of screaming girls in those last six months we had been together.

This Chris Jensen is well aware of the way he's affecting me. A man. No longer a boy. I search his face for some specter of the person I once knew, but I can't find anything. I can't quite figure out how that makes me feel, whether I'm relieved or disappointed or somewhere in between.

He doesn't say anything. I don't say anything. Years stretch between us, creating some semblance of distance. I'm grateful for it.

"Why did you marry him, Hallie?"

It's the last question that I thought he would ask.

He definitely doesn't know, then.

I'm not sure what kind of answer he wants from me. Does he want to hear about the two months that I spent in bed after London? The time when Ben came to Atlanta to kick my ass into shape? Or maybe he wants to hear about the fact that I've been trying (unsuccessfully) to avoid his face for years.

I've thought about his question an obscene number of times. There's only one answer, really, that makes any kind of sense. And it's the true one.

"I loved him."

His face falls, just for an instant, but it's enough for me to see that I was wrong, that the person that I loved is in there still. It breaks me down, but before the whole, terrible truth can come spilling from my lips, his façade returns. I close my mouth.

"I hope the two of you are very happy."
He didn't catch the past tense.
I don't correct him.

Chapter 4
CHRIS

Pretty much everything in my office is broken an hour after I get back from my little trip to her hotel. There's not a piece of glass that isn't shattered or an object that's intact. Some poor intern is going to draw the short straw and spend the next three weeks gluing things back together. I make a mental note to check their pay scale and double it.

I'm muttering incoherently to myself, and I wind my arm back to throw another gaudy statue against the wall, but I stop suddenly.

Jeff is standing in the doorway with his arms crossed.

"What the hell, Chris?" he asks. "Now, I've heard of celebrations before, but this doesn't look much like a party."

I am not in the mood for this. I called him in here for one reason, and it wasn't so that he could give me a frank opinion about my choice of festivities.

"What?" he asks, peering at me closely. "Seriously, what the fuck? We got the movie. We paid a little more on the back end than we wanted, but I'm pretty sure that doesn't warrant throwing a fit."

I glare at him, and he looks suitably humbled.

"My secretary said that you needed some background on the deal."

"That's right."

BFE that none of the emergency crews could get there in time to help. So, the amazing Ben Ellison starts pulling dozens of kids out of that bus, one by one. He's like Superman, at least according to some of the kids that survived. Before the rescue crews can even get there, one of the TV helicopters shows up, just before the bus blows him and a couple of the kids into a million pieces. So, it's all recorded for the world to see."

Oh, God. So, Ben Ellison actually was Gandhi and the Dalai Lama and Mother Teresa all rolled into one. And now he's dead.

"It would have been a big story anyway, but some genius in the copy room at one of the publishing houses released this crazy story to the tabloids—that Ben Ellison had a pen name, and that hero teacher was actually the same guy that had written the Carson Sellers books, the *Rage* books. The craziest thing is that the whole story turned out to be true." Jeff shakes his head. "It's rotten luck for him, really. He's like the van Gogh of the literary world, you know, without the whole cutting off the nose scenario. He never really got to relish his own success or even to spend any of the money that he made. Sure, some of the literati were already calling him some kind of wunderkind, even before the bus incident happened. But the fame and fortune? He got none of that."

"He wouldn't have wanted any of it," I say, so quietly that I don't think that Jeff even hears me.

"What's that? Chris?"

"He was plastered all over the news. His face was everywhere. For weeks. Months. If you turn on CNN right now, there's probably a story running on it."

"Hero teacher?"

"Seriously?"

I shrug. "Tell me."

"All right, man. I think it was about a year ago. Ben Ellison is this stand-up guy. I think he's even teacher of the year, a basically a saint by anyone's standards. He and the hot writer are the golden couple in this small town in Michigan and they're both so saintly that they spend all their weekend volunteering and building houses and shit on the weekend. They have the perfect life, you know, the kind of life that makes you wish you never heard the word Hollywood."

I close my eyes. I didn't need to hear that.

"So, he decides to take some kids from his school on a college visit, and they're driving to some no-name college in Michigan's Upper Peninsula, traveling on some deserted road with not a soul in sight except for maybe a stray lumberjack or two. Then, wham! Their bus gets blindsided by a semi. Everyone's screaming and bleeding and shit, and then someone realizes that the truck has a sign on it that says, 'Explosive Materials.'"

Jeff's taking pleasure in telling the story, dragging it out. I close my eyes again.

"The worst part is that the door's blocked, so everyone has to crawl through a window. I think someone calls 911 right away, but this shit is so far out in into it before..." Suddenly, he turns to stare at me. "Didn't Marcus tell you all of this?"

So, Ben and Hallie were a team, then. A little husband and wife writer team. Cute. It was just so fucking cute. I ignore the question about Marcus, who's probably cursing my name right now.

"Why didn't he write it? It's his brainchild, right?"

"Well, who the fuck else was going to write it?"

I am utterly confused.

"You really didn't know, did you? Jesus."

"What?"

"He's dead."

I'm out of my chair and on my feet. What is he talking about? Why didn't someone tell me? Why didn't she tell me?

"Who's dead?"

"Ben Ellison."

"Ben Ellison is dead?"

"Yeah, that's what I said."

My brain can't process that information. That means...

"Don't you think that's information that I should have had, I don't know, maybe when you sent the screenplay?"

"I assumed that you knew. Of course I assumed that you knew. The dude was fucking hero teacher, man."

I give him a blank stare, even though the phrase rings a faint bell.

I need to hear every gory detail. I still have some hope that maybe the image of her face, sad and wistful and lost, will remove itself from my brain. There's another option, one that I can't bring myself to own up to, the tiny little voice that's telling me that maybe everything is not so perfect in the Ellison marriage. I mean, he couldn't even bring himself to show up today. I need more information.

"What do you need to know? More numbers? I mean, the budget…"

I don't give a shit about numbers. "Not that. Why was she here?"

"I'm assuming that you mean the smoking hot writer that you couldn't keep your eyes away from. Not that I blame you. That's a piece of grade-A ass right there."

"Yes, that's who I meant." My voice is a growl, but he doesn't seem to notice.

"Well, it's her screenplay, so we needed her to sign the paperwork."

"It's his screenplay."

I can't say or even think his name. His words come rushing back anyways.

"*You'll never be good enough for her…I'll be there to pick up the pieces…*"

He had been right on both counts.

"Ben Ellison didn't write the whole thing. He didn't write any of the screenplay, actually. I mean, maybe bits and pieces, but I don't think he managed to get very far

I don't answer, so Jeff keeps talking. "I mean, you could look at it another way and say that the guy had great timing. The second *Rage* book had come out just a few days before the accident. After the hero teacher story broke, the publisher rereleased them under his real name, and the first two sold a few million copies in record time. Hero teacher, boy genius superstar writer. You should have seen it, man. Caused a firestorm among the big studios. That's why I didn't think we were ever going to have a chance at it."

My breath is caught in my throat, but I manage to gasp out the question I need answered. "And her?"

"Hot writer wife?"

"Don't call her that."

He gives me a curious look, but he answers anyway. "She was on the bus with them when they got hit. I think she was the school counselor. Psychiatrist. Something. She became the other story. Hero teacher's wife. There were pictures of her and the two of them all over the place. They were high school sweethearts, I think, which only made people crazier for her. The press went nuts. It's got everything—tragedy, heroism, romance."

A light comes into the corner of Jeff's eye, and he stares at me, eyebrows raised. "Someone should make a movie about it. Really. I mean, we already got her on the hook for the press junket. All we need to do is pay someone to do a mock-up of a script…"

I certainly don't have the patience for this. "No. Absolutely not. We are not parading her around and making some pathetic movie of the week about her life. Don't ever mention that idea in my presence again. Ever. Do you hear me?"

The menace underlying my words makes Jeff take a step back. He holds his hands up in surrender.

"Sorry, Jensen."

"Never mind. What else do you know about it?"

"That's about it. You can look it up online, but fair fucking warning—even I don't want to see those pictures again. They never found more than pieces of his body, or those kids' bodies. Terrible stuff. The bus got charred in the explosion, and they kept replaying it on CNN, with the smoke rising and then the investigators digging through the rubble. Honestly, the worst shots are the ones of her, from after she got out of the hospital. That shit will make your blood curdle."

"Why?"

"She got hurt pretty badly, which of course only made her more of a tragic heroine. Reporters and photographers and everyone else followed her around for months. I was actually surprised that she didn't have her own little paparazzi train here today."

Hallie, with her own paparazzi army?

Jeff corrects himself. "I guess not, though. She's been in hiding for ages. That's probably how come she looks hot again. Plastic surgery or something. Right after it happened, the big studios sent their best guys out, because they wanted to get the deal done right away. They wanted the sit-down with Oprah. Strike while the iron's hot and all that jazz. I'm not saying that the sit-down is off the table, especially since people are still curious about her, about what happened, but I am saying that some of the heat's died down a bit. There's always another story. That one is three tragedies ago."

"Shit."

"Yeah, it's shit. Especially since she is totally fuckable. I was going to think about making a real move, man, but I just kept thinking about her face when she got out of the hospital. It was enough to turn me off."

"Don't even think about touching her."

My voice is a growl, and under it lies a ferocity that Jeff recognizes immediately. I buy myself a few seconds to think as Jeff holds his hands up innocently.

How did I miss this? What had I been doing?

Right.

Michele. On a beach in France.

I'm the world's biggest asshole.

"Hands off, man. I still can't believe you didn't know about any of this. I figured that was why you wanted that script so badly. Hell, it's why everyone else wanted it so badly. I mean, the writing is good and all, but that's not really the story. To be really crass, everyone's going to go nuts over the movie. Add in the press, and you have a bonanza. Hero teacher's wife, selling her story to fulfill her husband's last wishes. The fact that the writing is dynamite, better than we could have ever hoped for, is really just a bonus."

The stony look that I give him is enough to send him scrambling for the door, and he pauses only long enough to give my obliterated office a quick look. "I'll send someone in after you leave to clean this shit up."

I bury my head in my hands and try to will my brain into working again.

I can't come up with a plan to steal her away from Ben Ellison, because he's already been taken.

I need to see it for myself. I type in "hero teacher" into the search bar on my computer. There are millions and millions of hits. I click on images first, because photographic evidence will give me what I need the fastest.

Each one is, in its own way, devastating.

The first one, the one that's repeated in a thousand different crops and angles, shows Ben pulling a bloodied kid from the rubble as flames start to lick at the bus.

The next is an abstract image of the gaping hole in the earth after it exploded.

However, the ones that I linger on the longest are the thousand fractured images of Hallie's face staring up at me.

Most of them show her leaving the hospital, and she's angry and sad and some other emotion that I can't quite read, probably because her flawless skin is covered in gauze bandages and red-streaked scars that curl angrily at the edges.

I keep clicking through the pages, unable to tear my eyes away. As I get further down, the pictures are less sensational, but no less painful. She and Ben look happy and beautiful on a beach, at a football game, from a school dance. In the last few, Hallie's wearing a long white dress and staring up at Ben and the two of them look disgustingly elated.

I pass over those last ones quickly.

The last image I see, on the twentieth page of results, seems vaguely familiar, and when I click on it, I realize it's a video clip.

I know instantly that I absolutely do not want to see this, and that it holds its own kind of pain. My finger hovers over the little red x, but every impulse towards self-destruction takes over instead.

Free from the constraints of time, a much-younger Hallie moves towards the camera, shaking her fist and grinning.

"Tell me, oh mysterious lady, what are your plans, now that you've captured the hearts of millions of lovers of art who've looked upon your beautiful face?"

She pulls her little black mask onto her forehead, revealing wide blue eyes under exaggerated black eyebrows. Of course. It was Sam's annual masquerade, the summer after Hallie and I had met. She had insisted on da Vinci and Mona Lisa.

She gestures wildly at Sam, and he lets out a low chuckle.

"Tell me, Sam. What are your plans, other than becoming a New York bum who occasionally goes to clubs to show off your dancing talents? Cheater. You didn't even wear a costume to your own party."

"Baby, who needs a costume when you've got a face like this?"

Hallie leans back her head and releases long peals of laughter. The camera shakes as Sam takes another step towards her. Her eyes are full of mischief as she opens her mouth, but Sam shushes her.

"Mona Lisa, right now, my plan is to take our little show on the road. You know, we'll find some sort of dance contest in each city and we'll just make our way from coast to coast. No responsibilities, no obligations. Whenever you realize that Jensen is a total clown, I'll be here."

Before she can offer a quick retort, another voice cuts in. It's a younger, happier version of my own.

"In your dreams, asshat."

I breathe a sigh of relief when I see myself step into the frame. At least I'm wearing a black mask that obscures my face. Thank god for small mercies. Otherwise, the press would have found this one a long time ago. But even though my face isn't visible, there's no disguising the fact that we belong to each other.

I watch as the other version of myself moves quickly to her side and lifts her off her feet after casually throwing a middle finger in Sam's direction. Despite the bulk of our costumes, Hallie and I are entwined together, dancing and staring into each other's eyes. Sam mutters something about the shot being ruined by my presence, but he keeps the camera zoomed in on us anyways as we begin to spin amongst the sea of elaborate costumes.

We are dazzlingly happy.

Correction. We were dazzlingly happy.

Chapter 5
HALLIE

After Chris left my hotel room, I was immobilized for long minutes that stretched into hours and maybe days. Time has seemingly lost all meaning for me. I check the clock and realize that an hour has passed, but the air is still filled with his presence, his scent, the faint whisk of something woodsy and masculine.

"One breath at a time. Find your strength." Thanks, Dr. Feelgood. That little mantra might have been fine a month ago, but it sure isn't working very well at this exact minute.

Finally, I manage to perch myself on the edge of the bed. As the annoyingly flowery comforter moves slightly with each breath I take in and out, inspiration strikes. I grab my phone from my bag and murmur a silent prayer that he'll pick up immediately.

"Hey, Hals. Just thinking about you, actually…"

I cut him off. "Sam, I need a place to stay. Now. Tonight."

I start shoving my stuff into the bag like a madwoman.

"You need a place to stay? Do you mean a place to stay in New York? Are you in New York? What's wrong?"

He's going to be angry, but it can't be avoided.

"Sam, I'm sorry I didn't tell you this, but I'm in the city. I really needed to get in and out as fast as possible, and I just couldn't face the thought of spending more than 48 hours here. You and Marie would have insisted…"

"The fuck? You're actually in New York? I thought you were joking."

Yep. He's totally pissed. Of course. Great. Just what I need right now. I reach for my hairbrush and shove it into the front pocket of the black leather bag.

"Yes, Samuel. I am in New York. And I need a place to stay for the night."

"Oh, so you didn't see the need to tell one of your oldest and dearest friends, who adores you, that you were making your first trip to his hometown in more than five years. Now, you need a place to stay? No, no, no. Where's the quid pro quo? Do you know how many times I've dragged myself out into the wilderness to see you? Into a variety of states which all look and smell the same, like pine trees and small-town lives…."

I manage to swallow the urge to berate him for the condescending comment.

"Sam, I saw Chris."

There's a sharp intake of breath on the other line. "What? When? Where?"

"The movie deal."

"Damn."

"Yeah."

He hisses in frustration. "You really should have told me."

"I know, I really should have, and I'm sorry about it."

"Do you want me to send a car for you? Where are you?"

"The Marriott in Times Square."

"They put you up in a dump like that?"

"The quality of the hotel is absolutely not important right now. I need to get out of here before he comes back."

"What do you mean, when he comes back? When was he in your hotel room? Why you would agree to see him if…"

"Sam, I promise that I will explain everything to you as soon as I get out of here, but time really is of the essence. I'm just going to take a cab, okay? Give me thirty minutes."

"You do know that Marie is going to kill you for not telling her that you were in town? She's in Africa right now, so you'll miss her. If you think I'm keeping something like this from her, you are absolutely, totally crazy."

"I'll just have to deal with the consequences."

Sam mutters something about sending a car, but I manage to brush him off before I hang up. After blindly throwing everything else I brought into my bag, I rush out into the hall. I don't even check under the bed and in the closet and behind the shower curtain, like I always do.

I'm looking back at the door to make sure it closed behind me when I feel a bit of solid flesh collide into my own.

Before I can look up, the pulse of his invisible force field envelopes me; there's always been and there always will be something in the air around Chris that announces his presence. It's unmistakable, even in my current state of disarray.

I grit my teeth and force myself to look into his face for the third time today. It's a miracle that I've found the strength to do it twice. This time almost breaks me entirely.

There's an ocean of regret in his eyes. Not pity. Just regret.

He knows, then. At least there's some relief in that. I've never had much affection for secrets.

He takes a step towards me, still not breaking eye contact. For a second, I'm afraid he's going to try to wrap me in a hug, or even worse, that he plans to offer some words of comfort. I must be made of clay, because I don't even attempt to move.

He neither lifts his arms nor opens his mouth to speak. Instead, his eyes still intently focused on mine, he reaches up to brush away the loose strands of my hair. It's an intimate gesture. What's worse, it's one that carries a thousand memories with it, most of them perfect and loving and wonderful and warm.

"You're the most beautiful thing I've ever seen."

I wish I could say that I hadn't thought about our first day together a million times, replaying it over and over and over again until memory began to play tricks on me and I couldn't figure out what was real and what was a shadow of the truth. But I had thought about it, memorialized it. The look on his face tells me that he remembers it too.

He removes his hand from my skin, but his palm is still raised, hovering around my face. His eyes are wide and questioning, and he looks like the old Chris, the one who taught me how to ice-skate and wasn't sure if he even wanted to be James Ross and made up funny stories about art and laughed at all of my bad jokes.

I turn my eyes down to the ground and move away, backing up against the wall. Physically, I'm as far away from him as I can get. He takes one hesitant step towards me and then another, and then he's so close that I can feel the warmth of his breath on my face.

Out of habit, of madness, or the need to shatter even the last piece of myself, I raise my arms slightly. I need…I need so much to touch him, to feel his arms around me, to throw myself headfirst into what I had always told myself I would never do again. I need the weight of his skin on my own. I need to forget. I need to remember.

I need Chris Jensen. To hell with it. With all of it.

As I hurl myself into his arms, I feel him shake slightly under the force of my embrace, but his skin closes around mine and I lose myself in the minefield of memory.

In that moment, we're no longer grown-up Chris and Hallie. We're eighteen and madly in love and lust and everywhere in between.

* * *

7 Years Earlier
Los Angeles

"Good morning, beautiful."

He hands me a cup of coffee as I glance down at the tangle of sheets around my feet. I stretch myself like a contented cat and grin at him.

"What are we doing today? Steak dinner? Sightseeing? Disneyland?"

He snorts. "Hallie, you really don't want to go to Disneyland, do you?"

I turn my face to his hopefully. I do, actually, kind of, sort of, want to go to Disneyland, but his incredulous face stops me from saying it aloud.

"No?"

"If you really want to go to Disneyland, we can go to Disneyland. Since today is our last day here and all."

"It's silly. Never mind. That's for kids."

He laughs. "Nope. That's it. To Disneyland we go. I won't hear any more arguments about it. You want to go, so we shall go."

"My hero!" I place my hands firmly on his face and give him a long kiss.

"One promise—we have to get the mouse ears with our names on them."

"That's a deal."

I laugh, and as he touches my cheek gently, I realize that he looks exhausted. I can't blame him, because the last two weeks had been a blur of costume fittings and read-throughs and meetings with Marcus and Alan. For me, the last two weeks had been a blur of long days hanging around the pool and working on my tan while reading romance novels and pointedly ignoring the pile of books I had ordered for my classes in Prague, which were still sitting neatly in their plastic wrap.

Despite the long days, there had been time for us too, to find the small things, the little quirks and the upward flights of eyebrows and little noises that made up the big things. I've tried to memorize every single one—the looseness in his body as he drifts off to sleep, his complete inability to remember that bottles of toothpaste have caps, the way he taps his spoon against a bowl of cereal.

People say that love is hard, and I guess that's true. The Sophia disaster had been hard. Delving into the wreck of long-forgotten memories of a fourteen-year-old girl who was changed, perceptibly and imperceptibly, had been hard.

Honestly, though, this felt easy. And more importantly, it felt right. Like I had found my perfect place in the world.

"Mama…ooooo ooooo."

Queen's "Bohemian Rhapsody" blares from my phone. Chris bursts into laugher as I cover my face in abject horror.

So, everything had been easy, except for one little thing—convincing my mother of the fact that I had found my perfect place in the world.

When I had called her from the Atlanta airport on the way to LA, she had screamed and cajoled and begged and pleaded for me to stay at Greenview. While I hadn't expected any less, her words still stung. *"Throw your life away, Hallie, throw away everyone who cares about you and loves you and only wants the best for you, and you'll regret it. This won't end well."*

Three weeks ago, I might have agreed with her. Now, I was all about the happy ending and totally converted into a true believer.

Chris grabs the phone and taunts me, holding it just out of my reach. "You're going to have to talk to her again sometime, you know."

I lunge for the phone, but before I can reach it, he gives me one last evil look and touches the glowing green button.

"I'm going to kill you," I mouth at him.

"What a way to go," he mouths back, handing the phone to me.

My mother's voice is an alarming screech. "HALLIE VIOLA CALDWELL! You have broken my heart. If you think that you can just traipse off with some boy you don't even know into the depths of Eastern Europe, where you'll probably be turned into a prostitute by the Russian mafia, you have another thing coming. You will take the next flight back to Greenview and enroll in the Philosophy of Confucius class that we discussed, along with statistics. No more questions, no more complaints."

She's picked up the conversation just where we left it the last time I talked to her. It isn't a good sign.

"Mom."

"Your father would be turning over in his grave if he knew that you were wasting all of your intellectual resources in order to go play house on some movie set with some boy. However, it's not too late. There's probably even still time for you to sign up for that history course covering Marxist theory and its role in shaping modern thought and the course of history."

I glare at Chris, who's laughing and pointing his finger at me. I flip him off and try one last plea with my mother.

"Mom, I won't have to read about history. I'll be living it. Prague has…"

"Prague has some boy who's bewitched my impressionable daughter with his good looks and empty charm. I looked up a picture of this boy on the internet, Hallie, and he has a salacious look about him. He will ruin you. Mark my words."

I sigh. There's no way she's going to let me get off the phone without another lecture. I keep talking. Better me than her.

"Mom, I am not impressionable. Why does everyone always think that? 'Hallie's so innocent. Hallie's naïve.' I am a grown woman. An adult in the eyes of the law."

I'm laying it on a little thick, but I need to get out of this call alive. I ignore my mother's snort and try another tactic.

"I am going to Prague. My whole life, Mom, I've always done everything that you wanted. I was the editor of the newspaper. I was even in that stupid musical. I went to Greenview, because it was your favorite school out of all the ones that I applied to. I took the dance lessons. Now, I want to do something for me. I want to go to Prague. I want to explore the city. I want to see Europe. I want to do all of the things that you and Dad did, once upon a time. If I remember correctly, you once dropped out of school for two whole years to hang out on a beach in Ibiza, selling homemade jewelry. Remember? You both used to say those were the best days of your lives. And I'm not going to be selling jewelry. I'll be going to school."

I get only another dissatisfied grunt. I thought maybe the reference to her own youthful indiscretions might work. Apparently not. I'm running out of options here.

Chris, who's been listening this whole time with his hand over his mouth to cover his laughter, whispers over my shoulder.

"Let me talk to her."

I stare at him and shake my head violently. With a naughty look in my direction, he grabs the phone and ducks into the bathroom, shutting the door between the two of us. I'm still pounding away furiously when he reemerges a minute later.

"We're all set. At the very least, she's not planning on calling in a kidnapping charge to the authorities, which would definitely be more than a minor inconvenience."

I gape. "How did you manage that?"

"I dazzled her with my salacious charm."

I punch him in the arm. "Christopher, that's really not funny. Seriously, what did you say to her?"

"I started by carefully outlining the course offerings at Greenview's partner university. I delved into the bountiful array of cultural experiences in Prague. I waxed poetically about music and art for a while."

I stare at him. There's something he isn't saying. He sighs.

"And we're going to see her tomorrow. Well, tonight, actually. I told her we would hop the next flight out. She requested at least three or four hours for a full-on inspection."

For a minute, I think that it's some kind of really sick joke, so I start laughing. Then, I look more closely into his face and realize that he's serious.

"No. No way. Nope. Not going to happen. You honestly have no idea what you're getting yourself into.

You'll regret it after three minutes. Three seconds. Maybe less."

Chris shakes his head and grins. "Why? You're afraid that all of your deepest, darkest, childhood secrets will come out?"

That hits a little too close to home, but I manage to force my facial muscles into a small smile. "I'm afraid your psyche will be permanently damaged. My mother is…" I try to find the right word. "Difficult."

It is a massive understatement. However, if we're really going to Ohio, he'll see for himself soon enough.

"I'm good with difficult parents. They find me charming."

Of course Chris would be good with parents. It made what I knew was about to happen with my mother seem slightly comical.

"We'll see."

He grins cockily. "No, you'll see."

"Confident much?"

"It worked on you, didn't it?"

"I'm an easy target."

He kisses me gently before leaning back onto the pillows. "Sorry about Disneyland. At least you won't have to worry about the impact of that particular brand of commercialism on your impressionable mind."

"I'm going to let that one go, even though it's killing me a little bit to let you slide with your unfounded assumptions. But I am only letting you slide because I know that you are so not ready for my mother. I'm going to enjoy this one. I'm going to enjoy this one a lot."

"I so am ready for this. It's really only fair. You got to see the baby pictures. Diana's probably given you more unsavory information about my childhood than even I know."

He definitely doesn't even know that I had seen the videos of him as Turkey #7 in the Thanksgiving play. But that's neither here nor there.

"Chris, you don't know my mother. This is going to turn into an intervention. It's a disaster waiting to happen. She'll drag in the cavalry. And by the cavalry, I mean her fully stocked arsenal of verbal daggers. You really have no idea. It's the worst. It's a miracle that I escaped that house alive."

But he hasn't heard a word I've said, because his hands have already started to rove over my body as he starts to play with the top of my tank top. A smile flickers across his face as I make an undignified noise.

"We have at least an hour before we need to get to the airport. That means…"

"That I have time to prepare you for the dragon lady?"

"That's not exactly the direction that my mind was going in." He lifts me effortlessly on top of him and drags his fingers through my tangled hair, gently finger-combing the knots, his eyes locked on mine. "I love you, Hallie. And if that means that I have to deal with the dragon lady once in a while, it's worth it. Anything would be worth it."

His lips meet mine hungrily, and I kiss him back, trying to forget that my mother is probably sharpening her knives.

"I love you, too."

"Actions definitely speak louder than words." His voice is low and teasing, and I manage to extract myself for just a second to stare at him.

"You think you deserve a reward right now, huh?"

"I definitely deserve a reward right now. I'm about to meet your mother."

I pretend to consider it for a moment before pouncing on him. "Just so that we make this very clear—I am not rewarding your behavior. This is pity sex. I pity you."

"Hey. A guy's gotta take what he can get."

"You're impossible."

"So I've been told."

I manage to hold him off for precisely one more second before he pulls me back under his spell.

Eight hours, a limousine, and a fancy private jet later (I harp on that one for a while and I'm ultimately just glad that my mother didn't see it), we're standing in my living room in Ohio. My mother flung open the door without a word to either of us, and she's currently standing with her hands on her hips, staring at Chris through narrowed eyes.

She opens her mouth to speak and I let out a little groan, because I certainly know what's coming when she grabs a folder from the table next to the sofa. Besides Ben's mother, her closest friend at work is a social studies teacher who does a little private investigation on the side. Her memory, while not photographic like Chris's, is firmly sharpened after years of working as a researcher, so she doesn't actually need the notes, but they make her look official and unapproachable. It's clearly by design.

The litany of facts starts. She and Chris are stuck in a stare-down as I look on powerlessly.

"Christopher Jensen. Parents are Agnes and Harry Jensen. Agnes's stage name is Lavinia Crawford, and she's an actress of some repute, I suppose, on the New York stage. Your father is recently deceased. I'm sorry for your loss."

Chris nods, but she continues, undeterred.

"Two sisters. One of them, a Diana Jensen, was a fairly successful features editor of a women's lifestyle magazine before she became a full-time caretaker. The other is in graduate school and studying sociology, which is a path I had once hoped my now-wayward daughter would travel."

She gives me a pointed look. I try my best to ignore it.

"Then, we come to you. Christopher Jensen. An actor." She can barely disguise her disdain. I close my eyes and look down. "Three films completed. The most recent one is a modest box-office success. I had to use one of those pirate sites to view it. I generally consider the use of those to be a base form of stealing, but sometimes you have to do unsavory things in the spirit of hunting down information about the child who has apparently stolen **my** child away."

Chris is trying to hide the amusement on his face, but it's unsuccessful. My mother gives a little harrumph as he nods again at her.

"It's a poorly made film, although you have a certain je nais se quoi, at least on the screen."

"Thank you, ma'am."

"It wasn't a compliment, Mr. Jensen. The more recent tabloid stories focus on your most recently obtained role as James Ross, which I assume is the reason for your imminent Prague trip. There's a string of flings with girls from Sampson Preparatory School, otherwise known as Sampson Prep, which you attended at different points during your high school years. You achieved middling grades, but excellent standardized test scores."

Chris shrugs.

"My least favorite kind of student. Gifted, but lazy. A tragedy, really."

I would try to stop her, but she's on a roll, and I know nothing that I could say could stop her now. It's best to just let it run its course.

"None of that tells me why you're interested in my daughter. None of that tells me why my baby, who has always had a fiercely independent streak and once promised me that she would never change her priorities for a man, would lose her mind and decide to follow you to the ends of the earth."

She stares at Chris expectantly. He draws in a breath and looks at me for a second before speaking.

"Mrs. Jensen, I wholeheartedly understand that you're upset about the fact that Hallie will be taking a brief break from Greenview. However, coming with me to Prague won't affect her studies at all. Study abroad programs look excellent on a resume, and before even asking her to come with me, I made sure that nothing would happen to her standing at school."

I stare at him in amazement. He hadn't told me that. I had just jumped headfirst into being with him, assuming he had done the same. Instead, he had thought, planned, calculated. I should have realized it when registering for classes in Prague required nothing more than signing a few forms and transferring my scholarship, but I had just accepted it, without questioning. I want to throw my arms around him, but another surreptitious glance at my mother tells me that it would be a very bad idea, indeed.

I see Chris take control, adjusting his vocabulary and the tone of his voice to match my mother's. I've seen him do it before; when he talks to Marcus, there are more "fucks" and "shits" and his normally musical voice becomes brisker, more urgent. It amazes me every time, that adaptability. I don't have it. Instead, I'll always be bumbling Hallie, words coming out in spurts and gasps.

He gives her a quick grin, the same one that charmed me, the one that will soon charm millions of preteen and teen girls and middle-aged women all over the planet. My mother, on the other hand, just continues to glower at him.

"I apologize, Mrs. Caldwell. I'm actually just evading your question, which in its most elemental form, is why I felt the need to steal your daughter away from her life."

"Yes, it is. The circumlocution is a nice trick, though."

My mother smiles wryly. She's trying her hardest not to like him. What she said about her least favorite students being brilliant but lazy? A total lie. Those with prodigious and undisciplined minds have always been her favorites, because they're the ones who have the power to surprise her, for better or worse. The look on her face tells me that Chris had surprised her.

"I love your daughter, ma'am."

Okay. Now, she's really surprised. She opens her mouth to speak, but Chris is the one who keeps talking now.

"I know it's selfish." He runs his fingers through his hair nervously, and I reach over to touch his hand. He takes in another breath before shooting me a grateful smile. "I know it is. But I've tried to arrange things so that she doesn't have to make a once and for all choice between school and me. Your daughter is the best thing that's ever happened to me, ma'am, but it's more than that. I can't live without her."

She's not going to take that well. I glance at her, see the beginnings of an explosion, and brace myself for fireworks.

Chris gives me an innocent shrug. "It's true, flip flops. Can't live without you."

"YOU ARE EIGHTEEN YEARS OLD! WHAT THE FU…"

My elegant and always perfectly composed mother is neither elegant nor perfectly composed anymore. Uh oh.

"I'm very happy that both of you think that you're mature enough to accept the consequences for your actions, but you have no idea what it takes to make a relationship work, over years, over time, over sickness and health and turmoil and tragedy."

Those words are an echo of my father's, the last pearls of wisdom that he imparted to me before he left us forever. She realizes it and her face colors as the realization hits her. Her argument, her intervention, has gone off the rails, but this isn't how I wanted it to happen. I'm struck briefly by the memory of her catatonic state, the days of staring into nothing which came and went for years after my father died. I'm not looking to go back to that. I move quickly to nestle close to her on the couch, looking at the tiny lines around her eyes.

"I don't know what it takes to make a relationship work, Mom. But I need to find out, and I'm certainly not going to find out in a class about Marx or Confucius. Dad wouldn't have wanted me to pass up a chance at anything, let alone this. Remember what he used to say? 'Be an explorer, Hallie. Find the strength in yourself by taking risks with your heart.' I haven't been very good at taking risks, Mom. I've never been very good at that. But I'm taking one now. And he would be proud of me for trying it out, for being an explorer. That's what he would have wanted."

She looks searchingly into my face. "Do you really that he would be proud of you right now, Hallie? Do you really think he would be proud of the fact that you've been sneaking around behind my back, that you're making decisions without even so much as consulting me? Hiding things from me? Running away?"

"He wouldn't be proud of the way I've handled things. No. But people make mistakes. Even you, Mom. I'm going to make a million more mistakes. And some of the risks won't pay off. But it's better than being afraid, of not taking the leap, of being so scared of consequences that you never even try to make a move."

Chris moves into the corner of the room to give us space. She's silent for a long time before she turns back to me. She shakes her head one last time before patting my hand.

"Please tell me that you've registered for enough credits so that your graduation won't be delayed."

It's a minor victory.

"I have."

"And what are these credits, if I may ask?"

"I'm taking statistics, just like you wanted, an art history class in place of the one I was going to take this semester anyway, sociolinguistics, psychology, and French."

She nods. "The psychology class will be good for your psyche. It might help you to understand why risk-taking behavior is so prevalent among eighteen-year-olds."

It's a little dig, but as she grabs my chin and looks into my eyes, I see fear, not censure, there.

"I want daily phone calls. Daily. Do you understand what that means? You need to call me every day. Not once a week, or never. Every. Single. Day."

I grin. "You got it. Every day. Daily phone calls."

"I don't approve of this little jaunt to Europe. I want you to hear me loudly and clearly—you're making a life decision with serious ramifications, Hallie Viola Caldwell. And I think it's a poor one. But only time will tell that. And thankfully, time is something that you have a lot of, baby."

She runs her fingers through her closely cropped blond hair to smooth it before turning to give Chris a malicious little smile.

"Mr. Jensen, while doing my research, I saw that you took a course in anthropology at that fancy high school of yours. I have to admit, that field has always held a special interest for me. Mind regaling me with some of your knowledge over lunch?"

He glances at me, and I give him a very small nod.

"I would be happy to, Mrs. Caldwell. We have about three hours before the car comes for us, and that should be enough time to tell you about some of the theories that I like best. And those that I don't."

She smiles slightly and raises her eyebrows at me before turning back to Chris. Because I know exactly what's coming, I groan inwardly and close my eyes.

"You can call me Dr. Caldwell, Mr. Jensen. I think it might be a few millennia before we address each other in more familiar terms. Archaeology might have been a better field of study for you, now that I think about it. Now, Hallie, I've had far too much take-out since you went away to school. Go make yourself useful while Mr. Jensen and I have a little debate."

With a mock-sympathetic look at Chris, I exit the room, laughing a little bit to myself.

After all, he was the one who insisted on meeting my mother. I know he was hoping for baby pictures, but my guess is that they aren't coming out anytime soon.

* * *

7 Years Later
New York

I've made a lot of life decisions with serious ramifications. Willingly making the choice to fall back into the wreck of Chris and me is one that I won't be able to take back.

I never wanted him to see me like this. I never wanted anyone to see me like this.

It's no longer a matter of what I want.

Just what I need.

I fall into his arms, no longer able to resist seeing if the real-life version of him can compete with my memories.

Chapter 6
CHRIS

Her fingers grip my neck, and she clings to me. No words seem right enough to actually put voice to, so I lift her into my arms and hope that it's enough.

I try to breathe in and out slowly, but she must feel the quickening of my chest. Then again, maybe not. She's oblivious to the man who emerges from his room, the way that his eyes widen with a flicker of recognition as he looks at me. I reach into her bag, praying that she still keeps the key in its own compartment, a habit that was particularly useful when we had banged mindlessly into a hundred different hotel room doors years ago.

I find it. In one smooth motion, I lift her limp body and carry her into the room, just as the nameless man starts to open his mouth. The door closes behind us, and I wrap her into me, allowing myself to breathe in her honey and mint and sunshine. I try to keep myself from wanting more, from doing more.

She was running from something; that was made clear enough by the presence of the black bag slung over her shoulder. Whether she was running from me or from New York, I'm still not sure. I hadn't surprised her when I had showed up at her door earlier, but this time, she had been shocked by my presence, and subsequently she was unable to cover the pain in her face.

I couldn't help myself from trying to provide some kind of comfort, regardless of the consequences. I had needed to touch her, and brushing her hair away had been the least intimate gesture I could find. It was the wrong choice. That one touch was laced with our history together, and she and I both knew it.

Backed up against the wall, literally and metaphorically, she fell into my arms. I don't know how or why that happened, and I really don't know if I'll ever be able to let her go again.

I shift her slightly so that I can touch her hair and as I do, I feel her muscles tense against me. She pulls herself away, and even the partial separation hurts.

Stop it, Jensen. Stop.

Her expression is inscrutable, but I'm so dizzy from the blue of her eyes that I don't even care to find out what secrets she's hiding. Then, she closes her eyes once more and moves closer, touching my hair with deft fingers. Other girls, women, have done that over the years, and it's always made me cringe. That gesture has always belonged to her.

I lean back and lose myself in the feel of her skin.

I don't know what she wants or needs. I don't know what it's going to cost me.

And I really don't give a shit.

I force my hands to lie at my sides as she gently touches my face. Leaning into me, she draws my lips dangerously close to hers.

"I want…" She stops mid-sentence before pleading with me, in a whisper, "I want to be the old Hallie. Just for a little while. Do you think you help me with that, Chris? Or is it too much to ask?"

I want to scream at her, "Of course it's too much to ask." But I don't. Of course, I want nothing more than for it to be possible to be the old Hallie and the old Chris, to move backwards in time. I've thought about it often enough. But we both know it's not possible, and I open my mouth to tell her that and she hears my words before any sound escapes my lips.

She's withdrawing back into herself, and I touch her check gently. As she gives me a wistful smile, I realize that she's not asking for time travel. She needs to get outside of her own skin. I know that feeling well enough, although I tried to conquer my own demons with alcohol and not with flesh. I don't tell her the lesson I learned— turning away from yourself won't work, not in the long term, but it sure feels good in the moment.

She slides herself closer to me. I want to crush my body and soul into hers, but I manage to hesitate for long enough to give her another moment to think about it.

She must know me well enough to see the answer, because she touches her lips to mine gently.

Fuck it.

I crush her mouth under mine, putting five years of loss and anguish into kissing her slightly parted lips. I slide the tip of my tongue into her mouth and she kisses me back, softly at first and then with real hunger, devouring me until I feel like I'm going to fall apart right there and then.

She arches her back and curves her body into mine and I meet her there, letting my fingers graze the outline of her face. It's an old rhythm, a familiar one, but the fragility of her slim body feels alien to my touch. She moans slightly and runs her fingertips across my palm, and I shudder at even that slight contact. I revel in the sweetness of her smell as she lets her fingers entwine with my hair, curling it under her fingers until I moan and manage to push back from her slightly.

Everything that I've ever wanted is right in front of me. And it feels all wrong. I start to open my mouth to tell her that I can't have her like this, that this is only going to hurt her and me, that I can't bear to be the cause of any more pain in her life, but she silences me with the brush of her fingers across my lips.

Her eyes hold a thousand memories, so many that I need to look away.

"I need this. I need you. Please. Just take it away. Take it all away." She pauses and her lips twist into a sad smile. "Christopher."

That's it. Reason and caution and pain be damned, I lift her in one smooth motion and clasp her close to my body. She's impossibly light, and her long, strong legs wrap around my waist with a certainty that takes me by surprise. We stand, locked together, kissing and touching and letting the months and years between us disappear.

When she yanks at my clothes, she tears the bottom of my shirt and looks up at me guiltily. I rip it all the way off, putting my finger over her lips and smiling gently.

The irrepressible need to be joined, to be inside her skin, takes over. She lifts her shirt over her head and unclasps her bra and before I even have the chance to drink her in, she pushes her warm body next to mine. Her skin has retained something of its lushness, despite the fact that she's far too thin, and as our limbs tangle together, none of that matters.

I had forgotten what it meant to be with someone, body and soul and spirit. Lust is different from love. However I managed to convince myself that they were one and the same, I'll never know. I won't make that mistake again. Not after this.

Her skin turns fiery under my mouth, and unable to wait any longer, I grab her and push her beneath me. I can't give myself time to decide that this is an extremely bad idea.

Her mouth is working overtime, devouring my skin with kisses, but she's not looking at me. I need to see her face. I need to feel her eyes looking into mine. I drag my mouth to hers again and brush against her soft lips, gripping her shoulders.

"Look at me, Hallie."

"I can't."

"You have to."

With that, I slide into her. As I do, I take her chin in my hand and force her to see me staring down at her. Her eyes are endless, down and down and down. There's shock there and thick desire, and a wisdom that belies her childlike wonder and tousled hair. I haven't seen her, not like this, in six years. She's a thousand times more beautiful than she was at eighteen. She's the most beautiful thing I've ever seen.

I'm shaking and I try to cover that small display of weakness, but she sees it anyway. She's always seen everything.

I'm trying to keep myself from making any sound, but it's impossible, because I had forgotten what it was like between us. I don't even know if it was ever like this. The years have made me hungry for her in a way that I never knew existed. I'm desperately trying to keep myself in check, but she's moving her hips against mine in a pulsing rhythm, begging me to move faster.

Her hair, still tied neatly in a knot on the back of her head, taunts me. I run my fingers through the masses of brown and red and gold waves, and it tumbles down around her face, making smooth waves onto the pillow beneath her. She reaches her hand up to brush it away, but I clasp it and hold it down.

"It's beautiful. You're beautiful."

She tosses her head and smiles, once, a real, genuine smile that holds a hidden sea of emotion.

I love her. I will always love her. The knowledge of it, and her warm body in my arms, makes me feel alive and heartbreakingly human.

I move again, within in, and she lets out a little moan, and I can feel her body tensing beneath mine as the first waves of the orgasm begin to hit her. My body is on fire, and I can't resist it for much longer. When her fingers dance across my face as she begins to contort herself, I feel myself slipping under, losing myself to this particular kind of madness. I'm so far gone and outside of myself that I barely realize it when we burst into flames.

* * *

Long minutes later, I'm still drifting in and out of consciousness. I've been trying to keep myself from leaving the glow of our love-making, to keep the feel of her in my arms so that it remains tangible, unlike the half-remembered dreams I usually wake up from. I reach for her to reassure myself that she's not merely an apparition, but I find nothing but a warm spot on top of the bed.

For a moment, I think she's already gone, but when I glance up, I find her huddled over the table, scribbling away furiously.

"Hallie."

She looks back at me, but she doesn't quite meet my eyes. Bad sign. Fuck. I want to cross the room and pull her into me, but her arms are crossed firmly against her chest and her eyes are solid steel. It's clear that she's built a protective barrier around herself, one that I can't penetrate.

I attempt to wipe my face of any trace of emotion, but apparently, I've been making my living in the wrong business, because it's not working.

"Chris."

"I…"

"Please don't say anything."

Unfortunately, I've seen that particular brand of tension in her body and that exact look on her face before. I know what they mean. And I know that there's nothing I can say that will make her stay.

She lets the paper drop to the table in a flutter and gives me a sad smile.

"Thanks for not rejecting my advances, Chris. I appreciate it."

She might as well be talking about the book deal.

"Anytime." It's barely audible.

Her eyes soften slightly, and her hand flutters upward as if she's going to reach out and touch me. At the last second, she recoils and pushes her hand away, like it moved on its own. "Chris, I…"

"I know, Hals."

I silence the voice in my head that's telling me to drag her back into bed.

I thought I would be able to give her this thing, this moment of being able to forget about everything else. I thought I would be able to leave this room with some kind of closure, knowing that I couldn't bring myself to harm her again.

But I want more than that. I want her. I want to make her feel whole again, because it's obvious that even though she's badly broken, she's not beyond repair. And, because we're all selfish creatures, to one degree or another, I need her to make me feel whole again, too.

"You don't have to leave, Hals." I keep saying her name, as if to prove to myself that she is actually still here. I know she'll refuse, but I still need to say it.

"I was leaving anyway. I need to go, or otherwise, Sam will wonder if I decided to jump off the Brooklyn Bridge or something. I mean, I know we're not in Brooklyn, but Sam always manages to come up with some crazy story. You know how he worries…"

She stops abruptly and takes another step backwards. She certainly didn't mean to let that piece of information slip out. I tuck Sam's name away in the back of my head. I can't stop her from leaving, and I won't. I need to tread carefully, to figure out how and why and if it's even possible to make her fall in love with me again.

"Chris, I'd appreciate it if you didn't share the fact that we knew each other, way back when. The press hasn't managed to make the connection between you and me, even though there are some pictures of us still out there, and I'd really like to keep it that way, especially with the movie coming out and the fact that I have to do all of the interviews, and it would probably be better for me if no one ever found out that I was linked to you. I mean, not that we were ever really linked together, since Marcus insisted that we shouldn't be or anything, but now it would just be such a disaster…"

She moves to cover her mouth with her hand, and the gesture is accompanied by a frustrated shake of her head.

At the tumble of words, at the tiny echo of the old Hallie, I grin.

I can't tell if she's going to throw something at me or break down into tears. To my surprise, she smiles.

"Verbal diarrhea. You can take the girl out of the Midwest, but you can't take the Midwest out of the girl. We all talk too much. New Yorkers have nothing on us." She even tries a little Brooklyn accent, and I almost laugh before I realize where we are. What we did. What we are, or aren't.

"That's a lame joke, Hals."

"Yeah, it is." She shrugs her shoulders and throws on a jacket and a scarf.

She takes one last look at me before she opens the door to leave.

"Stay as long as you want," she adds, brushing her hand across the air in the room. "I have the room through tomorrow. If we happen to run into each other at any of the preproduction meetings or on set, I promise, I'll try to keep my hands to myself."

If we run into each other? Nice try, Hals. Make that when.

"I make no promises about such things."

I try to pass it off as a joke, a visible display of my carefully cultivated public persona, but I'm deadly serious and we both know it. She doesn't even address my words when she speaks again.

"Thank you, Chris."

It's more of a goodbye than a thank you, but it's accompanied with a soft, genuine smile.

"You're welcome."

And with that, she's out the door and out of my life.

I give myself five minutes of breathing in and out and remembering the feel of her on me. I languish in the memory, letting it roll over me. It's an old trick I learned from Hallie. She used to call them photographic moments. We had a lot of them, once.

If I have anything to say about it, we'll have a lot of them again.

Chapter 7
HALLIE

I should want to bury my face so deeply in the sand that I'll never have to bring it out again. I just begged Chris Jensen to have pity sex with me, and as if that wasn't bad enough, I am definitely going to have to look into his face again, because I just signed a bajillion dollar contract that guarantees me a specific amount of face time with the producer and star of the movie that my dead husband wrote. It's the worst Shakespearean tragedy/screwball comedy mash-up I've ever heard of.

It's my life.

For some reason, the Bon Jovi song playing a loop in my head makes me smile. "And it's now or never." If I wasn't standing in a cab line, I would be singing at the top of my lungs and whipping my hair back and forth. A quick glance at the man standing in front of me, dressed in an Armani suit, assures me that it wouldn't be a good idea.

I do a little head-banging anyway.

I don't feel ashamed, although I'm sure that that particular emotional response is waiting somewhere around the next corner. It doesn't matter. Right now, I feel strong, myself, in control, alive. I'm more than the shadow of a person I was this morning.

There will be consequences, because there are always consequences. Every action causes an equal reaction. But for now, I feel relieved.

That would be in more ways than one. I had forgotten that mind-blowing sex has curative powers. More specifically, I had forgotten that Chris Jensen and I had been born to make love to each other. My knees are still shaking.

My foot taps out a quick rhythm as the person behind me taps my shoulder.

"Ma'am? There's a cab waiting for you." The man's voice in tinged with annoyance, which probably means that I've been allowing myself to relive that love scene for just a few moments too long.

Also, when did I become a ma'am?

"Thanks."

The man gives me a slightly bemused grin and I wave at him as I hop into the back of the cab.

"88th and Columbus," I tell the cab driver. He gives me a curious look in the mirror before turning his head to stare.

"Hey lady, do I know you from somewhere?"

He probably does. He's probably seen the pictures of my ravaged face, like everyone else in the country. Thanks, 24 hour news cycle. I merely shake my head in response and manage to give him a toothy grin, hoping that if he has recognized me, the stark difference in facial expressions between the person in the pictures and me right now might throw him off.

My phone buzzes as we start to pull away from the hotel. I see Eva's name, groan, and pick it up.

If there's a dotted line somewhere that I forgot to sign, I'm just going to tell her to screw it all. I'm planning to keep this little happy buzz, no matter how short its lifespan.

"Hallie, is there anything you happened to conveniently forget to tell me about why you didn't want to do this deal with FFG studios? Any little piece of *incredibly important information* that seems like maybe it slipped your mind?"

Damn it.

"Um…"

"I was curious as to why one of my most beloved friends, not to mention my favorite client, was eye-fucking the soon-to-be star and producer of *Rage*, the little multi-million dollar movie franchise that you and Ben and I have agonized over for the last four years. It was especially disconcerting given the fact that I've barely seen you look at anyone, let alone a man, in over a year."

She's gaining momentum with every word and there's no stopping her. She and my mother share that particular trait.

"You know, at first, I thought maybe he was your adolescent crush. Everybody has one. I thought, maybe you were the president of a fan club. Maybe that was your deepest, darkest, little dirty secret. Maybe you made some YouTube videos professing your love for him. Maybe that's why you were looking at him with starstruck eyes when you're the last person in the universe with a tendency to be starstruck. So, you know what I did?"

I really do not want to know what she did.

"I dug through the dregs of tabloid archives, thinking maybe I would find a blog post or two from a young and idealistic Hallie Caldwell. 'Oh, Chris Jensen, he's so sexy. I want to have ten thousand of his babies.' Did I find that?"

"My guess is that you probably did not find that."

"Thanks, smartass. By the way, when did you decide to open your own comedy troupe? The Hallie Caldwell I know doesn't make jokes. She's taken a vow of solemnity."

My foot is still tapping out pop songs in the back of the cab, despite the forthcoming lecture. I can't help it. Sometimes, sex just really is that good.

"You're killing my thought train here, Caldwell. Let me tell you what I did find. You can probably imagine my surprise when I used my friend Google to search out all traces of your past. Somewhere, in the depths of the Internet, someone posted a snapshot of a young, idealistic Hallie Caldwell looking up at a young and idealistic Christopher Jensen. But that's not the crazy part. The crazy part is that she's looking at him like he is the only person who ever existed, and he's looking right back at her with the same expression in his own eyes. So, then I told myself, "Eva, this is crazy. Maybe Hallie was a model. Maybe that's your little dirty secret. Maybe it was a posed picture.' But then I kept digging. And I found another one. And then another. Jesus, Hallie, you were with him. With Chris Jensen. You were together. You were maybe even in love with him?"

I am so not answering that.

"I did tell you that I didn't want to do the deal, Eva."

"I thought you didn't want to do any deal! I thought you wanted to pretend that you were still the guidance counselor at Two Rivers High, and that your life was still exactly the same as it was two years ago."

"I did say that there were some other reasons that FFG wasn't a good choice, Eva, or don't you remember?"

"Clearly!" She's indignant, and I can practically see her rolling her eyes. "I wasn't aware that you and Chris Jensen had history."

"It was a long time ago. I didn't even think I would have to see him. After everything I've been through in the past year…"

It's a dirty trick, bringing up Ben, but I'm desperately trying to hold onto the memory of Chris looking at me like no time at all had passed, like we really were kids again, in love and happy and teasing and fighting and making love all morning and day and night. My buzz is drifting away, and I can't come back down to earth. Not yet.

"I know what you're been through, Hals. I do." Her voice is understanding, but there's an undertone there, one that clearly lets me know that there's no way she's letting me get away with my bullshit. "I went through it, too. I loved Ben. Hell, everyone loved Ben. But you and I both know that this has nothing to do with that. Christ, you and Chris Jensen. You should have told me. I need to know if you're contemplating suicide or fuckacide."

I could try to give her a snappy retort about needing to deal with my grief. But then Eva would just come back at me with an equally snappy retort about how it was time to stop using my grief to get out of telling her things.

I laugh instead, and the sound of my long, loose peals of laughter surprises even me. It also causes the driver to snap his head around to stare. I can't blame him. It certainly sounds like the laughter of a madwoman.

"Hallie?" Eva's voice is cautious.

She definitely thinks I've lost my mind. She may be right.

I manage to stop laughing. "No, I'm okay."

She takes in a deep breath. "I'm sorry, Hals, I didn't mean to accuse you…"

"Yes, you did. I was laughing at the fuckacide comment and not losing my mind totally. I promise, if I decide to enter a never-ending descent into total madness, I'll let you know first. I wouldn't want the crazy to come out on any nationally televised talk shows."

"Oh, Caldwell, tell me you didn't commit fuckacide with Chris Jensen. Please, lord, just tell me this one thing and I promise I'll never tease your ass again. I'll never yell at you for keeping things from me."

I can hear her holding her breath.

"So what if I did?"

"Hallie. I was joking about that getting back into the saddle comment. And the Chris Jensen comment. I didn't mean for you to...I hope this is a joke. Please."

"I don't think you were joking when you said it yesterday. And I'm certainly not. Joking, that is."

"You didn't. No."

"Yeah, I did. It's done. And the seriously wacky thing is that I think I'm okay with it. Honestly. Come on, Eva. You're the one who told me to go out and find myself a one-night stand. What were your exact words? 'Hallie Viola Caldwell Ellison Caldwell, what you really need to do is to go down to Chelsea and find yourself an artist/playboy/model child and fuck his brains out.' And in a matter of speaking, that's what I did. So, I think I should actually blame this on you."

"I never thought you'd actually take me up on it! Not Miss Wallows-Around all day."

I laugh again, wishing I could reach through the phone to punch her arm. For the past year, everyone else had been whispering, soothing, touching, talking, their voices and faces and movements so careful that I had become fairly certain that I was surrounded by a field of landmines and broken glass. Everyone but Eva, who's had faith this whole time that somehow I would return to myself.

"I have not been wallowing." So, that isn't true. "Not for the last three months or so." Still not totally true.

"Mmmm hmmm. Tell that to someone who's buying." Her voice lowers again, and her next words are careful. "Hallie? Are you really okay?"

I think about it. I honestly have no idea of whether I'm okay or not.

"I don't know. I feel better than I did this morning, and better this morning than I did yesterday, so I think that counts for something. Right?"

She starts to speak, but I hear the hesitation in her voice, and she asks a question instead. "Where are you right now?"

"On a cab on the way to Sam's."

She breathes a sigh of relief. "Good. Maybe he can talk some sense into you. But you need to know that we have to talk about this and about what it means for the movie. It definitely means something, but whether that's keeping you away from Chris Jensen or throwing you directly in his path, I don't know."

"I don't want to see him again."

I don't. I don't want to see his electric green eyes or the way that he touches the top of his left ear when he's nervous, or the way he rubs his fist against his eyes to keep the morning light away, or...

"Okay, Hallie. Okay. We still need to talk about the best way to make that happen."

"Fine. We'll talk soon, but I need to head home in the morning, so maybe you can come up to the cabin for a few days. I can try to explain it all to you."

"That's going to take a whole lot of explaining. You and Chris freaking Jensen? How did I not know about this? It's my job to know things like this. As your agent and as your friend." She sounds like a petulant child.

"I don't think it makes for a very good story, but I'll do my best. I owe you that."

"You most certainly do owe me that." She makes a little grunt. "We're supposed to have a round of meetings with some of the production people next week in Chicago. FFG is trying to get a crew in place to start scouting some locations, and they want it done yesterday. I need to be at those meetings to make sure they don't try to butcher your work, but maybe I can come up at the end of the week to spend some time at the cabin? You should probably come to Chicago, too."

"I'll let you know if I can." I pause. "I'm sorry for not telling you, Eva."

"You should be. You know, this stuff, these pictures of you and Chris Jensen, they could be an issue, Hals. Fair warning. If I found them in an hour-long internet hunt, that means someone else could, too. I'm frankly surprised they haven't been found already, with the media storm after Ben's…"

She pauses.

"You can say it, Eva. Ben's death."

She draws in a breath, sharply, because she knows that I haven't said that word, or so many other words, death or dead or widow or explosion or accident or tragedy, in over a year.

"Okay. I just don't think it can stay hidden forever. Someone who knew you, who knew Chris, will talk. Someone will make the connection."

"I consider myself warned."

I can't think about that right now. I can't think about what it would mean for anyone else to discover another one of my long-held secrets, to come marching into my life again with cameras and microphones to ask me about the young Chris Jensen.

It won't happen. I've gotten good at denial, so I push the thought of the possibility to the furthest reaches of my mind.

"Take care of yourself, Caldwell. Love you bunches."

"You too, Eva. See you soon."

Click.

The rest of the cab ride is mercifully short, and when we arrive at Sam's building, I hand some money to the driver and quickly get out of the cab. He speeds off, as if hysterical laughter and possible madness were a contagious disease. I seem to have that effect on people. At least recently.

I glance up at the opulent building, and an overwhelming wave of déjà vu passes through me. I haven't been here in years.

The momentary high is starting to wear off and the total embarrassment is starting to seep in.

What the hell am I going to tell Sam?

Chapter 8
CHRIS

After I allow myself a good fifteen minutes of laying in the sheets and breathing in the still-lingering scent of her, I consider the possibilities.

I could go to Sam's apartment right now, but the paparazzi would follow, and I can't imagine that Hallie would appreciate that.

I could call the private investigator that FFG uses. Not yet.

Then, it hits me. It hadn't made sense the week before, when Marcus called me to scream that optioning the *Rage* series was career suicide.

"You'll ruin your career, Jensen, the career I've carefully made for you despite all of the dumbass moves you've made in your life. It's trash. Who wants to read about some asshole who takes a journey through post-apocalyptic America with his dog, his best friend, and some zombie-vampire hybrid things?"

"The millions of people who read the books?"

"It'll never transfer to the screen."

"The millions of people who fucking loved that book and that dog would beg to differ, Marcus."

"I'm not doing it. Use Jeff as your agent, if you want. You know he'll never be able to get half the deal that I would have gotten, but that's not the point. I am out. And you better hear me on my next point, because it's important. If you choose to do this, you have to

realize that this is going to cause a serious fucking problem between the two of us. So, you better ask yourself whether this movie is worth it, Jensen. Whether it's worth throwing away almost ten years of a partnership. Whether it's worth losing your agent and your best friend."

I did think about it. But my desire, my need for the Rage *series was too powerful. The last movie I produced had been a box-office hit, but it was trash. I was on the verge of becoming Alan, someone who made movies that were nothing but explosions and bombs and aliens/zombies/vampires/spies. Of course,* Rage *and its sequels had those elements, too, which was why we could spend a hundred million or so on each of the movies, but the screenplay had something different, an element of truth, of reality, that my last films had lacked. It was my chance at redemption, my chance to create something that would do more than make money.*

It had gone on like that for a week, back and forth between us, until he and I had finally exchanged a series of words that had seemed to destroy everything.

"I'm out, Chris. I'm tired of corralling you, of treating you like some fragile object that I'm afraid to break. You know I love you, man, but this is the last straw. I'm done. End of the line. Go it on your own. You've always done that anyway, haven't you? You've known what's best, and I'm just here to help you make a quick buck."

"I think I helped you make a quick buck, too, unless you've totally forgotten about one whole aspect of our little relationship: the fact that I'm the talent, and you're nothing but an agent. You need me."

Marcus took a deep breath, and his next words were a whisper. I heard each one, as if my photographic memory had suddenly transferred into one that audio records voices.

"That makes this easier. You've turned into a world-class prick, Jensen. World-class. And I can say that with absolute certainty, because I work in Hollywood, where there are a higher percentage of pricks per capita than anywhere else in the world. It's impressive, really. Sayonara."

Those words stung hard. We haven't spoken since.

He must have known about Hallie. About Ben. About all of it. I grab my phone.

U have 5 mins to call me and tell me about H. After that, ur fired. For real this time.

My phone rings almost immediately.

"Fucking shit, Jensen. I was in the middle of a goddamn meeting and you spring that shit on me? What the fuck? Don't you know that I'm trying to do serious work here?"

"She's the reason why you wouldn't do the deal for the *Rage* series, isn't she?"

I wait for Marcus to say something, but he's utterly silent until his next words come out in a gasp.

"Who told you?"

"I saw her. At the meeting for *Rage*."

He mutters incoherently under his breath and his next words come out garbled. "I was hoping she wouldn't be there. Are you okay?"

"Why didn't you tell me about her and Ben? About Ben?"

"I was hoping you wouldn't ask me that."

There's a little click coming from his line, and I can practically see him grabbing a cigarette from the pack he keeps in the bottom-right drawer in his desk. He doesn't smoke, hasn't in years, and thinks it's a disgusting habit, but he keeps them around in case his latest conquest has decided to exist on a diet of cigarettes and pills. I've only caught him smoking one once, after his second wife left him for a producer at one of the big studios. It only serves to underline the seriousness of the conversation.

"I know exactly why I didn't tell you, Chris."

The certainty in his voice takes me by surprise, even though he doesn't offer any other explanation.

"I'm waiting here, Marcus."

He draws in a long puff. "It was simple, really. I asked myself how I was going to tell you that she had gotten married and widowed. I said to myself, now Marcus, how exactly are you going to say that? Maybe, 'Jensen, the fucking love of your life has made herself a little fairy tale ending while you were lying in a pool of your own vomit. Oh yeah, and by the way, her fairy tale has been smashed to smithereens.' It was the wrong question, but in thinking about how you might have responded to that statement, I asked myself another question. This time, it was the right one. What would Chris Jensen do with this information?"

"I would called her. I would have gone to the funeral. I would have created a Ben Ellison foundation. I would have tried to pick up the pieces."

Marcus's laughter is clipped. "Right. You would have done all of those things, but in the end, it wouldn't have mattered, would it have? He still would have been dead, and you still would have been the guy who broke her heart five years ago. I'm not blaming that all on you, because as I remember, she can give as good as she gets, and I think she did a fair bit of heart-breaking, too. But it wouldn't have changed anything." He stops and inhales again. "You didn't see her face. You didn't fucking see her face in those goddamn pictures."

I did, actually. Her face has been immortalized in the endless repository of cyberspace.

I wish I hadn't.

And I wish he wasn't right. But he is; nothing I could have done would have made any difference. It would only have hurt her.

I focus on the way his voice is breaking instead, trying to make sense out of it. Marcus has always told me that Hallie leaving was the best thing that ever happened to me. He's called her any number of uncharitable names on any number of occasions, but his voice is wavering now. His fondness for her is almost visible, even through the phone.

"You don't think she's a vapid, ugly bitch, do you?"

"No, Jensen. I never thought she was a vapid, silly, ridiculous, ugly, prideful, spiteful bitch. She made you happy, which I thought was career suicide. People who are truly, honestly happy don't need to fight for their careers. They just don't have the same hunger as the miserable types. So, the fact that you were happy and not miserable was an issue for me, but you get over that kind of thing when the girlfriend can squeeze studios out of a couple of extra million by beating the boys on the golf course."

"Then why did you say all of those things about her? Why did you keep telling me those things, so many times that I was almost able to forget that they weren't true?"

"Professionally, a broken-hearted, alcohol-addicted actor is an even worse thing that a client who's in love. We had to pull you out of that, and I figured a little Hallie hate could only help. And personally? A broken-hearted, alcohol-addicted friend is never a good thing, either. So, I conveniently tried to forget that Hallie was the best thing that ever happened to you."

There's a long pause, and Marcus's voice is softer now and filled again with a familiar tease.

"Jensen, I know that you've gone and fucked this whole deal up. You're probably paying eight times too much for these fucking books, and you need a real agent to look at the contracts to see if there's any way the situation can be salvaged. Besides that, you really need a good ass-kicking, which is something I just can't do from

California. So, we're going to fucking get a couple of nonalcoholic beers, we're going to go over the details with a fine-toothed comb, and we're going try to get you out of the worst financial deal I'm sure you've ever made. I'm on the next plane to New York, asshole."

He's slipped back into his normal voice, all bluster and macho enthusiasm, but I know why he's coming and I'm grateful. It's not like I'm a sad sack or anything, but I could use his devious brain. And I could definitely use a beer. Even if it is a nonalcoholic one.

"A good ass-kicking sounds like exactly what I need right now."

* * *

The light is just starting to disappear below the horizon line as I stand on the perfectly manicured terrace outside my apartment. Hallie and I had stood on a million terraces just like this, glancing over the city lights and making up stories about people and places and things, but the night I'm remembering is the first night I met her. She had been hiding behind a planter, trying to pretend like she was invisible. Of course, she could never be invisible.

I had always hoped that she had found her own little corner of the world and made a beautiful life for herself. No matter what, no matter how many times I had fantasized about finding her in a crowded restaurant or in the middle of the busy street and picking her up and throwing her into my arms, the past and my mistakes and her mistakes be damned, I wanted her to be happy. I couldn't make her happy, not five years ago, and she had deserved better than that. Of course, my visions of that beautiful life all involved her being a nun (an actual nun), but nonetheless…

But Hallie hadn't found her happy ending, after all.

And I was going to have to do something about that.

Suddenly, I hear a knock at the door, a muffled, "Fuck it," and the click of a key turning in the lock. Marcus bursts through the door, throwing his jacket over one of the chairs. I spin around, open the glass doors, and grin at him. He must have pulled some serious strings to get his ass here so fast.

"What did you do, Marcus, steal a plane?"

"Called in a serious favor. You owe me one. Or two. Or fourteen." He flops onto the horsehair sofa. "Shit, Jensen, this thing should come with a 'do not sit' warning. It's a couch, for chrissakes, and it's stabbing me in the ass."

"It was a Lena purchase. Sorry, man."

He pulls a few long white hairs from his sweater, cursing every one. "Just once, you could have screwed an interior decorator and at least gotten something of worth from one of your little flings. This place looks like shit. I'm guessing it's probably some of Lena's doing. Tell me this, Jensen. How'd you get rid of Lena ballerina? I'm assuming you are rid of her, of course. I think that's a fair assumption since you just called me about Hallie Caldwell."

"Don't ask."

"Oh, I most certainly will ask. You have no idea how many times I've had to throw the sluts out into the streets. It's always the same—the crying, the shrieking, the desperate pleas for just one more chance with you. It's my greatest pleasure in life to see you doing your own dirty work for a change. You have to give me this. Just once."

"It was expensive."

"Come on. Details, Jensen."

"She gets three all-expenses-paid weeks at the Ritz Carlton while she finds alternative living arrangements. I think that managed to soothe her aching heart."

"And? You can't tell me that you got off that cheap. I don't buy it."

"And a shopping spree at Tiffany's."

"Don't tell me you gave her your credit card. Please. That would be too good."

I look at him blankly. Had I?

I was in a total daze when I arrived home from the hotel. The only thing I could think about was Hallie and how she had fallen into my arms. And, unfortunately, how she had promptly fallen back out of them. It was an extremely unpleasant surprise to find Lena, my latest conquest, making plans for the redecoration of my apartment. She was hustling the delivery men around like she owned the place. Honestly, I didn't even remember giving her the key. It must have been an oversight in my eagerness to get the *Rage* project up and rolling. After a certain amount of hollering and shrieking and one serious slap that's probably left a permanent mark on my face, I managed to extract the key I had given her before slamming the door. I wasn't so sure about the credit card.

Marcus's laughter is coming out in gulps and spurts now, and he's struggling to get air.

"Cancel it. If you didn't give it to her, she probably stole it. You never give them the credit card. Never."

"I'll try to remember that."

He's still howling as I walk over to the bar. Although it had been devoid of any actual alcohol for more than two years, the fancy bottles remain, filled with water and food coloring. I pour him a glass of water from the sink and hand it to him.

"Wouldn't want you to choke, now."

Although he's still only barely able to cover his laughter, Marcus finally manages to get some words out. "I warned you about shitty bitches, man."

"A dime a dozen."

We both say it at the same time, and he raises his glass before peering into my face more closely.

"Time is money, Jensen. And every minute I'm here is fucking thousands of dollars going down the drain. So, tell me. How's Hallie?"

I can't even think of how to begin to answer that question, so I sigh instead.

Marcus groans. "Fine. At least tell me if she's still fucking hot."

"She's beautiful. A thousand times more beautiful than she ever was. And sad. Grown-up. Sophisticated. Alluring. Infuriating. Lovely. Devastated. Broken into a million pieces but unwilling to let anyone make it right. Fuck."

"So, where is she? Wouldn't mind laying my eyes on Hallie Caldwell, all grown up."

"She's gone."

"Hallie remains immune to your charms? I know I'm shocked." Marcus gives me a knowing look. "Jensen, we've been through this. You and she were like a fucking Rockwell painting, minus the weird little dogs and the 1950s tableau of the perfect happy family. You were perfect for each other. And then you fucked up and she fucked up and it was a downward spiral of anger and jealousy and alcoholism. You can't go backwards, man. That will never work."

"I know that, Marcus. Of course I know that."

I shake my head in annoyance and look away, burying my head in my hands. He's incredulous as the realization hits him.

"Oh, shit. Tell me you didn't sleep with her."

I don't say anything, but I do give him a measured look. We've been friends for long enough that he knows what it means.

"No way. You have got to be the dumbest person on the planet. Not this time, bro. I'm not about to spend the next five years of my life trying to help you get over Hallie Caldwell. Again. That is definitely not what I signed up for."

"What do you want me to say? It just happened."

"What just happened, Jensen? You just fell into bed with her? Yeah, of course you did. You two could never keep your hands off each other. Damn it. Fuck."

He jumps up from the chair and starts pacing across the carpet, muttering to himself, before he turns to me.

"Just tell me one thing. Is it over? Can the healing process start, or am I really here to help you come up with some half-cocked plan to dive back into the wreck of you and her?"

"It's not over for me."

"You still love her."

His voice is resigned, not surprised, but there's still a question there, one that I need to answer, for him and for myself. For the first time in a long time, I don't have to think about whether my next words are the truth or just another manifestation of whatever person that I'm pretending to be.

"I thought that I could live without her, that I would be satisfied just knowing that she was out there somewhere, living her life and being happy, and I wouldn't have to know anything about what exactly was making her that way. But I saw her and she isn't happy. I might just be fooling myself, but I think I can do that. I think I can make her happy."

"You are one dumb motherfucker, Jensen. You have everything any red-blooded male could want. Fame. Money—lots of it. You can have any girl or woman that you want."

"I want Hallie Caldwell and I need you to help me figure out how to get her back."

I cross the room and reach into the drawer under the bar and pick up an old Polaroid that's worn around the edges. It's a damn shame that you can't buy those cameras anymore, because there's something comforting in touching the white edges and feeling the thickness of the picture in your hands. It makes it more real.

Every time I've wanted a drink, every time I thought maybe a swig of whiskey or the quick buzz of tequila would soothe the temporary pain of bad box office numbers or a lost part or, more frequently, the realization that whichever girl was occupying my bed was never going to suddenly morph into Hallie, I've looked at that picture. It's from that stupid party at Sam's, the masquerade. Our masks are pushed up onto our foreheads, and she's grinning up into my face like I'm the answer to every question she'd ever thought to ask.

It hurts, every time, to look at it. But it reminds me of what I've lost. More importantly, it's kept me from trying to drown away all of the sorrows in the bottom of a bottle.

"I want her back," I repeat. "You have to understand that."

"I've had a couple of Hallie fantasies myself, so I guess there's some very tiny part of me that can understand the impulse. But are you sure, really sure, that you want to go down this path? I know you don't remember much from London, but I do, and I'll tell you right now, it wasn't pretty. Neither was LA. Or Morocco. Or any of the places we went after she left you. Any places for about three years. Not a good scene, man. Not good at all."

"Let me ask you this, Marcus. You've seen me almost every day for the last five years. Whether this ends all tied up in a neat little bow or not, who am I now? Who am I without her? Is that any prettier than what happened in London, or Morocco? Or after?"

"I can tell you right now who you are. You're a fucking movie star."

"And what does that mean, exactly?"

"What does that mean? Have you lost your damn mind, Jensen? You're on your way to being one of the most bankable stars in Hollywood, and let me tell you, that shit don't come around often. Not the twenty-five million a picture kind of bankable, and that's what you've got going for you at this very instant. I know you hate those shit movies that we make, but they make you and me a hell of a lot of money. So, the way I see it, given that you want to keep on being a movie star, and you'd have to be a fucking idiot to not want that, you have a couple of options. You can make more shit movies and stick the cash away in a bank account. Then, you can just pay someone to punch the lights out of anyone saying that you're a sell-out. But, hey. If you're not happy hearing the whispers about selling out, you can lose thirty pounds to play the crackhead brother in one of those boring-as-shit art movies. You might even be able to snag yourself an Oscar. Then, you can make some more boring movies about 'real life historical situations' and somewhere along the line, you can direct one. Everyone will call you some kind of genius."

"Those are possible career paths, Marcus. That's not a life."

"It is a life. Do you really think all those people in the suburbs with two and a half kids and an early midlife crisis have lives? Hell no. They're buying cheap red convertibles and trying to pretend they're you. I can't think of anyone who wouldn't trade places with you in a heartbeat, Jensen. Why do you think we sell so many goddamn tickets to your shit films? We're selling you. The lifestyle of a young, rich, ridiculously good-looking New York kid who hit the big time and went through some bad shit to emerge as America's hero. Even the rehab thing was just a bump in the road. Everyone goes to rehab these days."

"Even if I'm buying all of that nonsense, and I'm not saying that I am, I've still only got another ten good years of getting the parts, as long as I make the right choices and don't send my career into the shitter. What then? Twenty years of playing the dad in some bad comedy about taking care of the kids while Mom goes on a girls' weekend? Eventually, if I'm really lucky, I get to put the old tux back on and head out to a bunch of stupid banquets where they put my name on a trophy and call it a lifetime achievement award. All the while, you and I are sitting around in some uppity restaurant, reminiscing about the good old days, when I was a real movie star, and you were a real agent. We do all of these things to avoid talking about the fact that we've become old hacks who are past their prime and can't stop telling stories about girls and booze and all the shit that goes along with it. Do you really think that's enough for me? Would it be enough for you?"

"It was enough five years ago."

I take a deep breath.

"It's not now. Jesus, maybe I'm getting old."

Marcus claps a hand on my back and smiles faintly. "I think I see some wrinkles. I know a guy who can take care of those for you."

"I'll let you know."

His smiles falls away and his face darkens. "Are you sure about this?" He shakes his head in disgust. "Captain fucking obvious over here. I don't know why I even asked. Of course you're sure. You win, Jensen. If I know you, you already have some kind of grand plan to convince Hallie Caldwell that you've changed. And if I know me, I'm going along with it."

"As a matter of fact, I do have a plan. What would you say to a little party?"

"You know I'm always down for a good party."

I pull the embossed invitation that I managed to extract from the garbage can. I flash it at him.

"Want to be my plus one?"

Chapter 9
HALLIE

As I step out of the cab, I see Sam standing outside in the garden, with understanding and a faint expression of sadness on his face. I take a deep breath and collect my things, ready to face the firing squad. He opens his arms and I collapse into them.

"Let's get you upstairs." He breathes it into my hair, and I nod at him gratefully. Hoisting my bag over his shoulder, he pulls me behind him, and we don't say anything, even when we reach the impeccably decorated living room.

Marie's photographs are everywhere, enormous blown-up shots of slightly abstracted faces and full-length portraits of people who've managed to capture her attention at one time or another. My eye catches on the one over the grand piano in the corner, and my breath hitches instantly.

The three figures are blurred and hazy, but she's manage to create the illusion of movement, the passage of time perfectly frozen in a moment of kinetic energy. It's as if the subjects could leap out from the canvas.

If only.

I look first at Sam's image. He's making a goofy face into the camera, sticking his tongue out and reaching into the air for Marie. Even though I know it's going to hurt badly, my eyes hone in on the pair on the other side of the frame. A man with thick, sandy-brown hair and a brilliant smile on his sun-warmed face is leaning over to tie the shoes of a curly-haired little girl with enormous blue-green eyes. She's giggling and touching his face. It's clear that they adore each other. It's clear that they belong to each other.

Ben. Grace.

Grace.

Damn it.

I forgot to call my daughter to say goodnight. It's been hours since I've spoken to her, and this is the first time I've left her for more than a day since she was born. She must be panicked. I reach down for my phone before I realize that it's past eleven o'clock.

I must have lost my mind.

All notions of tapping my foot to an inaudible rhythm are gone. But even with Ben and Grace staring down at me, the warm memory of the hotel room is still bubbling in my throat, the taste of Chris's lips is still lingering in my mouth. I can't regret it, what we had. I swallow the shame and force myself to look at what had once been my family.

Sam follows my stare, and he leans over to touch my arm. He takes a deep breath.

"I'm sorry, Hallie. I forgot about the portrait and what it would..."

I don't smile, but I don't avert my eyes from the picture, either. "Don't be. It was a good trip. Do you remember the look on Grace's face when she first saw the ocean? Ben was teaching her how to swim. That was our last summer at the beach house."

"She kept looking up at Ben and saying, 'Do you think it goes on and on and on forever?' She sounded like an old woman, not an extremely precocious toddler. That whole week, she kept asking, again and again and again," Sam says, watching my face carefully.

I slow my whirring brain and try to make sense of what happened to Ben, the fire and the noise and the screaming and the horror. It doesn't make any sense. None of it will ever make sense.

But the picture of the man and the girl beside the ocean does. I take solace in the memory, and I'm almost able to feel the warmth of the sun, the grittiness of the sand beneath my feet. I can almost hear Ben's deep voice and throaty laugh.

"And he kept saying that yes, every ocean goes on and on and on forever. Until you crushed her dreams by telling her that there is an end of the ocean," I say, as Sam touches my hand.

I smile and turn my face to him. There's a question in his eyes that he finally manages to put voice to.

"What took you so long to get here, Hals?"

The picture of Ben and Grace looms large above us. It makes it impossible for me to tell a lie.

"I was with Chris."

"Please, Hallie, tell me that scumbag didn't…"

"He's not a scumbag."

"He is."

"I made my fair share of mistakes, too. You only picked my side because you needed a dancing partner and Chris has two left feet."

Sam lets out a dramatic sigh. "Yep, that's it. I picked you so that I wouldn't get all embarrassed up in the club." He grins at me and nudges my side. "What happened today?"

I can't tell him and I can't lie to him, so I focus my eyes on his deep brown ones and lift my hand slightly. He groans.

"Hallie. You know I want nothing more than for you to start living your life again. It's what I want. It's what Marie wants. It's what your mom wants, and what Eva wants, and it's what everyone else who cares about you wants. I can tell you right now that Chris Jensen is not the answer."

"I think it's the only answer I was able to figure out right now."

Sam's phone buzzes before he can offer a quick retort. He hands it to me with a wry look.

"Saved by the bell. This is Marie's fourteenth call. You better figure out a good excuse for not telling her that you were coming to town."

"Where is she?"

"Africa. Shooting some fashion spread with wildlife. She's been there for a week."

"So, she'll be exhausted. She'll be begging to get off the phone. You know what she's like if she doesn't get at least nine hours of sleep every night."

Sam chuckles, conceding my point with a little nod as I pick up the phone. Marie's lilting tones are raised in frustration, but just the sound of her voice puts a smile on my face.

"Samuel, if Hallie is already there and you didn't call me the second she arrived, I really will kill you this time."

"Marie, it's my fault."

She shrieks and I can almost see her arms dance around her, the way they always do when she's excited.

"Hallie, you have no idea how much I have missed you. But, how could you come to New York and not tell me? I would have come home a day early."

"I don't know." I throw up my hands helplessly, even though she can't see me. "I really am sorry for not telling you I was coming. I know it was a mistake. I was trying to keep this trip as business-like as possible with the movie and all, and..."

"Ah, so you are in my city for a movie deal. I knew there had to be a reason. I also know you hate New York, Hallie. Half the days, I hate New York, too. Of course, half the days I think it is the most beautiful place on the planet. So dirty. Such energy. So heartless. So alive. I do not blame you for not wanting to tell us that you were coming. You wanted to return home quickly, and we would have held you captive, because we love you and we do not see you enough."

Sam grabs the phone from my ear and shouts into it. "Baby, you know I don't like it when you talk shit about my city. I'm a New Yorker. I can talk shit. You're not a real New Yorker, even though you live here, so you cannot talk shit."

When Sam first told me that he was dating a half-French, half-Ethiopian model-turned photographer, I was prepared to be skeptical, particularly after the last four model girlfriends had turned out to be empty-headed (albeit decorative) gold diggers. All of my doubts were quickly dismissed when Marie had walked in to Ben's and my house in Michigan and promptly said, "Now, where is this Hallie who lives in the flower house?" right before throwing herself into my arms.

"So unfair, Hallie. He is always telling me this." She says it loudly enough so that I can hear her and Sam yanks the phone away from his ear to soften the blow. "Now, put Hallie back on the phone, love."

Sam reluctantly hands the phone back to me. I hear Marie trying to stifle a yawn.

"Is it finished? The deal? They will finally leave you alone?"

"More or less."

"And they gave you money? Which studio? Someone Sam knows?"

I sigh. "FFG."

She clucks her tongue before releasing a very slight sigh. "Well, since I am well aware of who owns FFG, I can tell you now that this sounds like the beginning of a very long story, Hallie. And long stories and red wine go together like, how do you say, peanut butter and jelly?"

She sounds decidedly French at the end of her sentence, and I laugh at her. "Bordeaux, I think. A very nice Bordeaux. You and Sam can raid my wine cellar. Tell him that for you, there is always an exception."

"Fair enough. But only for the first bottle. Then, we can dig into the cheap stuff."

"And this is why you are my favorite. No, go, and drink lots of wine with my husband and laugh and try to be merry. There is a tomorrow waiting around the corner."

Sam must have heard her, because both of us grin at the same time. Marie's always scattering her grandmother's slightly ridiculous expressions in all the wrong places. Still, I can't deny that the sentiment is appealing.

"Love you, Marie."

"I love you, too, Hallie. Call me when you get home and we can talk and giggle into the phone all night like teenagers. And tell my dear husband that if he drinks another one of my good bottles without you there, there will be hell to pay when I get home."

"Yes, ma'am. Get some sleep."

I hang up the phone and glance at Sam, who's rolling his eyes in exasperation.

"Let me guess. She recommended Bordeaux?"

"Yep. Sure did."

"Bordeaux sounds like a grown up drink, and I am most certainly not a grown up. Not yet," he says, tousling my hair affectionately. "I say we go straight for the tequila shots."

I laugh. "Maybe later, Sam. Maybe later."

"Well, we need to dig in to the wine, at the very least. I know you're a total lightweight, but I would hate to risk Marie's wrath when she returned home to find all of her bottles of Bordeaux lined neatly in a row. I know it's a sacrifice, but we should at least drink one bottle."

"You get the wine, I'll get the glasses."

"You're a guest!" He's mock-horrified.

"I think I stopped being a guest a long time ago, even if I never make it to New York."

He holds his hands up in surrender and disappears into the room behind the kitchen as I reach into the cabinet and pull out two long-stemmed glasses. When he comes out, he opens the bottle in one deft movement and pours the thick red liquid into the bottom of my glass. Feeling slightly ridiculous, I swirl it around and around.

"What the hell are you doing, Ellison?"

"Um…" I'm desperately trying to remember the right words for it, from that terrible road-trip movie about wine snobs. "Letting it breathe?"

He gives me a long sideways look. "Seriously?"

"Screw you! I might be a secret wine aficionado."

I take a long gulp of the sticky liquid and almost spit it out. So, maybe not quite an aficionado. Sam merely laughs and beckons me back into the living room. There's an old plaid chair in the corner, Marie's only concession to Sam's decorating prowess, and I plop onto it and throw my feet on the ottoman. The glass rests, heavy in my hand. I take another sip and there's an immediate lightness in my head. I've never been a big drinker, but it's been a hell of a day, and I can't begrudge myself the little indulgence. I take another sip.

"Penny for your thoughts, Ellison."

"Haven't you ever heard of inflation?"

The look on Sam's face tells me that he's not letting me off the hook. His next words, however, do buy me some time to think, which I desperately need.

"How long can you stay?"

"I have to leave tomorrow morning."

"If you stay another day, you can see Marie. There's a big party for Evenstar tomorrow. I know your favorite things in life are champagne and making small talk, so it should be right up your alley."

"Oh, you know me so well. I'd rather go water-skiing with alligators than go to that party."

"Figured it was worth a shot."

"I'm glad you've kept that fighting spirit, Sam, now that you're a big-shot music man."

"Shut up, Hallie."

"Gladly."

We lapse into a comfortable silence. He knows me well enough to realize that I need some time to think.

Sam and I became friends, real friends, the kind that don't dress everything up in fancy words and the kind that demand answers instead of asking for them, during the first summer that I spent in New York with Chris after we got back from Prague. Chris was shooting a cop movie in Brooklyn and was on set for what felt like endless hours every day. Of course, I didn't know a soul in the city besides Sophia Pearce, and I would rather make friends with the Central Park pigeons than call her. Luckily for me, after a very long night in which we drank too much champagne at one of his parties, Sam and I found ourselves singing the "Star-Spangled Banner" and dancing a little Irish jig on his rooftop. I had found a summer soul mate.

The friendship was eventually cemented over a love of early 90s hip-hop (Jurassic 5 was a personal favorite of both of ours) and long days spent wandering around the city and long nights tearing up the dance floor. Despite his connections to Sampson and Sophia and all of the bad memories of my first trip to New York, the friendship had survived, probably because of Ben, who had been Sam's real soul mate. Marie and I used to take bets on how long they would sit up and play video games when we went to Sam's father's beach house in North Carolina. She used to say that as long as they didn't beat the game, they would still be hammering away on the controllers when we woke up. I usually went the conservative route and bet on 3 or 4 am. She always won.

It hadn't all been sunshine and rainbows, of course. After Ben died and I was released from the hospital, he and Marie spent two months with Grace and me, holed up in Ben's father's house on Lake Geneva in Wisconsin, and we had played endless rounds of Chutes and Ladders and Pretty Pretty Princess and Barbies. They had saved my life. My sanity. He and Marie had been married there, in our garden, because Sam hadn't wanted to waste any more time. Or, as he asked me, who knew if there was time to waste?

The aimless playboy had also turned into something of a workaholic. He had eventually given in and followed his father into the music business. To anyone who would bother to listen, he described his job as being little more than an overpaid nursemaid who had to follow a bunch of half-naked assholes around to make sure that they didn't get caught doing drugs in foreign countries. In reality, he did something with promotion and marketing, at least until his father had retired a few months before, leaving Sam the apartment and a position as the head of the pop division of Evenstar Records. Even though Sam is always moaning about the lack of music in the music industry, I know he loves it.

Sam glances up again at the picture of Ben and Grace and grins. "How's my princess?"

"Obsessed with her Uncle Sam's new band, 4Sure."

"You really shouldn't let her listen to that garbage. It will rot her brain."

"I lost control of Grace when she turned two. She's a monster. She thinks the lead singer is, and I quote, 'the most darling thing she's ever seen.' His name is Noel. I can tell you his favorite color, the name of his pet rabbit, and his ten deepest desires."

Sam hoots, pumping his fist. "She sure knows how to pick 'em."

"Oh, no. He's a jerkface?"

"Wow. Wow, Ellison. Did you really just use the word jerkface right now? You're what, twenty-six? I'm fairly certain that's the first time I've heard that word used by anyone over the age of four. And I'll bet my life that even your own daughter could come up with something better than that."

I throw an embroidered cushion at him. "Jerkface."

"I don't even have a comeback prepared for that one. You…" He searches for a word and eventually gives up. "You win. But you better come prepared next time. I'll have to ask the members of 4Sure for some juvenile insults to throw at you. However, in response to your earlier question, Noel's not that bad. A spoiled, self-centered, annoying, preening, drama queen, but not as rough as some. At least he's making me money. Maybe I'll arrange a little birthday phone call for Miss Grace."

"She's already impossibly spoiled, Sam."

"She doesn't have a spoiled bone in her body."

"She will start to rot from her insides if the lead singer of 4sure calls her for her birthday! She'll be the talk of preschool."

The thought of that makes us both laugh.

"Oh, no. We wouldn't want that, now. She'll develop a reputation."

"Fine. You win. Have the whole band call her to sing happy birthday. I know you'll do it anyways."

"You're damn right I will. Plus, you have no idea how much satisfaction I'm going to get out of telling the pretty boys that they need to suck up to a four-year-old. Maybe they can even write her a special birthday song. Something about how Grace is their queen. It's gotta be good, though. Humbling."

He rubs his hands together, lost in thought, before realizing that he's letting me off the hook.

"That's neither here nor there. And you're avoiding the subject."

I lean back in the chair and meet Sam's eyes. "Let the interrogation begin. But I'm only answering five questions about Chris. It's all I can do right now."

"Seven?"

"Five."

"Five. You win, but it's an empty victory since I was only banking on getting three out of you. First question— why did you have to pick his company, Hallie?"

I let out the breath I've been holding. That one is easy. "You know that I'm only making this stupid movie because of Ben. As an extra bonus, maybe the vultures will leave me alone after I sit on a few couches. The FFG deal is the one Ben would have wanted."

"He would have wanted you to take a deal with Jensen? I don't think so."

"He would have wanted creative control. FFG was the only company willing to do that, to make the movie on Ben's terms. Or my terms. Or our terms. Whatever you want to call it. Okay. Enough. That's your first question."

"You think that's the end of it? That Chris will be happy to make Ben's movie and that you can leave the cabin and move back to Michigan and no one will bother you or Grace?" Sam raises his eyes to the ceiling and clenches his fingers into a fist. "You're one of the smartest people I know, Hallie, but you can be extraordinarily stupid. He'll never leave you alone. Not now. Not ever."

"That's question number two."

"You're a cheater. Plus, you didn't answer it."

"He's left me alone for five years."

"You changed your name when you got married. You've practically been in hiding for the past five years. Maybe he couldn't find you."

"Come on, Sam. Do you really think that he couldn't have found me if he wanted to? He once flew a plane to Prague to get me some cookies for my birthday. And he's infinitely richer and more powerful than he was at twenty."

"Maybe he wasn't ready to find you."

"Or maybe he just didn't want to. He's a different person now. Maybe he's just not interested in seeing me. Maybe he was never interested."

"Nice logic, Hals. He comes to beat down the door of your hotel room twice, and you two rekindle the old flame, which I don't think ever really stopped burning, from his side, at least, and he's just going to fly away and forget you ever existed? Sure. That's a leap."

"I never admitted that anything was rekindled, Sam."

"You never said anything to the contrary, Hallie."

We're locked into a staring contest with each other.

"You're impossible." We both say it at the same time, and before I can open my mouth, he sneaks in a quick "Jinx."

"Breakfast tomorrow is on you." Sam cackles and touches my arm. "Some things never change."

I smile at him sadly, and look up again, once more, to see Ben's eyes watching carefully over us.

"And some things do."

"That's the shit, isn't it?"

I take another sip of the wine and make a face at Sam.

"Tell me what happened, Hals. Just talk."

He makes it sound so simple.

I could laugh it off and clink my glass against his and talk about music and movies and dancing and Grace's latest adventures until the night melts into the morning, after dodging a few more questions about Chris, of course.

But it's been so long since I've talked to someone about something real, since I've let words come out of my mouth in the hope that I'd say something true. For months, words hurt when I said them aloud, so much so that monosyllables became my primary mode of communication, even with my precocious and beautiful and wonderful little girl, who deserved more, so much more. I poured my heart into transforming Ben's words into something that he would have been proud to call his own, but the way words form themselves on paper is so very different from the way they sound, tumbling out in rounded edges and musical notes.

Sam pats his hand over the spot next to him on the couch and I slide into it. In looking up into his familiar face, I feel strong enough to start with one word, and then another. In halting, screeching starts and stops, I start to speak, about Ben and Chris and Grace and fear and loneliness and sorrow.

Of all the things that I thought I had forgotten how to do, laughing and smiling and dancing and playing, I think I missed talking most. It is, in itself, a kind of healing.

Chapter 10
CHRIS

Marcus is giving the entrance to the museum a dubious look.

"You sure about this, Jensen? You know I'm not a big fan of mingling with the commoners."

"The elite members of the music industry aren't exactly commoners, even by your lofty standards."

"Oh, sure they are. Everyone wants to be in the movies. Especially the pop stars. Have you even been to a movie recently? Filled with pop stars."

"I try to avoid that trash whenever possible. You know I don't ever go to the movies. Not even my own premieres."

"If you did, you would know that pop stars all want to be movie stars." He groans. "Let's get this over with, man. I hate this shit. In and out, like you promised."

"Hopefully in and out, I said."

I present the invitation to one of the security guards and he looks at us in surprise, but then he pulls aside the velvet rope without even checking the list. We're immediately ushered into one of the main galleries, which is decked out in white orchids and a smattering of gold stars. It looks like a bad high school prom. But then again, Sam's always been a fan of over-the-top.

I force myself to smile at a couple of adolescent girls wearing too-tight leopard print dresses and my eyes scan the room with a fair amount of trepidation. I don't know why I'm so nervous about seeing Sam. I still see him occasionally at parties. Usually, we avoid each other, with the only acknowledgement that we had once been good friends consisting of an empty wave or the tilt of a glass.

It makes much more sense now that I know he and Hallie have stayed close, which was clearly a fact that he wanted to keep to himself. It also made my current task more difficult. I was going to have to do a lot of fast talking to get anything out of him, but I had to take the chance.

Out of the corner of my eye, I see a woman in a red dress making a beeline for us. She looks familiar, and I know I've seen her before, but I just can't place the face. She looks angry. My immediate assumption is that we hooked up at some point and I conveniently forgot to call her. I take a step behind Marcus, as if he could provide some protection.

To my great amusement, I realize that her eyes are full of the kind of fury that only Marcus can initiate. It's not me that she's coming to see. She makes a full-out stop in front of him.

"It's been a long time, Marcus."

Her nose is tilted up, and she's looking down on him with a mixture of rage and condescension. She's easily six feet tall, and Marcus has to stand on his toes to put himself at eye level, which he promptly does. The grin starts to spread across his face.

"Eva. A long time since our little island getaway, a long time since you fucked my brains out on the yacht, a long time since you whispered sweet nothings into my ear? Take your pick. That's a lot of long times."

"How about…a long time since you screwed me over on the *Crossed* deal? You stole my client right out from under my nose and left him dreaming about A-list movie stars and eight-figure advances. And then you promptly left him with nothing but a script sitting in a drawer somewhere, collecting dust. Oh, so you conveniently forgot that one? Typical."

I try to sneak away, but she turns to me then. I cower under the rage of her stare.

"Mr. Jensen. How lovely to see you again."

I have absolutely no idea who this woman is. However, we've apparently met before.

"It's nice to see you again, too. How have you been?"

"Since you obviously don't remember me, I'll take pity on you and help you out. Eva Larson."

Oh, shit.

"I'm Hallie Caldwell's agent."

Of course she is.

"It looks like you and Marcus made nice, then. I have to admit, I was happy to hear that I wasn't going to have to deal with your pig shit agent on this deal. I was told the business break-up was permanent. Clearly, I was misinformed."

"Hey, hey. Stop harassing my client, now, Ev. Your sources must not be as good as they used to be. A little bit of misinformation goes a long way."

"Did you learn that from personal experience?" Her eyes narrow. "Furthermore, I have absolutely no desire to put my hands on your client. Unless, of course, I have to. If he continues to harass my client, I will personally kick his ass."

Marcus's hackles are raised, and I let him take over my defense. They're just starting the first round of what appears to be a long battle, and I definitely don't want to get into all of the ways that I plan on harassing Hallie. I start to slip away, but Eva's watchful eyes pick up on my sideways movement towards the buffet before I manage to get more than a foot or two from the pair of them.

"Yes, Mr. Jensen, I am going to let you escape, but don't let that make you think that we're done here. We have unfinished business. However, you lucked out because Marcus and I also have unfinished business, and I don't have any kind of guarantee that I'll be seeing him again anytime soon. You, on the other hand…"

"I'll look forward to it."

I take her hand and kiss it. Marcus's face has turned an alarming shade of red, which amuses me greatly. I don't think I've ever seen him so angry. If my own unfinished business wasn't a matter of serious urgency, I'd stay and watch the show. As I make my way through the crowd, I glance back. She's gesticulating wildly into the air as he munches on a canapé, but there's some serious anger behind his blasé expression. A match made in heaven.

I spin around to find a tray to put the little wooden stick that had held the bacon-wrapped scallop, but instead, I find Sam holding two glasses of champagne with a sardonic little smile on his face.

"Chris, I could say that I'm surprised to see you here, but I think we both know that would be a lie. Anyways, I asked them to let me know when you arrived. I wasn't disappointed." He offers a glass to me, and just as I start to shake my head, he adds, in a low tone, "It's just grape juice, Jensen. Let's get out of here, okay?"

I take the glass and give him a wary look. "This isn't one of those 'take him out into the alley and shoot him' things, is it?"

"You've been in too many bad movies, old friend."

His tone does nothing to convince me that this isn't going to end in an alley. However, I do follow him up a stairway until we come to a stop in a room full of enormous canvases with naked men. There are a few sculptures scattered in the corners of the room, and my heart skips a beat when I see a familiar pile of orange and brown candy wrappers on the floor. Apparently, that guy was still making money. Hallie would have loved it.

"Time's treated you well, Sam."

His suit, obviously made on Savile Row, along with the flashy watch, tell me that maybe he's doing a little bit better than just well, but I decide to leave that alone for now.

"It has. But then again, time tends to treat you well when you have a trust fund with a lot of zeroes, connections to some of the most powerful people in the world, a chair at a boardroom with your name on it, and a board of directors just waiting for you to finish up your wild ways and file into the same pattern as your old man."

I concede his point with a nod. "We used to say that it was total hell to have the weight of great expectations on our shoulders. We wanted to make our own way in the world, to step out from our fathers' shadows."

"And yet, here we are, carbon copies of them. I'm running Evenstar and it's just a matter of time before you step into the director's chair."

"I hope not."

"We'll see." Sam shrugs his shoulders and gives me a small smile. "Let's get this over with, Jensen. I have a room full of people waiting for me to give a speech so that they can cheer all of the great work I've done, and I've got a hunch that there's somewhere else you would rather be, too. Aren't you going to ask me how she is? Where she is?"

That's exactly what I was going to ask him, but I'm not planning on giving him the satisfaction of knowing that he's nailed it.

"Did you see her?"

He sighs. "Yes, I saw her."

"Is she all right?"

"That depends on your definition of all right. And you're assuming that I think you deserve to get that information, which I don't."

"Sam."

"You know, obviously, I knew you were going to show up here. I've been thinking about what I was going to say to you all day. I pretty much covered every possible scenario. First, I thought about my own, more painful version, of your alley. And then, for a while, punching you in the face seemed like it might be the best idea. That would have been temporarily satisfying, but ultimately, not really good enough. I even thought about having your name removed from the guest list, but that wouldn't have worked, either, because I wanted to look you in the eye, Jensen, to tell you what I really thought."

"And that is?"

He starts to say something, but he abruptly changes his mind. "Ben was my best friend. Did you know that?"

I shake my head.

"Yeah. I didn't think so. Do you want to know how I met Ben?"

I don't, and I don't really want to know.

He gives me a pointed look. "Normally, I would say that there's no use dredging up painful memories, but I think you might just deserve a little bit of pain, so you're going to listen to every word of this particular story."

He has a point.

"It was probably what, five years ago? Imagine my surprise when a young and very beautiful Hallie Caldwell shows up on my doorstep in the raging August heat when she's supposed to be in London with you. She wouldn't say anything, and the only sign that something was wrong was the simple fact that she was too upset to go dancing with me. So, I asked. And she wouldn't dare besmirch your name by saying a bad word about you. She tried to put a happy face on it, to say that she was just going back for her junior year and the two of you were figuring some things out, but nothing about it smelled right."

What is he talking about? We had never talked about figuring things out. She said that she never wanted to see me again, that it was over, that she didn't love me anymore. And I had said... *"You need to get your own dreams, Hallie, instead of hanging around me like some stupid puppy dog. You need to figure out who you want to be in life, because I can tell you right now that I don't need a nursemaid, or a mother, or another person trying to tell me how to live my life. You've spent enough time hanging on my coattails. I mean, really, don't you think it's time that you figured out how to have a life outside of me?"*

Fucking photographic memory. I can even see the look on her face when I said those horrendous words, each of them hitting her like a ton of bricks. Why did she tell Sam that we were just trying to figure things out?

"So, she was obviously upset about something, but I barely got the chance to ask her about it before she ran off to Atlanta. It was pretty obvious that you had finally revealed your inner asshole. Let me tell you, I was shocked."

He doesn't sound shocked. I open my mouth to try to defend myself, but he continues to talk, so I promptly close it again

"I needed to see if she was all right. It's funny, how everyone who knows her is always running around, trying to figure out if she's all right. There's something about that girl. I don't know, man. And the funniest thing about all of it is that she's never really needed anyone to make sure she was all right. She would be better off if we would just all leave her alone. But again, there's something about that girl, man."

I tense. Maybe he and Hallie…

"Get your mind out of the gutter. I'm a happily married man. Hallie and I are friends. We'll always be friends. There's never been anything else. There will never be anything else."

My body relaxes.

"That's more than I can say for you and her. So, anyways, she leaves, my inner caveman takes over, and I need to see that she's not wasting away in some fucking dorm room somewhere, so I fly my ass to Atlanta. It's worse than I ever could have possibly imagined. I mean, she's a hot mess, all ratty hair and old sweatshirts and really bad poetry. I mean, Jesus Christ, she's playing the *Rent* soundtrack on a loop. Of course, she's still trying to say that nothing's wrong and that she'll be okay and that she just needs to make it to class. And all the while, she's still getting straight As, because it's just like Hallie to be crawling around like a little lost puppy while writing beautiful manifestos about Freud's role in current psychiatric practice."

I smile at that. Sam temporarily forgets that I'm the one he's talking to and he actually smiles back before a frown crosses his face.

"I've never seen her like that, before or since. I could make her laugh and smile for a second or two, but then the smiles would disappear and she would go back to moping. She wasn't even a shadow of herself. But then Ben showed up, and he kept prodding her, teasing her, making little jokes with her, and then she started smiling again for real. He was..." Sam clears his throat. "He was special. To her, to me, to everyone. The kind of special that doesn't come around twice. He made her happy. She made him happy."

It feels wrong to hate a dead man, but irrationally, I want to hit something. To be more specific, I want to hit Ben Ellison. *"I'll be there to pick up the pieces."* Of course he had been there.

Sam's staring at one of the paintings on the wall and twirling the stem of the glass in his hand carelessly. He eventually turns to me with a wistful smile.

"Ben and I developed a little bromance, drinking beer and teasing Hallie and staying up all night to ponder the mysteries of the universe. We were young, but we weren't, you know? Sometimes, it felt like we were a hundred years old, and everything since has just been aging backwards. I thought maybe life was going to be one long series of late-night conversations with a few bong hits sprinkled in to liven things up a bit."

Sam's poetic waxing about Ben Ellison isn't improving my mood. He seems to sense my impatience, and he revels in it, in making me squirm.

"Ben managed to talk Hallie into transferring to his school in Ohio, and I was glad for it. Anyone could see where the two of them were heading, and I thought, finally, Hallie was going to find someone who wasn't going to crush her heart into a million pieces. And I managed to find myself a best friend. I thought that the three of us would have a million more nights like that. And I guess we did, in a manner of speaking."

He looks upward for a second. Yep, I'm a douchebag. I try to remove all thoughts of hitting a dead man, but they're still there, taunting me.

"You probably know what happened next." Sam peers at me for a minute. "At some point, he made a move, or she did, and their happily ever after started."

"Is this entertaining you, Sam? Is this fun for you? What do you want me to say? Sorry? I fucked up? I did. And I am fucking sorry."

He watches me closely as I stare at the candy wrappers in the corner. I reach down and pick a stray one up and twist it between my fingers.

"Ben was my fucking best friend and he was a prince of the human race, a real goddamn American hero, even before the bus."

"Clearly. And I'm an asshole."

"Maybe." Sam looks at me contemplatively and shakes his head. "Jensen, I wasn't going to tell you this, but I think you need to know. Even as I was standing up there with my best friend on his wedding day, waiting for my other best friend to come out all smiling and happy in a long, white dress, I thought that you were going to come and screw it all up for her. I was just waiting for the minister to say, 'And if there's anyone here who has just cause for why these two should not be wed.' I really thought that you were going to show up on a white horse to steal her away. But you never came. And they got married and got themselves a little house and…"

He lets the sentence trail off, lost in thought.

"It sounds like they were the perfect couple," I say, bitterly. "And we all know that I'm not the knight in shining armor type. Even if I had shown up, ready to make my objection, I would have ended up with egg on my face."

"Come on, man." Sam slams his glass down on one of the side tables in frustration. He gives me a long, cold stare. "Seriously?"

"Tell me, Sam. You're standing there, telling me how happy they made each other, that Ben Ellison was the once-in-a-lifetime kind of guy. And you're actually trying to tell me that you were worried that my drunk ass would have waltzed in there and fucked everything up for the two of them? That's bullshit, and we both know it. I'm the second choice for her now. It was probably always Ben that she was in love with. I've thought that for years. You have no idea how many times I've thought that."

He doesn't respond at first. I'm shaking with it, the old fear that I would never be good enough, that it wasn't me that she actually wanted to be with.

Sam's voice is cold, and full of certainty and anger. "I said that Ben was the kind of guy that doesn't come around twice, and I meant it. I said that he was my best friend, and I meant it. I said that they were happy together, and I meant that, too. On paper, were they perfect for each other? Sure. But I never once saw her look at him the way she looked at you. It just wasn't that kind of love between them, Chris. It was the comfortable kind, the sharing of socks kind, the making breakfast for each other in the morning, the shared history and memories kind of love that makes you grateful that someone can put up with you for so long."

I take a breath.

"But it wasn't the kind that wraps you up and spins you around and makes you want to scream and yell and never let go. I've had that, and I'm telling you right now that I would never be happy with anything else. I think you and Hallie had that, too. I don't know if she was ever going to be truly happy with anything else."

"What are you saying to me, Sam?"

"You never listen, do you? Hallie Caldwell was always going to be in love with you. Always. It doesn't matter how perfect for each other she and Ben might have been. It doesn't even matter that the two of you were always going to be a powder keg of wrong. What I'm saying to you is that you could have waltzed into her happy little home and busted it wide open. Yes, I think that. She would never have left him, not once they were married, but I think she was always going to be at least a little bit in love with you."

"That's just you, making things up. Seeing things that aren't there."

"No, I'm not. It's what Hallie thinks, too."

"She thinks that I should have come and ruined her marriage? No, Sam."

"Not like that. I'm not explaining myself very well right now, am I?" He looks to me for confirmation, and I don't give him the satisfaction of a response. "For some reason, she thinks Ben's death was all her fault. It's insane, of course, but she thinks it's all some cosmic joke, that he knew that she was never going to love him the same way that she loved you, and that's why she lost him, that's why he was taken from her. She thinks that she didn't deserve him or their life together."

"What?"

"She thinks that she didn't deserve him or their life together, and that's why he was killed." He speaks slowly and clearly, like he's talking to a small child. "You can't carry that kind of weight without letting it fall in on you, man."

I look at Sam.

"So, what do I do now?"

"See, I thought you were just going to ask, 'How do I find her?' My response, before I started telling old stories, was that it was never the right question. Instead, you need to think about what you're going to do when you do find her. And the answer to that is definitely not to fuck her. Even I understand that people have needs, but sex isn't going to solve anything here. There are other issues at play, ones that you know nothing about. It definitely isn't my place to get into those right now, but you really need to trust me when I tell you that sex is not the answer. So, Chris, what are you going to say? What questions are you going to ask?"

"I need to know whether the crazy kind of love that lasts lifetimes and makes you want to rip all your hair out and crawl inside the other person's skin and never let them go is worth fighting for. I know what I want. I just need to know what she wants."

Sam takes in my words, and long moments pass. "She'll be in Chicago next week, for the production meeting. The only thing that I'm asking of you is to think about it, to think about whether your latent desires are worth possibly destroying her for good. You also need to think about whether it's worth possibly destroying yourself for good. Because I don't know. I just don't know. I think if anyone ever managed to figure out this whole love thing, they'd have to shun society and live alone on an uninhabitable mountaintop to keep the people from beating down the door. If you've heard of anyone who's ever actually done that, it might be worth taking some uninhabitable mountaintop climbing lessons."

That makes me laugh. "Uninhabitable mountain climbing lessons, huh?"

"It was the best analogy I could think of. I'm not the wordsmith. Ben was."

"I'll remember that."

"See that you do."

I extend my hand to Sam, and he shakes it tentatively.

"Thank you, Sam."

"You're welcome, Jensen. And if you let it slip to Hallie that I told you any of this, I will kill you. No alleys needed."

I take one last glance at the pile of candy wrappers and nod my head at him before we make our way back to the main gallery. As we reach the bottom of the stairs, he turns to me and shakes his head.

"You're a prick who doesn't deserve a woman like that. You do know that, right?"

"Does any man ever really deserve a woman?"

I tilt my head towards a brown-skinned knockout wearing a silver dress who's tapping her watch and giving Sam a death stare. They obviously belong to each other.

He takes a look at her and grins back at me.

"Fair enough, man. Fair enough."

I see the way that Sam's hand rests on the woman's back as they move into the waiting crowd, and I try to ignore the familiar twinge of longing before turning to scan the room for Marcus. I find him and Eva tucked away in a corner. She's gesturing with an animated expression on her face, and he's matching her, waving his frenzied hands in the air. People have moved away to give them a little bubble of space in which to air their anger. I think about going over to rescue him, but I decide against it.

Even Marcus needs a good ass-kicking sometimes.

Chapter 11
HALLIE

The plane ride from New York to Wisconsin is just interminable enough that I manage to indulge all of my wildest fantasies about Chris and me before slipping into a melancholy state that's only enhanced by the clouds passing by outside of my window. I read somewhere that planes make you nostalgic. Something about the lack of fresh oxygen.

I should have taken a bus, because that nostalgia is making me forget all of the reasons why I should forget everything that happened in New York. Instead, it makes me remember.

Once upon a time, there was a boy who loved me. I loved him back. I thought that was all we needed. All we would ever need.

The worst part about it, even after life intervened and taught me that it can never be that simple, is that maybe I still believe that it's enough.

I should know better by now.

* * *

6 ½ Years Earlier
New York

"I have to go back to Greenview."

The last thing in the world I really want to do is to go back to Greenview. Eight months with him isn't enough. I need more. However, my mother's nagging, insistent voice plays like a broken record, saying, "Hallie Viola Caldwell," over and over again. Of course, she just has to add the middle name each time. It takes me back to my kindergarten self, standing, with my hand literally caught in the cookie jar. Damn it. Moms.

Chris twists a long lock of my hair between his fingers. "I know."

"And you need to go make a movie. The cop movie doesn't count. It won't be seen by enough people to be a real follow-up to James Ross, and you really have to think about your career. I know I sound like Marcus right now, but you really need a new project that will keep your name on everyone's radar. A big-budget film is the only real way to do that."

"What if I just want to play house in Atlanta with you? You know. We can see how dirty the dirty South really is?" He wiggles his eyebrows at me, and I laugh at his cheesiness.

"Don't even joke about things like that. We've had eight months, of Prague, and here, and everywhere in between. We were only supposed to have a week together, if you remember correctly, and we've managed to extend it for this long. We should just take that and be grateful. Besides, it won't kill us to spend some time apart. People do it every day, you know. You can't get rid of me that easily. Long distance relationships do not have to be complete failures. We'll be fine."

The nagging sense of worry that's plagued me for months starts to surface again, but I push it away. We would be fine. We had to be fine.

"I would argue that we have not had eight months. Hell, we've barely had eight days this summer. It's not like I've seen much of you." Apologetic green eyes bore into my own. "I'm sorry about that. I know I promised…"

I put a finger to his lips. "It's really okay. I've been fairly productive myself. Sam and I have now mastered pretty much every dance there is. I can even do a pretty mean Thriller at this point, although I'm not sure if that's the kind of cultural experience that you promised my mother. However, I do think that even MJ himself would be proud."

"Hey. You never know when knowing those moves might come in handy. What if you're kidnapped by some unscrupulous characters who will only let you go if you do the Thriller dance perfectly a hundred times in a row? You wouldn't be laughing about your lack of cultural experiences then."

That makes me giggle. He touches my chin and draws me close.

"Okay. Forget Thriller. What would you say if I told you that I found the perfect little house for us, just a few blocks from Greenview?"

"I'd say that you're crazy. Please tell me that you didn't."

"I even have the perfect plan--I'll put on my beret and you can pretend that I'm some Eastern European prince that you picked up on your fabulous adventures. Best of all, we can garden and get a dog and let it roam around and get muddy paw prints everywhere. We'll be an old married couple."

"If we're still playing the what if game, I would tell you that you're absolutely nuts and that Marcus would never approve of this plan."

"And then I would tell you that he already did. There's only one condition—you have to read all of the scripts and tell me which one to pick. As Marcus says, and I quote, 'Jensen, your taste in screenplays is shit, at best, and fucking shit, at worst.'"

"Did he really say that?"

The Marcus stamp of approval fills me with a ridiculous sense of pleasure, especially given the fact that I ostensibly dislike Marcus. Kind of. So, maybe he's grown on me. A little bit. Still. I shouldn't care if he approves of my taste in screenplays. Jerkface.

"He did. And he also approved the Atlanta plan."

"Seriously?"

"Seriously, silly. Just you, me, and Buster, chilling in the garden."

"But…"

"But nothing. You know how this argument will go. You'll protest, I'll make a dazzling argument filled with logical claims that even you won't be able to poke any holes in, you'll change the subject, like you always do, and we'll waste a couple of hours fighting until you eventually give in to my desires. Then, we'll kiss and make up. Let's just skip all of the foreplay and kiss and make up instead. Plus, I already have the winning argument, one that you absolutely can't fight."

"And what would that be?"

"I already put the deposit down on the house. You, me, and Buster will be chasing each other around in no time. If you say no, that's a lot of money down the drain. Wasting money drives you crazy."

"It's nonrefundable?" He had convinced me before he had even mentioned the deposit, but I wasn't planning to give in as easily as all that. "And cheap enough so that I can pay my half of the rent?"

"And it's nonrefundable. And cheap enough so that you can pay your half of the rent. See, I already anticipated your silliness. I thought you would be proud of me for knowing you so well."

"Let me guess. You already found Buster, too."

"No, that one I leave up to you. The womenfolk get to pick the dogs. It's probably written on a tablet somewhere."

"I don't think they had dogs back in the Stone Age."

"I don't think they wrote on tablets back in the Stone Age. Now, get your ass over here so that I can do a proper job of convincing you."

"I'm curious to know what you think a proper job consists of."

"Baby, I've got moves you've never seen."

"And don't think that just because you've found a perfect house that you can call me baby."

"Yes, ma'am."

* * *

6 Years Later
Lake Geneva, Wisconsin

"We're now arriving in Lake Geneva, Wisconsin, where the current temperature is a balmy seven degrees Fahrenheit."

The flight attendant's cheerful voice snaps me out of my daydream. We never did find exactly the right Buster, I think to myself, with a little smile. What if...

"Hallie Caldwell, you'll only drive yourself crazy playing the what if game."

It was something my mother used to say, whenever I peppered her with questions. The same questions that my own daughter peppers me with on a daily basis. And my response is an echo of my mother's. I chuckle to myself. It is true, the old adage. We all become our mothers, given enough time.

The wait to disembark is painfully long. As soon as I hit the end of the tunnel at the gate, I break into a run. The airport is tiny, and I can see both of them standing just beyond the glass.

I bust through the doors.

"Mommy!"

She's running towards me on steady, chubby legs. It takes everything I have not to run towards her with the same determination that I see in her face. But Grace would hate that, so I force myself to stand still. I settle for scooping her up and closing my arms tightly around her tiny little body as I ignore the rush of people hustling past us with their bags and cell phone and tablets and signs.

The smell of baby powder really is the best smell in the whole wild world, as Grace would put it.

"Mommy, you were gone for so long. So much has happened."

I chuckle and touch the tip of her nose.

"Like what, sweet girl? Tell me everything."

"I got a new pink shirt and a truck and a real trucker hat."

I give my mother a sideways glance as I set Grace back down again.

My mother sighs and grabs the black bag from my shoulder as she leads us into the parking garage.

"It's not good for little girls to fall into masculine and feminine stereotypes. She wanted the pink shirt, so I told her the only way I was indulging that wish was if she agreed to wear the trucker hat along with it."

I look down at the camouflage cap covering Grace's riot of dark curls and tousle the ends with my fingers. She grasps my hand with surprising strength and beams up at me.

"Uncle Sam called to tell me almost happy almost birthday and we sang together and he said we need to go to the beach, him and me and you and Aunt Marie and maybe Aunt Eva and maybe Grandma and we'll get shells and swim in the ocean. He said that we went swimming in the ocean a long time ago, but I can't 'member."

"We most certainly did go swimming in the ocean a long time ago. And Uncle Sam is right. He and I talked about the beach while I was in the big city, and we both think it's time for another trip. And maybe Grandma and Aunt Eva will want to come this time, too, since they had to miss it the last time we went."

"I'm a good swimmer. Probably even better than Uncle Sam."

"Uncle Sam has a deathly fear of sharks, so I think it's probably safe to say that you are a better swimmer than Uncle Sam."

"See, Grandma? I told you she would want to go to the ocean."

I lift Grace into her car seat and ignore the surprised look on my mother's face. Unfortunately, I can't ignore the questions.

"You saw Sam? And you want to go to the ocean?"

Her voice is incredulous, but I try to make my answer as matter-of-fact as possible.

"We didn't go last year. And I think it's probably time to go again. Grace doesn't even remember the ocean. It's my duty as a mother to rectify that."

"I really just want to swim. With the sharks. And the jellyfish. Miss Oona says that the jellyfish aren't made of jelly, though. But she might not be telling the whole truth."

"I promise, we shall swim. But hopefully not with any sharks. Or jellyfish, for that matter." I take the cap off and ruffle her hair. "There will be lots of fish, though."

My mother drives, and I sit in the back seat with Grace as she babbles away. She's filled with long, winding stories about preschool and Grandma and a boy named Derek and everything else that happened while I was gone. I catch my mother casting a wary glance in my direction a few times, but my attention stays focused on my daughter instead. There will be time for questions later, even if I'm still not sure about the answers.

I do know one thing. For the first time in a long time, I'm able to watch every toss of my daughter's head and every little grin without feeling every ounce of the weight that Ben will never be here to see it again. The ache is still there, of course, but it's not the stabbing, breathtaking pain that I've felt for too long.

When my mother stops at the end of a long, curving driveway, I breathe a sigh of relief. I unbuckle Grace, but before I can lift her from the car seat, she wiggles away and dances up the stone steps.

I take a long look at the cabin, our little sanctuary. It's like something out of a storybook, nestled amongst the trees and lake. The grass has grown wilder in my brief absence, as it always does, but it makes sense here, among the explosions of flowers and color covering the front yard and porch. The dusting of snow on the ground doesn't change that. Grace grabs the key from behind one of the flowerpots and opens the door as we lag behind her.

My mother places a strong hand on my back. "I'm getting too old for this. That girl wears me out."

"I think you used to say that about me, too."

"At least you used to look before you leaped. That one is a world of trouble."

Grace takes a tumble over the hardwood floors in the entryway, and before I can check to see if she's all right, if she needs kisses or a pink Band-Aid to make it better, she's up again, running into the kitchen and tossing her trucker cap into the air.

"Thanks for looking after her, Mom."

"Of course, baby. We had dinner before we came to get you, so it's just the bath now. I'll heat something up for you if you want to take on story duty."

I give my mother a grateful smile, and she touches my arm.

"Do you have the contract? I'd like to take a look."

"It's in my bag. I'm sure you'll find a thousand places where there's something that I didn't think of. And I'm also sure that Eva's going to love talking to you on the phone tonight about how you should be doing her job."

I shoot a warning look to my mother. She and Eva have never seen eye-to-eye on anything and my mother's never been one to mince words. I think she might even scare Eva a little bit.

"I know I'll enjoy that conversation." She shoots me a wicked little smile right back. "You know, I think I could have handled the deal. I've gotten pretty good at contracts."

"Mom, the only thing worse than doing business with friends is doing business with family. It's certain disaster."

Before I can say more, Grace interrupts us by tugging on the bottom of my coat.

"Mommy, can you read the story about the moon tonight? And then, I can read the one about the bears all by myself. I know all the words. I don't need any help."

"Moon and bears. But that's it. There's no way you're getting more than two stories out of me."

"Three?"

"Two."

"Four?"

"Two."

When she nestles her tiny body next to mine in the narrow twin bed with its princess canopy, and pleads with me for just one more story, I can't resist. Moons, bears, tigers, lions, and princesses it would be. So, one bath, two cups of cocoa, and six stories later, Grace finally falls into sleep. Exhausted, I tiptoe down the stairs to find my mother poring over endless sheets of paper.

"There's soup on the stove and a bowl on the counter," she says, obviously distracted. Before I can sit down, she looks up at me with wide eyes. "Hallie, you didn't tell me that the company you were planning to work with…"

"Yeah, Mom. I know."

"He…"

"I know that, too, but thanks for the reminder."

"Did you see him?"

"Are you sure there aren't some numbers you want to talk about? I know there has to be something in there that didn't pass muster. Something about on-set catering for the screenwriting team? A percentage point on merchandising? Foreign rights? I know. I forgot to ask for a luxury trailer so that my mother can make extended set visits."

"Is that my daughter, making a bad joke? What have you done with the gloomy-faced woman I've come to tolerate? This uncharacteristic sarcasm is making me think that we might not have lost you to the dark side, after all."

"That's totally unfair. I make lots of jokes."

She gives me a long, hard look. "I don't think so. Not lately."

"Well, I don't even think that counts as a joke. It's a feeble attempt, really."

"I would have to agree." She leans her head forward, letting her glasses fall to the tip of her nose, and examines me more carefully. "But it's an attempt."

I figure I might as well keep going, since one joke apparently qualifies as being on a roll. "So tell me, any more mud fights at preschool? The first one practically gave me a heart attack. The teacher got on the phone, and was all, 'I'm so sorry to have to tell you this, but your daughter has been the cause of a fairly serious ruckus here at school.' And then I was like, 'Oh no. Is anyone hurt? Wouldn't want to cause a ruckus, now.' And then she said, 'No, but there's mud all over the clothes of another little girl. I believe that you might be getting some angry phone calls from parents in the upcoming days, and I wanted you to be aware so that you could prepare a response.'" In my frantic attempt to change the subject, I mimic the high-pitched voice of Grace's teacher. "I mean, seriously. What are we teaching our children? No more playtime. Mud is evil."

My mother just continues to stare. "A joke and a bad anecdote?"

"Fine. You win. I saw Chris Jensen. Let me guess. You have some questions?"

She smiles slightly. "Will you answer any of them?"

"Um, no. However, you're going to ask anyways, so I figure I'll at least speed that process up."

"Is he still as handsome as always? Have there been any surgical alterations?"

"What happened to his salaciousness? I pretty clearly remember you saying that any genetic abnormalities leading to a pleasing appearance were clearly outweighed by his empty charm."

"One of the few luxuries of getting older is having the freedom to just say whatever you're thinking. Wisdom, respect—that's a load of baloney. Don't let anyone ever tell you otherwise. But the loosening of the tongue? Pure gold. And thankfully, my tongue's loosened enough to be able to tell you one thing—that boy was the best-looking specimen I've ever laid eyes on in my life. Even Ben, God rest his soul, and you know how I adored him, couldn't hold a candle to Chris Jensen. You have to give me this very small concession. Botox? Rhinoplasty? Chin implants?"

Because I'm too shocked to do anything but laugh, that's exactly what I do. "None of the above, unfortunately."

"Well, I have to say that is very disappointing. Although…"

"Although what, Mom? Spit it out."

"Although nothing. It's just nice to hear your laugh again, that's all." She pauses for a moment and pats my arm affectionately. "I love you, kid. And I love that child upstairs, too, even if she does have a certain knack for turning gray hair to white. I won't ask you anything else about it. You must be exhausted, so I'll get out of your hair and head up to bed."

"You know, you told me once that it's the fate of mothers and daughters to fight and rage through the teenage years, but eventually, we'd be talking men and life and children at the kitchen table. How did you get to be so wise?"

"Lots of living. I had my own mother once, too. I think the appropriate phrase there is 'god bless her soul.' However, I don't know how much I would bless her soul." My mother crosses herself and gives me a wicked grin.

"I love you, Mom."

"Don't disappear again, Hals." Her voice is urgent. "I don't know if I can lose you, too. Not with all I've lost."

I take the dishes from the table and place them in the sink. As I hear her leaving the kitchen, I turn to give her one last look. "I'll do my best."

"That's all you can do. That's all any of us can do."

Chapter 12
CHRIS

I stare out at the endless blue of Lake Michigan as the car passes the sea of people pushing strollers and running alongside the lakefront and generally living their lives. When I see a jogger run past with a sweater-clad dog, I smile. Dogs remind me of Hallie. The lake reminds me of Hallie. The snow-covered sand reminds me of Hallie.

Who am I kidding? Everything reminds me of Hallie. For the past week, every cup of coffee and seemingly mundane task has turned into a hidden minefield of memories. It's exacerbated by the fact that my ridiculous photographic memory makes it possible to examine my mind for little details that I thought I had forgotten long ago. I'm considering a lobotomy. An exorcism. Something.

"She's not going to be there, is she?"

There's uncharacteristic panic in Marcus's tone, and I know that he isn't thinking about Hallie. That makes one of us.

"Considering that Eva is Hallie's agent, I think it's probably a pretty good bet that she will be there."

"Don't mention that spider's name in my presence again. She probably cast some kind of spell on it. She's just waiting with her little poisoned apple. I need a food tester. Isn't that what the kings of England have?" Marcus accompanies his words with an exaggerated shudder and wink, which brings some much needed comic relief.

I manage a small grin in response, but my fingers fiddle nervously with my phone. I've been nervous for a week, and I'm never nervous.

The car stops abruptly.

"We've arrived, Mr. Jensen. Is there anything else you'll require today?"

The driver is peering at me expectantly through the rearview window. There are plenty of things that I'll require today, but I'm pretty sure the man in the front seat isn't going to be able to provide any of them.

"No, we're all set. One of us will call if we need a ride."

"Very good, sir."

He comes around to open the door. After thanking him, Marcus and I step under the awning and into the hotel.

"I'll check us in. You just try to stand over there and look inconspicuous. If anyone recognizes you, just play dumb. Maybe Chris Jensen has a twin somewhere. Go with that. You know, if you had just listened to me about the security team, we wouldn't have to worry about staying incognito this weekend. But no. No security. Dumbass."

"It will be fine. Just check us in and spare me the lecture, okay?"

He rolls his eyes before making his way over to the check-in area. I pull the knit cap over my eyes as I look for a good spot to hide out. I've been to this hotel before, years ago, when my mother had dragged Diana and me on one of her little shopping expeditions. It seems like nothing has changed. Well-dressed women pass me with bulging bags holding the spoils of a few hours of shopping on the Magnificent Mile, just as my mother did, so many years before. I ignore them and make a beeline for the darkest corner of the lobby instead.

I scope out an empty couch but before I can reach it, I hear two very familiar voices. I duck for cover.

"That jackass."

"He's not a jackass, Eva."

Shit. I'm not ready. I need a minute to prepare to see her, but I have to know who isn't a jackass? Me? That might be too much to hope for.

I can't see the pair of them, but the voices are tantalizingly close. They must be somewhere behind me.

"Oh, fuck yes, he is a jackass."

"Eva, come on. There are kids around here."

"Well, their fucking mothers should know better than to bring their grubby children, no offense, to a fucking grown-up hotel where grown people have too many fucking martinis at lunch."

Hallie laughs, and it's not the clipped laugh of the woman I saw in New York, the Hallie-but-not-Hallie. Instead, it's filled with mischief and happiness and teasing. It takes every scrap of will in my body not to spin around and yank her into my arms. I murmur what I hope is a silent thank you and strain to listen to her words.

"You are so drunk right now. I never pinned you as a girl who couldn't hold her liquor."

"Oh, so now you want to be spunky again? All of this teasing is starting to freak me out. I forgot that you even knew how to make a joke, and here you are, coming back with zingers left and right. I miss the old Hallie. Put on the mopey face. For old times' sake."

"You are not even about to turn this around to make it about me. Not this time, drunkface. I cannot believe you didn't tell me that you had history with Marcus. I also can't believe that it took a three-martini lunch to pry that out of you. You were the one harping on me for neglecting to mention certain historical events."

"I wouldn't call it history."

"Oh, then what would you call it?"

"A youthful transgression."

"That you've been repeating for, oh, just the last ten years or so?" Hallie clucks her tongue. "For shame, Eva. For shame."

"It's seven years, not ten. With the jackass. I swear, there's a special place in hell for him and his kind."

"Marcus isn't all bad."

"We'll see about that at the meeting tonight. Just wait until he starts shredding your screenplay. He'll make mincemeat out of Ben's work. He's going to try to turn it into a Chris Jensen vehicle. That man's career is the only thing in this world that Marcus cares about, other than making money and chasing tail. Even when we were in bed, it was always, 'What do you think about this for Chris's career? What about that?' I swear, those two should just get married and be done with it. It would save us both a lot of trouble."

"Save you a lot of trouble, you mean. I don't have a horse in this race."

Marcus suddenly appears before me with his arms crossed, and I raise a finger to my lips. He shakes his head and points behind me to an oversized pillar. After pulling the hat further over my eyes, I turn around and sneak a quick look in the direction of the voices.

I catch a clear glimpse of her face as she turns around to glance down at her phone. It's only been a week since I've seen her, but she's transformed. She's still too thin, but her shoulders are ramrod straight and her hair has regained some of its luster. Even from this distance, I can see some of the old light, that sense of wonder at the world around her, reason # 482 that I had fallen in love with her in the first place.

She glances once in my direction, and I inch behind the pillar. When I look up again, she's absorbed in her conversation with Eva, seemingly oblivious to my presence. I breathe a quick sigh of relief.

"No horse in this race, huh? So, you're telling me that it's just a magical coincidence that you decided to return to the land of the living after your little rendezvous in New York. That none of this newfound snarkiness can be attributed to Chris Jensen."

"Yep, that's what I'm saying."

"Sell it to someone who's buying."

"Be careful what you wish for."

"Be careful what *you* wish for. If I were more informed on the subject, I might back off a little, you know. You still won't tell me what happened between the two of you. Was it a whirlwind romance gone bad? A steamy love affair that ended in tears? Did he cheat on you? Run away with your best friend? Was it Hollywood that dragged the two young lovers apart?"

"You're getting Hollywood endings confused with reality again, Eva. I'm sure Marcus could whip you into shape. But for your information, it was none of the above."

"Don't you dare mention that man's name. You're too cruel. You at least owe me the short version. I'll get the long version another time."

"I will tell you the short version under one condition. Two conditions. You have to promise that you'll get a few cups of coffee before tonight's meeting and you have drop the subject completely for the next month. No more badgering."

"I promise on both counts, even though the thought of not badgering you is unpleasant."

"We were together. It was great until it wasn't."

"Come on. Not fair. That's a non-story."

"He's Chris Jensen. He's colossally talented, looks like a Greek god, and had the whole world wrapped around his little finger, even back then. I thought…"

Her voice catches and I can hear the sharp intake of breath from across the lobby.

"What?"

"I didn't realize that I was living in a fairy tale. The jackhole broke my heart."

Her voice is suddenly filled with naked emotion and I lean back. I want to disappear.

"Every girl's got one of those in her past. What doesn't kill you makes you stronger." Hallie's voice is teasing again, but the barely concealed hurt is still audible. "And bad breakups are the best diet ever. They need to put that one in the magazines."

"Unless your break-up strategies involve a lot of Ben and Jerry's."

"Fair enough."

There's a bit more teasing back and forth and then I hear the rustling of chairs and I know that they're leaving. As they pass our hiding spot, I take a deep breath and move closer to the pillar, even as my eyes follow the pair of them. I'm not alone. A number of interested onlookers watch as Hallie bends down to rustle in her purse for the key card.

I hide my face as she glances in my direction. She can't know that I was listening to that. Marcus lets out a long, low whistle as the elevator doors close on them.

"Damn. Hallie Caldwell, all grown up. I take back what I said, Jensen. If I knew she was going to look that good, I wouldn't have tried to talk you out of your machinations. I would have helped more." He shoots me a sympathetic look. "But look on the bright side. She called you a jackhole. Means that there are still strong emotional feelings there."

"You're the jackhole, you know that?"

"I would let Hallie Caldwell call me a jackhole any day, but I'm not taking that kind of abuse from you. Listen, I have to meet with one of the set design guys at the restaurant in a few minutes. You think you'll be able to make it to your room without assistance? Or, do I need to come along to wipe your ass for you?"

"That's really funny, Marcus. Original, too. Go."

"Eight o'clock. On the dot, man."

"Got it."

With a quick wave, Marcus darts off to the restaurant. The sounds of him barking orders at some hapless assistant over the phone echo throughout the lobby. Voice modulation has never been his strong suit. I shake my head and yank the cap down over my face as I join the crowd that's waiting at the elevator bay. When the bell dings, I move towards the open doors and take a sideways step to avoid the rush of people tumbling out.

The elevator is nearly emptied when a woman and her a half-asleep Pomeranian careen into me in a rush to squeeze themselves on. The dog lets out a sharp bark as the woman's arms loosen and instinctively, I reach out to catch him. I put him safely back into her arms with a little smile.

"Thank you. I don't know why I'm so clumsy today. Buster says thank you, too."

The woman's arm flutters over mine in a gesture of appreciation, and I smile at both her and Buster, although hearing the dog's name rips a tiny little hole in my gut.

"No problem, ma'am."

When I try to get on, I realize the elevator filled to capacity while I was busy rescuing the damn dog. I wave off the woman's protests.

"I'll catch the next one."

"Oh, you're such a dear thing. Say goodbye to the nice man, Buster."

I'm still watching Buster when I feel a pair of eyes on my face. Great. It's probably a fan. I quickly pull up the collar of my shirt in the hope that I can remain incognito, but the heat of the stare is still there a moment later.

Hesitantly, I look up. It's not a fan.

Hallie Caldwell, in the flesh.

"Of course, that dog would be named Buster," she says eventually. "The universe sure has a great sense of humor."

"Or a lack of one."

"Or that. I can't figure out why anyone would want to call a Pomeranian Buster. I can't figure out why anyone would want a Pomeranian, period. A yellow lab, a pug, maybe. But a Pomeranian? Named Buster?"

She chuckles nervously and when she meets my eyes, I smile at her.

We say the next words at the same time.

"Buster's a good name for a beagle."

Atlanta
6 Years Earlier

Her voice, full of unbridled enthusiasm, rings through the tiny house.

"I found him. The most perfect Buster ever to walk this earth. I saw him at the shelter when I went to drop off the donations from the fundraiser and I almost just got him and put a little red bow on his neck and brought him home, but then I thought, a dog is a big grown-up move and I shouldn't be making these kinds of decisions on my own. But he's Buster. There's no doubt about it. We need him. I mean, he has the name Buster written all over him. Buster's a good name for a beagle. A beagle is a real dog, not like one of those…"

Her talk abruptly stops when she finds me in our little kitchen. I tap my foot on the stone floor and glance up at her.

"What's wrong, Chris?"

"Nothing. Nothing's wrong." I quickly try to assuage her worry, but a line crosses her brow anyways.

"I know that look. That's a 'Marcus just called me' look." She sighs and places her hand over mine and moves to sit across from me at the rattan table. "Just tell me."

"No. Finish the Buster story first."

"No way. Out with it. Marcus said what exactly?"

I sigh. "There's a part that I wanted, and I didn't tell you, because I knew it was going to go to someone else. And it did, of course. Go to someone else, I mean. Except…"

She knows what I'm going to say before I say it. She tries to cover her disappointment, but it's written all over her face.

"The actor they cast had to drop out and the movie starts shooting in a week. They need someone to step in."

"And they want you." It's not a question.

"Yes."

"What's the movie?"

"It's an adaptation of a play that was on Broadway a few years back. About club kids from New York."

"*Ecstasy.*"

"Yeah."

"The Danny Mills project."

I look at her in surprise. "How did you know that?"

"Marcus and I talked about it a few months ago. He sent me the script, and I read it for him, because I'm still not convinced that Marcus even knows how to read. I guess this was probably when they were casting it the first time."

"I'm fairly certain that Marcus does not know how to read."

"Maybe not. His taste in scripts isn't much better than yours." She gives me a wicked look. "Hmmm…a movie about rich, bored kids who party too much. What's the tagline? 'If you live life in the fast lane…you learn to live life in the fast lane.' There's your deep thought for the day."

"Yeah. The tagline sucks. But the movie should be good."

"I don't know why they would ever think of you. It's not like you have any firsthand experience with being a bored rich kid on the Upper East Side of Manhattan."

"I'm from the Upper West Side. Get your facts straight."

"Oh, that's right. You have East Side envy when you're not pretending to be just like the rest of us. Tell me about that again." She raises her hands to shield herself before I can even throw the napkin that I have waiting. "I surrender. You once bought a shirt at Goodwill. You're a regular guy. I totally believe you."

"You're such a reverse snob. What do you think of the play?"

"The writing's great, except for the tagline. Story's fine, I suppose, but I think the characterization is really what made the play. I'm guessing you'd be Garrett."

"You guessed right."

"Are you going to take it?"

"I don't know. I thought the plan was to hide out here for the rest of the year and then to see if I could find a movie this summer before we have to come back to Atlanta next year."

"Before I have to come back to Atlanta, you mean. I still haven't decided whether or not I'm letting you come with me. But that's a conversation for another time. You should take the part, Chris."

"But what about Buster?"

"We can't actually get a dog. You travel too much, and I'm trying to take this overload so that I can finish school early. I'll be at school for about twelve hours every day for the whole semester. I wouldn't be here to train him, so it would be highly irresponsible to get Buster now. Maybe next year."

It's a rational argument, but her disappointment is palpable.

"I don't have to take the part. I can stay here and I can train him."

"Come on. You're bored out of your mind here, sitting around and waiting for me to come home from school. All you do is read scripts and putter around the garden. And honestly, I've been meaning to tell you this, but you're not a very good gardener. I can't have you killing another one of my rosebushes."

She's right. My thumb is the color of ink. Besides that, I really hate gardening. But I refuse to let her win on that one.

"Like you could do better. It would take a ninja to keep those things alive. A gardening ninja."

"Which you are not." She smiles. "We both know that you should take the part. Besides, James Ross comes out in a few months, so it's not like we could waste away in our little haven forever. You have to think about the rosebushes. Maybe another one can avoid death. Take it."

I reach out to touch her hair, which is coming out of its messy bun and making tiny curls all around her face.

"I love you."

"I love you, too. Now, are you going to take the part willingly, or am I going to have to kick you out of our house?"

"I'm going to take it. But that doesn't mean that I have to like leaving."

She stands up and nestles herself into my lap. I take her face into my hands, crushing my lips over hers.

"When do you leave?" she whispers into my ear.

I stiffen slightly and look up to meet her eyes.

"When, Chris?"

She runs her fingers through my hair, mindlessly curling it between her fingers, a vague expression dancing across her features.

"Tonight. I have to be in LA by tomorrow morning to go through the contracts with Marcus."

She breathes in once and gives me a rueful smile. "If this is going to be the last time I'm going to see you for months, then I better ravage you good, then."

"I like the sound of that."

"I thought you might."

She laughs and throws her head back. I try to capture her in my mind, just like that, but all I can concentrate on is her touch on my skin and the fire that's building deep in my gut. I lift her and carry her into our sunny bedroom, watching her face with every step.

She pushes me back onto the bed and places feathery kisses over my torso and abdomen, moving lower and lower until she slides her body over mine and I move into her. I let her set the pace, slowly at first, until the slowness starts to drown everything out of me and I push her urgently beneath me.

My lips meet hers for a long, deep kiss. Our tongues tangle together, harder, deeper, until we are consumed. I try to put all of my fears about leaving and coming back to find that she's changed without me, that she's left me behind, into that kiss, because I can't say them aloud. I feel her entire body tense and I slide more deeply into her, letting her warmth envelop me and pull me under.

We stay just like that, locked together, pretending that the rest of the world never existed, until the sun dips below the horizon.

An hour later, I'm still lounging against the pillows as she carefully folds clothes and stacks them neatly into my suitcase.

"Are you really packing for me?"

"You don't like it when your clothes are wrinkled." She grins. "But you never learned how to fold your own clothes, and I don't see an army of personal assistants around here, so I guess you're stuck with me."

"I thought it went against your feminist principles to play housewife."

"When did I ever say that I was a feminist?"

"Is that supposed to be a joke?"

She grabs an old hoodie from the closet and places it gently on top of the second suitcase.

"I guess. If we're talking equal rights, equal pay, I'm all about it. Give me my sign and I'll show up for the march. But honestly, I think you should take care of the people you love. And if that means doing some cooking and some cleaning and some packing, then I'll do those things, whether they're excluded from some feminist manifesto or not. I don't think ideologies should be an excuse for getting out of chores."

"Is this some kind of test? Am I supposed to jump up and start packing my own clothes or something?"

"Stay in bed, lazybones. I hear Danny Martin works his actors even harder than Alan does, so you'll have enough work to do soon enough."

She leans over and places a light kiss on my forehead. I breathe in the faint smell of honey and mint and hold my breath until she laughs and tosses the hoodie at me.

"You'll want to wear that one, I bet."

"Did you wash it?"

"I did. Say thank you, domestic goddess."

"Thank you, oh heavenly domestic goddess. Now, let me get out a gigantic piece of meat and I'll slap it on the grill."

She laughs before giving me a pensive look.

"Promise me that you're going to take care of yourself, okay?" Her tone is light, but there's an urgency in her eyes and something else. Fear. I tread lightly.

"You mean when I pull out that piece of meat or when I slap it on the grill? Afraid I'm going to get burned? I can handle myself. I know we've never used the grill in the backyard, but that doesn't mean that I'm a novice with the barbecue."

"That's not what I mean." She bites her lip, and I can tell that she's trying to figure out if she can say more. "I read the play, Chris. Garrett's an alcoholic, which means that you're going to spend the next three months trying to get into the head of someone whose whole life is dominated by alcohol. You have some history with that. We never talk about your dad."

"Why would we want to talk about my dad?"

"Because he died."

"I'm well aware of the fact that he died, Hals."

"Are you?"

"Yes."

"I'm not so sure about that. There are times when I lose you, when you stare out the window or play in the garden or you're reading, times that you just drift away, and I wonder where you've gone. The movie worries me. That's all. Danny Martin is notorious for making his actors fall into the characters, for making them live the lives of the people that they play. I just don't want you to…"

I tense. "What? You don't want me to become an alcoholic? I can assure you that it's not going to happen."

She stands up and backs away from the bed. "I'm not saying that. I'm just saying that I want you to take care of yourself. You get so wrapped up in the characters. Remember? When we were in Prague, your nickname for me was 'Boss,' because James Ross went around calling everyone that. I'm not saying that you're like some crazy method actor that only talks in tongues because he's playing some psycho killer who thinks he's an ancient Egyptian or something, but you just get so absorbed in the characters you play. That scares me a little bit. It's like you can't step out of the movie world."

I bristle at the presumption. "So, what you're telling me is that you think I can't handle myself without you. That you think I'm some kind of baby who needs protection. That playing a character who drinks a little too much is going to turn me into an alcoholic. Alcoholics are born, not made."

She gives me a long, measured look. "I never said that, and I don't think you're going to turn into an alcoholic. But playing Garrett in this movie isn't like playing James Ross. It's fraught with history for you, and it's going to be personal."

"History. Always with the history. Why can't you understand that being in a movie is a job? I swear, people, even you, think that the movie business is some kind of magical place where people become trapped in Neverland. Such a ridiculous notion. You're being ridiculous."

I'm angry, and the words were harsher than I intended, maybe because somewhere, deep inside, there's a tiny piece of me that thinks that maybe she's right, that maybe taking this role isn't such a good idea after all.

"I'm sorry, Chris. I couldn't let you leave without at least trying to say something. It's not you that I'm worried about. It's the character. And the industry."

She doesn't sound sorry. She sounds terrified, which, for some reason, makes me angry.

"That's all a part of me, too, you know. The me who makes movies is part of the same person who's been sitting with you in this house for the past four months. Maybe you think that it can just be the two of us, playing house, while I watch you troop off to school every day. That just ain't going to happen. It couldn't last forever."

"I never said that. You're being completely unfair."

"Maybe I am."

"I'm the one who's been trying to talk you into getting back to work. I want you to make movies. It's what you were born to do, and I would never try to come in the middle of that. Never. I love you. I love you so much that I worry about you, and maybe it's not even you that I'm worried about. Maybe I'm worried about me. Maybe I'm worried that you'll be off in Hollywood, dancing all night and making friends with your costars, and you'll forget about me. And maybe that's the way it should be."

"Stop."

I stand up and take her into my arms, putting my finger across her lips.

"I don't want to fight with you, Hals."

"And I don't want to fight with you."

I take her chin in my hand and watch her face as the light dances across her skin.

"You're beautiful. Did I ever tell you that?"

"About eight million times a day."

I feel her relax in my arms.

"I should tell you eighty million times a day, then."

"That might be overkill."

"I don't have to go."

"Yes, you do. It's just three months. I really don't want to hear anything else about it. You're going. That's that."

"You probably won't even notice that I'm gone."

"Nope. I'm planning on forgetting about you completely."

"Well, that's not going to work. We'll talk every day. Twice a day. We can make plans for a summer trip around the world. Maybe we can go backpacking in Nepal."

She scrunches her face up. "I'm not really the backpacking type. You know, the camping, the hard ground, the making your own meals, the no showers for a week, none of that sounds very appetizing. I used to camp, back in high school, and I hated it every time. If you turn the tent into a fancy hotel in Nepal, maybe I would be more easily persuadable."

"Okay, so no backpacking. I'll let you plan the trip."

"I'm a very good trip planner." She hesitates. "You'll tell me if anything is wrong while you're on set, right? If there's anything that you need. I can be in LA in a matter of hours. It's not like I have to take the Pony Express."

I try my best Darth Vader voice in an effort to lighten the mood. "I promise. I will tell you if I think I'm crossing over to the dark side."

It's apparently a poor approximation, because she bursts out laughing before her face turns grave again.

"It's only three months, right?"

"Three months, and I'll be right back here with you. Or on a mountaintop with you. Or on a beach with you. It doesn't matter where. Absence makes the heart grow fonder, right?"

"Right."

Still, she doesn't sound entirely convinced.

* * *

Chicago
6 Years Later

"Jinx, Hallie."

She's staring off into the distance and she doesn't hear me.

So, Buster wasn't meant to be.

When she turns to me with a wistful smile, I allow myself to hope that she and I don't have to share that fate.

Chapter 13
Hallie

I'm only able to find my voice once the shock of seeing him wears off slightly. I smile and clutch my purse to my side.

"Buster is certainly not a good name for a Pomeranian."

He's wearing a ratty old hat that covers his mass of black hair, but it doesn't manage to dim his attractiveness. I'm melting. Crap.

"Hey. To each his own. Or her own. And I think you're ignoring the fact that I called jinx. You owe me a cup of coffee."

I must have missed that. It's probably because I was staring at the way his taut muscles ripple under his t-shirt. The reflection of his insanely green eyes. The way his body leans slightly to the right when he starts talking. The little quirk of his eyebrows when he's trying not to laugh at me.

I toss my head to the side and scowl at him, which only makes him lift his eyebrows further. Ugh. I suck at life. What did he say? Something about coffee? Hell no. There's no way I'll make it out of that coffee shop without pouncing on him. I scramble to find an excuse.

"I don't think that's a very good idea. I just came down to the lobby because I forgot my jacket. I have very important things to do. Like getting ready for this dinner tonight. I mean, meeting. Dinner meeting. I have a meeting. It's a meeting about things. Movie things. And I need my jacket. To do those movie things. It might take a long time for me to find it. My jacket. Not movie things."

I think I just said that. I could crawl into a hole and die. Right now. Movie things?

He has to turn his head to the side and he doesn't make any noise, but his whole body is racked with laughter. Oh no. He's definitely laughing at me. Not with me. At me. To his credit, he manages to keep a straight face when he turns back to me. He points to the table where Eva and I had been sitting with a victorious little grin.

"So, you grab your jacket, and I'll ask the concierge if there's a coffee shop around here."

I follow the direction of his finger, and he's right about the location of my jacket. But…

"How did you know that?"

Now, he's the one who's caught by surprise.

"Um, isn't that the same one that you were wearing in New York?"

"No, it certainly isn't." I stare at him, my eyes narrowing as I realize what happened. "You were eavesdropping. You…you…sneak!"

He rears his head back and laughs. "Really? Sneak? I know you can do better than that."

"Now, you're making fun of me. A sneak and a…a laugher."

I am going to find that hole and die right now. A sneak and a laugher. I don't think either of those are real words. I try to recover what's left of my dignity by shooting him a haughty glare just before I stomp off across the lobby to retrieve my jacket. He follows me, catching my hand just as I reach for it. He takes it and holds it out with the arms open.

"I'm sorry, Hals. I shouldn't have listened to your conversation. I heard you talking about Marcus and figured I should get some recon in. It was a favor for a friend. You can't begrudge me that."

"Oh, yes I can."

I snatch the jacket back from him and struggle with it for a minute. He takes it back silently and holds it out again.

"Hallie. Stop. Let me help you."

People are starting to stare at us. There's a guy at a table in the corner who's adjusting the lens on an expensive-looking camera. He stares a bit longer than the others, and I give him a quick once-over. He looks fairly normal, like a regular person, but my brief stint as the most pitiful person in America taught me that the paparazzi come in all shapes and sizes. I can't take the chance. Muttering obscenities under my breath, I slide my arms into the jacket, and Chris's hands briefly touch my uncovered skin. I think I manage to squeak out a thank you as the little tremble in my spine starts. Turning abruptly from him, I march across the lobby and press the button over and over again, praying that this is the one time that I don't get stuck with the slowest elevator in the history of mankind.

I feel him behind me, or at least I think I do.

I don't wait long for confirmation. When he spins me around to face him, his eyes are filled with good-natured laughter, and I'm torn between wanting to smack him and wanting to fling myself into his arms. He draws me close and whispers into my ear, his lips brushing against my hair.

"You know, coffee is really good for doing movie things. It helps with the things. And I'll even let you cheat on the jinx, as long as you forgive me for the eavesdropping. It wasn't even really eavesdropping. I would call it overhearing. Definitely overhearing."

I push back, giving him my best angry face before crossing my arms and turning in the opposite direction. I've apparently become a pouty four-year-old. What's worse, I can tell that he's still doing the silent laughter thing and stubbornly refusing to move out of my way.

The elevator door dings and mercifully, it's empty. I step inside, but before the doors can close, he steps right beside me.

"Get out."

"Oh, I don't think so. You don't own the elevators, you know."

As the doors close and the lobby disappears, I take a look at him. He's sticking his tongue out at me and has an absolutely ridiculous expression on my face. I want to be mad, to maintain some semblance of my ice-cold façade, but I can't help it. I lose it, and before I even know what I'm doing, I'm laughing so hard that I have to lean against the back of the elevator for support.

He lets his eyes wander the full length of my body, and a small, hunger-filled gasp escapes his lips.

"You drive me crazy, do you know that? Especially when you talk about…things."

Don't say it. Don't say it. Don't say it, Jensen.

"Hallie."

It's one long moan.

Shoot. I'm a goner.

It's all instinct, the reaching of my hands up to encircle his neck and my unconstrained movement into the crook of his arm. My mouth finds his immediately and I stroke his hair, pulling it under my fingers and letting my whole body turn into jelly under his grasp. He lifts me and pushes me against the elevator wall, his hands grabbing at my waist with greedy fingers. I gasp as he sucks my bottom lip into his mouth, releasing it only after I feel like I'm going to drown from the lack of air.

I don't even notice when the elevator doors open to the top floor, but he manages to brace them with his foot just as they start to close on us.

We tumble out.

"Something about this feels extremely familiar," he whispers, the laughter rumbling in his chest. He reaches into the back pocket of his jeans and pulls out his room key. "We're moving on up, though. The presidential suite."

He's trying to hide it, but there's a prideful undertone there.

"So, that's all you got? The presidential suite?"

His face falls slightly, and I want to tease him more, but the sight of his disheveled hair and slightly annoyed expression are too much. He's the one who looks like a pouty four-year-old now. I kiss his cheek and run a lone finger down his neck, which causes him to wrap his arms around my back as we make our way down the hallway, knocking into walls and falling into each other.

We're in serious jeopardy of not making it to the room, but he manages to slide the key into the little slot in the lock just as I'm about to make the security guy's day by ripping my shirt off.

As we stand, joined together, in the center of the enormous suite, he pulls back to look at me before crushing his body into mine.

"Don't run, Hals. Please."

I should say something in response. I should say that I need to run. I should just run. But the naked vulnerability of his plea breaks down even my last defenses. I need to be with him, not as someone who's trying to escape from life, but as someone who wants to throw herself headfirst into it.

He's tracing my collarbone with his fingers and planting slow kisses down my neck and without warning, he spins me so that I can't see his face. I'm twisting in his arms, and as he wraps his arms around my back and runs his hands over my chest and waist and jeans, I make a whole series of undignified noises that I forgot could even come out of my mouth. He needs an answer.

"I'll try not to run. I can't promise, but I can promise to try."

"Good enough. For now."

He twirls me around to face him and his eyes widen as I lift my sweater slowly over my head before unhooking my bra and letting it fall from by body. He stares for a long time, his lips pressed into a tiny line. Afraid I've made a monumental mistake, I reach for the sweater. He pushes my hands away roughly.

"Hals, you are so beautiful."

He says it in one long breath, in the way that tells me that there's no argument to be made. I don't want to. I want to feel beautiful. I want to know that I am beautiful. I smile gently at him and place my hands under his shirt and run them up and down, in the way that I know drives him craziest.

"Thank you for saying that."

"There's no need to thank me." He grabs a piece of my hair and grins at me. "At least, there's no need to thank me with words."

His hands cover the small of my back, kneading insistently, grabbing at skin. I tremble slightly and kiss him again, needing the warmth of his mouth on mine. I slide myself into the bend of his arm and let him kiss my neck, slow, slow kisses that grow more urgent as I touch more and more of him.

I reach to lift his shirt over his head and as I do, he cups my chin in his hand and exhales a shaky breath. He is so, ridiculous, obscenely, out of control handsome. The intensity of his stare burns my skin and I try to turn my head, embarrassed, but he refuses to let me, instead looking deeply into me, so deep that I'm afraid that I'll never be able to let go.

He lifts me and I turn my face to his even as he carries me into the bedroom, keeping our eyes locked together. I manage to wrest myself free from his grasp to kiss the little dimple on his cheek that's only barely visible before moving my head lower to kiss his chest. He wiggles beneath me impatiently, but I'm planning on taking my time.

"Hallie, what are you doing?"

"I'm thanking you. Isn't that what you wanted?" I glance at him with wide eyes and flutter my lashes until he reaches for me and pulls me in for a long kiss.

"Not exactly."

He lets out another frustrated gasp as I push him back down. I continue my slow caresses, covering every inch of his flawless, golden skin. I reach for the zipper of his jeans and he lifts his hips, ostensibly to offer his help, but I take achingly long minutes, inching the last piece of clothing from his body with deliberate slowness.

I'm starting to regret my newly conceived plan of torture when he starts to graze my arms with his fingers. I lean over him, straddling his chest and rocking back and forth.

"You forget that I know you so well," he says, tracing my jawbone. "You're the most impatient person I've ever met. My turn."

With that, he reaches up and pulls me beneath him, sliding my jeans and underwear off in one smooth motion and caressing the delicate skin on my legs with his incredibly patient fingertips.

I growl at him, but he only moves his fingers more slowly, studying my face carefully with each movement. He kisses the skin behind my knee gently before covering the rest of my skin with soft, wet kisses. I lift myself from the bed and beg him with my eyes, and sighing, he moves to cover my entire body with his own.

"Make love with me, Chris."

I watch his eyes as I say his name, knowing that it, if nothing else, might push him over the edge. I'm not disappointed.

He closes his eyes tightly, his eyelids wrinkling, and whispers, "Damn it."

I run my fingers up and down his spine as he takes a long breath once and eases himself into me. His movements are tantalizingly slow and I start to move my hips more rapidly, but he just shakes his head and kisses the inch of skin behind my ear.

I let a long, guttural sound escape from my chest.

"You know I hate that."

"I know you love that."

He's right. I do love that. I grip the back of his neck and pull his lips to mine, tilting my head so that he can drip his tongue into my mouth as he fills me entirely.

His breath is ragged and I let out a strangled moan as he starts to pick up the pace, rocking in and out. His eyes stay firmly focused on mine and when I try to look away, he touches my skin softly and brings me back. I cling to him, feeling the first waves of the orgasm start to tear at me. I cry out, twice, and I feel his skin start to vibrate as he moves faster until he empties himself into me.

He doesn't move. We stay, skin on skin, until he rolls to the side and props his hand against his elbow, still not removing his gaze from mine.

I had forgotten the way he once looked at me, as if he was memorizing the landscape of my skin. I let him do it now because it feels unspeakably good to let him.

Finally, when I'm burning from the intensity of his stare, I lean back against the pillows and tear my gaze from his. I reach down to pick up my shirt, but he pushes my hand away.

"Not this time, Hals. Not this time. We need to talk."

I sigh, knowing that he's right, that this, a real conversation between the two of us that involves more than a shadow of the truth, has been a long time coming.

I'm still afraid of what I'll find when I look back at him.

I was right to be afraid.

Any notion that this, whatever is happening between us, was nothing but a few tumbles in the sheets is instantly removed from my brain when I see the expressions that are dancing across his features. There's latent desire, a sad smile, a dreamy bliss that's a direct result of our lovemaking. But there's something else there, too. There's love, the kind that goes on and on and on forever and doesn't stop, despite the years between now and then. What's worse, there's a tiny tremor of fear that he's not even bothering to hide.

Unless I'm mistaken, and I'm pretty sure I'm not, he still loves me. He still wants me.

I have to ask. Words can be lies and faces can be lies, but I have to hear the words spoken aloud. I have no idea what I'm going to do about it, but I need to know.

"What do you want, Chris?"

It's a question, not an accusation, and it's one that I desperately need the answer to. His answer is immediate.

"You."

"It's supposed to be as easy as all of that?"

"It is as easy as all of that. You. Me. Us. For the foreseeable and unforeseeable future."

I release a long, shaky breath. "It's not easy. I'm not easy."

Wrong choice of words. He laughs, once.

"Ugh. You know what I mean."

"Do I?"

"Chris, there are things that I need to tell you about, there are things that you don't know about me, there are things that I can't even figure out how to say. I'm not eighteen years old anymore. My life story no longer consists of high school parties and dancing on rooftops."

"I don't think that was ever what your life consisted of, Hallie. You forget that we once had a life together. A real one."

"And I had another life. Without you. A real one."

A pained expression crosses his face and he turns away.

"I'm well aware of that, Hallie. I had another life, too. But it wasn't a real one."

"Well, mine was. Don't try to…"

I bite my lip and look away.

"I didn't mean to say that it wasn't." He reaches up to touch my hair softly. "I don't think that."

"This isn't easy for me. My life hasn't been easy, and I don't want to talk about it right now, because I still can't find the right words to make you even understand a tiny sliver of what it's been like for me."

"Try, Hallie. Please."

I owe him that much. "When I saw you in New York, it broke my heart." I shake my head, because it's not the right thing to say. I try again. "Seeing you, looking the same as you always did, made me remember that I had once laughed and teased and loved something so much that it was possible to get my heart broken. I needed to do anything that might help me to be okay again. I needed to do anything that might help me feel again, period. I wasn't trying to go back to the way we were, or back to the person I was, because that will never happen and I realize that. I know that. I was just trying to be someone who could make it through one day. The kind of person who could see a school bus without having a meltdown in the middle of the street. You have no idea how badly I was broken. Not partially broken, all the way broken. I think I wanted to forget all of that for a little while, to try out what it would feel like to be normal. I think I needed to forget, and you've always been able to do that for me. To make me forget that there's a big bad world out there."

My voice is wavering uncontrollably and I have to bite back the tears. I'm leaning on the edge of a precipice, and if he says the perfectly wrong words or the perfectly right ones, I will shatter.

He takes my hands and kisses them. "It won't work, Hals. Forgetting about the big, bad world. I knew that's what you were doing and I let you do it anyway. I was complicit in it. I can't tell you how sorry I am about New York. It shouldn't have happened, not like that. I never should have let it go that far."

I turn to him with a ferocity that surprises even myself.

"I'm sorry that you wish it didn't happen. Because I'm not sorry about it. I'm not sorry about this."

"I'm not sorry about this, either. But I am sorry that I took advantage of you then."

"I don't think you're remembering correctly. I'm pretty sure that I took advantage of you."

"The onus was on me, and we both know it."

"No, it wasn't."

His only response is a vehement shake of his head, and I know that he's not hearing me. I want to make sure that he understands my next words very clearly, so I say them slowly, looking deeply into his face.

"I needed you. I needed to make love with you. Then and now. So please don't tell me that you're sorry. Be sorry if you have to be, but don't say it to me, because I don't want to hear it. You can at least do me that very small favor."

He nods, but I can tell that he's still torturing himself. I graze the side of his face with my fingers and take a long, shaky breath.

I've managed to pull myself back together. It seems like a small thing, to pull myself back from the edge of the cliff, but it isn't, not when I know what it's like to lose all control over what I say and think and feel, when I've had no way to figure out what my reaction to a particular piece of music or picture will be. A large part of regaining that control is due to him.

"Thank you, Chris."

I don't think he realizes what I'm thanking him for, because he gives me a remorseful smile.

"You're leaving, aren't you?"

"I have to. I need some time to think. Furthermore, if I don't show at this dinner, Eva will kill me."

I reach down and slide my shirt back over my head before turning to look at him one last time.

"You should go. You really should. You're right. You need time to think."

"I meant it. I just need some time. There weren't any alternative meanings there. I'm not running away. Just taking a moment."

I take his face in my hands and give him a long kiss that contains everything that I don't have words for, gratitude and love and pain and lust and heartache.

He gives me a bittersweet smile in response before looking at the door. "It was grand to be young, wasn't it? There weren't so many things that we had to be sorry for."

That sounds too much like goodbye, and that wasn't my intention, so I measure my response carefully.

"There weren't so many things that we were proud of, either."

"Fair enough."

"I think I might have to exempt the breakdancing movie from that. What was it called? *Breakdown*? I wouldn't be too proud of that one, if I were you."

He throws the pillow at me and I narrowly avoid it with a well-timed duck.

"Chris, I'll see you at dinner, okay?" When he doesn't respond, I prod the side of the bed with my hand. "Okay?"

"Sure."

I don't entirely believe him, but staying in this room for one moment longer might make me say something that I'll regret.

So, I leave, but not without leaving a piece of myself behind.

Chapter 14
CHRIS

I slam my hand into the headboard as I hear the door shut behind her.

The hunger for the head buzz, the loose, easy feeling, the release of obligations in favor of blackness, fills my gut.

I want a drink more than I've ever wanted one in my life.

And for an alcoholic, that's saying something.

She shouldn't need time to think about me. When had it all started to go wrong? How had I managed to screw this up so royally?

But I know the answer to that question. Ultimately, London.

But it had begun long before that.

Ecstasy. New York. The apartment. Chelsea.

* * *

5 ½ Years Earlier
New York

I turn the key in the lock as one of the girls behind me giggles maniacally. I spin around to face them.

"Shut up!"

"What, is your mom going to be mad?" she says, intentionally raising her voice, which causes even more giggles.

My annoyance level is reaching monumental proportions.

"My girlfriend. And yes, she will be very mad."

"You have a girlfriend?"

Adam, my costar from *Ecstasy*, looks totally confused. "You still have a girlfriend, man? The same one? Really?"

"Yes, the same one. Really. And she's going to be pissed if we wake her up at 5 am."

My buzz is starting to wear off, leaving me with nothing but a gigantic headache and what feels like cotton balls in my mouth. Suddenly, bringing Adam and my newfound friends from the club for breakfast on the terrace doesn't seem like such a good idea after all. The three blond girls in the back are still giggling as we stand in the entryway. The sound of their tinny voices combining is only making the headache that much worse.

"You all seriously need to shut up. Adam, do you think you can remember how to make coffee?"

"You have one of those instant press machines, right?"

I look at Adam and his friend Charlie, whose eyes are starting to roll back in his head. He's obviously coming down from some sort of high. Shit. I have to get them out of there before Hallie sees.

"Never mind. There's a table on the terrace. Grab the fruit from the fridge and the bagels from the counter and head out there. I'll put the coffee on," I say, rubbing my temples.

"This place is a freaking palace," one of the girls (Ami or Abby or Allie or something or other) shrieks. "You must be rich! I mean, I know you were in that movie with the prom and everything, but, I mean, you must be, like really, really rich."

Adam throws his arm around my shoulders. "This is the next movie star, ladies. I'm talking private jets and meetings with kings and prime ministers and billion-dollar fundraising dinners. Just wait until the end of the summer. James Ross. I'm just planning to ride his coattails all the way to the bank."

My head is really starting to throb now. I feel the bile rising in my throat.

"Terrace. Now."

I run to the bathroom on the lower level of the loft and place my head directly over the toilet and empty the contents of my stomach a dozen times. The vomit reeks of alcohol. I reek of alcohol and vomit. I hate vomit. I hate everything about it—the shaking in your gut, the nasty breath, and the way that you can still taste it even after you brush your teeth. Shit. Why do I keep doing this crap?

I brush my teeth three or four times, but I finally give up on trying to get the grit out of my mouth. I'll settle for making the fastest breakfast ever. I dump grinds into the top of the coffeepot and some spill over the sides, but I'll leave it for now. I've been bugging Hallie about getting a maid, anyways. This will just be another good reason on top of all of the other good reasons. I reach for the sunglasses on the counter and place them over my eyes, because even the fluorescent light from the kitchen is making me want to die.

"You're the prettiest one!"

"No, you are!"

"I think you're both pretty!"

Their voices are getting progressively louder. By the time I make it to the bottom of the stairs, they're hollering and screaming and singing funny songs at the top of their lungs.

Great. Hallie really is going to kill me.

It had almost taken an act of God to get her here. Our summer plans included a trip, maybe to Nepal, maybe to France, maybe to Costa Rica, maybe to the mountains somewhere, but the *Ecstasy* reshoots and all of the *James Ross* press had made that a total impossibility. She wanted to stay at Greenview while I took care of my business, but I had begged and pleaded and cajoled to get her to New York instead. The Chelsea apartment, all sharp corners and modern furniture and geometric pieces of art, was supposed to be a love nest that would make her forget about all of the midnight phone calls and drunken rages from the set.

But she hated the apartment, my new friends, even *Ecstasy*.

I never should have taken that part. The shoot had been utter madness—late nights of rehearsing scenes again and again until they were absolutely perfect, and long nights of going out and dancing and drinking. There were always clear plastic bottles with pills that never seemed to belong to anyone in particular (and which I couldn't keep myself from indulging in). Then, I would wake up and repeat the same thing all over again. I couldn't seem to stop it. I kept going out, and then there were later and later nights, and the cycle kept repeating, over and over. New York has been more of the same.

A distance is starting to grow between Hallie and me, one that I'm currently trying desperately to ignore.

I glance down at my shirt, which is clearly wearing the signs of the all-night binge. I tear it off and tiptoe up the stairs. Hallie's curled up in a tiny little ball at the corner of the enormous bed, making little noises like she's trying to stay in the middle of a really good dream. I grab a shirt from my closet and put it on. I make the decision to kick these people out of my house with Styrofoam cups of coffee. Maybe she'll never have to know. But, when I look back and see her twisting and turning in the sheets, I can't resist moving back to the bed, and planting a quick kiss on her forehead. She stirs slightly, and turns her face to look at me.

"Chris?" she whispers, stretching her arms. "What are you doing?"

"Shhh. Go back to sleep."

She's already sitting up in the bed. "Did you just get home?"

The peals of laughter from downstairs are impossible for her to ignore, even though she usually needs a good twenty minutes before she's cognizant of anything other than coffee. Her eyes narrow.

"Are there people with you?"

"Just Adam and a couple of people we ran into at the club. I told them that I would make breakfast, but I'll get them out of here as soon as I can. I promise."

"Marcus called a dozen times last night. He said something about talking points for the press junket and requirements for the August premiere," she says, rubbing her eyes. "You should call him before he has a heart attack."

She pulls the covers off, and I see that she's wearing a pair of my boxers and her favorite t-shirt, a retro Greenview one that Alan had found somewhere and given to her after his daughter, Lily, had decided to go to college and not to join a cult.

The sight of her disheveled hair and sleep-filled eyes fills me with an unexpected rush of love. I pick her up and kiss her over and over again.

"Chris, you smell like the bar. Gross. Put me down. I love you, but you really, really, really, need a shower right now."

"After breakfast. I need to feed these people so they'll get the hell out of here."

"Okay." She glances at the clock. "Chris! It's 5 am. You were out all night?"

"You know how it is. An hour turns into two, and then you want to leave, but you get stuck in a conversation, and then it's the morning before you even realize it."

I don't tell her about the party favors that changed my perception of time, but the suspicious look in her eyes told me that she probably knows anyway. She opens her mouth but then promptly shuts it again, instead motioning to the stack of books on the bedside table.

"I don't really know what you mean, Chris. But sure. An hour turns into two. Look, I'm going to try to get this reading done. My final for my NYU class is in a couple of days, and I don't think I have a good grasp of constructivism and positivism."

I have no idea what she's talking about. I vaguely remember her telling me about a class at NYU, but I didn't realize that the class had already started.

"You know, the class I've been in for the past six weeks? I had to stay up for three days straight last week to write that paper?" She takes a long look at me before shaking her head. "Never mind. You were busy with a hundred other things. Go. Take care of your friends."

"I'll make it up to you. I promise. We'll talk all about constructivism and positivism and whatever other isms that you want to tell me about. We'll take a trip. Where do you want to go? Paris? Africa?"

"How about Nepal? Remember? You, me, a mountaintop tent? Oh, wait. There aren't any clubs there." She covers her mouth and groans. "Sorry. I didn't mean that. Seriously. Go. Shower."

I can't shake the sense that I've broken something, possibly beyond repair, but I've suddenly become so hazy that I can hardly form a coherent sentence, let alone a heartfelt apology.

I think I was going to make breakfast but I suddenly need to wrap myself in a curtain of warm water. Maybe it will take some of the sickness in my stomach away.

I stumble into the shower and let the water run over me until I can't find the edge between where my skin ends and the water begins. I shake my head to clear it, but the blurry line between the sink and shower and water and me grows dimmer and I slam my hand into something sharp and there's a stickiness and a thickness and my vision is narrowing. Everything is white and gray and somewhere in between.

I groan, loudly. Suddenly, there's a panicked voice coming from somewhere, from a fog, but I can't hear it and I can't make sense of it and I can't make sense of anything, words or noises or sounds.

"Chris? What's wrong? Are you okay?"

There's a loud crashing noise and then there's a warm body next to mine in the bathroom and she's wrapping my hand in a towel and whispering something softly.

That's it.

Blackness.

* * *

Chicago

5 ½ Years Later

I still have the little half-moon scar, just above my thumb, where I gashed out a piece of my skin with the mirror, and I can still see Hallie's face as I came around in the hospital bed, the fear in her eyes. The fear that I had put in her eyes.

No wonder she needed time to think tonight.

The only thing I can't figure out is why she would even entertain the thought of giving me a second chance, after New York. After London.

I pick up one of the tiny glass bottles from the minibar and twist it around in my hand. That, at least, would be simple. There would be one drink and then another and then another, until the burning in my gut was nothing but a foggy memory.

I open it, lift it to my nose, and take a long breath in.

I hear voices, Hallie's and Marcus's and Dan's, from some foggy memory, screaming at me instead.

I set it back down again and pick up my phone.

Marcus starts yelling before I even say a word.

"Jensen! What the fuck, man? If you're calling to tell me that you can't make it to dinner, I really am going to kill you this time."

"I can't make it to dinner. I need to find a meeting."

The sharp anger switches instantly to concern. "Chris? Are you all right?"

"I'm fine. Fine."

"Hang on. I'll be right up."

"No, don't. I'm going to call my sponsor and see if he can find out where the closest meeting is. I just can't do dinner. Not right now. Make my apologies, okay"

"What do you want me to say?"

"Anything but the truth."

"Chris…"

"I'll be fine, Marcus. I promise."

I grab my wallet and eye the little glass bottle that's sitting on the table.

Unable to resist, I pick it up and place it in my pocket.

My fingers close around the cool glass as I twist it again and again, knowing that it, too, contains a kind of history.

Chapter 15
HALLIE

I have bigger problems than finding something to wear for dinner. I could try to figure out whether I want to throw myself into the Chris Jensen abyss. Again. It might also be a good idea to consider how I'm going to tell my ex-boyfriend (and apparently, my current lover) that I have a four-year-old daughter.

Instead, I'm thinking about whether I want to go for paisley innocence or candy apple red sex. I wonder if it's too late to burn all of the clothes I own and take advantage of the Magnificent Mile? I glance at the glowing red numbers on the clock. 7:55. Yep. Definitely too late.

There's a knock on the door and I allow myself to hope for one second that it's Chris. But light tapping isn't his style, and there's only one other option. I open the door, clad in nothing but my undergarments, and Eva takes a long look at me.

"What was it that you said? No dog in this race, huh?"

The taunt of her voice causes me to make an immediate and executive decision not to tell her about the elevator. Or the hallway. Or the hotel suite.

"I think what I said was that I didn't have a horse in this race. Not a dog. And shut up."

She picks up a green silk dress and runs it between her fingers, taking in my total state of disarray with a bemused expression.

"Touché. More importantly, you didn't tell me the mopey period was accompanied by the purchase of some incredibly frumpy outfits."

"Thanks. I'm glad you think I need more encouragement right now."

She chooses to ignore my comment and focuses on the frumpy wardrobe instead. She arches her eyebrows before moving into full-on stylist mode, tossing aside my two best options without so much as a second look. She picks up a short black dress from the bed and eyes it with more interest.

"What about this one?"

I give the dress a long, cold stare. I'd thrown it into my bag at the last minute. Chris had insisted on buying it for me on one of our weekend trips to Paris. Of course, I had never been able to bring myself to wear it. Or return it, for that matter.

"Hallie, darling, this is gorgeous. It's begging to be worn. Now, we just need to figure out what to do with your hair."

She fusses behind me, coaxing my curls into some kind of harmony while I stare at the dress.

"Ok. That's the five-minute special, but it will have to do."

She pulls back and inspects her handiwork. Even I have to admit that I'm starting to look halfway human.

"Thanks, Eva."

"It's an agent's job to be a master of all trades. Now, go be a good girl and put the dress on. I thought I was going to have to do some serious last-minute shopping, but at least you had the sense to buy one pretty thing for yourself."

"I didn't."

"Well, Ben didn't give two shits about clothes, so I know he didn't…" The realization hits her and a sneaky little grin crosses her face. "No, it's perfect. Wear it. He won't remember anyways."

I don't really have any other options. I slide the dress over my head and glance in the mirror. I look like a tart. An expensive tart.

"I feel like Grace, playing dress up." And I'm whining like her, too.

"You could use some of Grace's fashion sense." Eva grins at me. "Where's my munchkin, by the way? I forgot to ask you earlier. I know I said that I would make it up to the cabin, but…"

"But you were too busy having sex with the asshole." I finish her sentence, and we both laugh.

"Fair enough. I deserved that one. But that doesn't answer the question about Grace. I thought she might want to go to some of the museums."

"My mother's bringing her up early tomorrow morning, after the meetings are all finished."

"She'll love it. And I, for one, am filled with enthusiasm at the thought of seeing Claire again."

Eva's voice is filled with anything but enthusiasm. I wag my finger at her.

"My mother is going to hop a flight back to Michigan just as soon as she drops Grace off, so you might just miss the pleasure of her company." I sigh. "I didn't want to drag Grace into all of this. I couldn't take the chance of someone snapping her picture."

It's true. But what I neglect to tell Eva is that the thought of keeping my daughter in the same hotel as Chris Jensen fills me with dread. As far as I know, he's completely unaware that she exists. I've done everything that I could possibly think of to keep her out of the press, and while a few people with cameras managed to snap pictures of her with me in those awful days after Ben died, the paparazzi have been surprisingly well-behaved when it comes to her. Maybe even the vultures have hearts.

But that just means that unless he did some serious digging, which I wouldn't put past him, he doesn't know about her. I had wanted to tell him, back in the suite, but something about the mixing of different worlds made me run instead. If I can't even bear for them to be in the same hotel, what does that say about any possibility of a future for him and me? Was there even a future there to begin with?

"Hello! Hallie, wake up. Where are you taking Grace when she gets here?"

"Sorry. Sorry. I promised her a trip to Lincoln Park Zoo before we head back up to Lake Geneva. You should come with us."

"Oh, good. I brought the most darling little…"

"No. No more gifts. Sam already turned her into a monster last week by having all five members of 4Sure call her for her birthday. They even wrote a song for her. 'Grace of My Heart.'"

Eva looks appropriately horrified. "Sam's title, I suppose?"

"I think it was all his idea. I promise, it's even worse than it sounds. I'll have to get the recording for you. Of course, Grace thinks that it's the next masterpiece. She's probably right. It has just the right mix of pop and rock. That's what Sam said, anyways. And Marie send clothes that were 'straight from the Paris runways.' The saddest thing is that I think her favorite gift was this hideous trucker hat that my mother gave her last week."

"The kid is on trend. Trucker hats. Chic again. Who knew? Randomly, that's the only late 90s trend that I did not want to come back. But that's fashion." She gives me her best runway pout. "Enough about Grace. We don't have time to argue about my spoiling of my favorite preschooler. You know I'll win anyways. Now, how do I look?"

She's wearing her signature red and does a little twirl to show off the dress to its full effect.

"Marcus will die when he sees you in that."

"As long as it's a long, slow, painful death, I'm fine with that." Eva touches my arm. "You look gorgeous, Hal, and we both know it. Ready?"

"As I'll ever be."

The dress keeps riding up on my thighs, and I yank it down at least five times in the elevator ride, trying desperately to make it cover more of my body. When we reach the maitre'd stand, I notice that a couple of the diners are staring blatantly at me. Of course. I look like a total slut. I'm too old to pull off something like this. Just as I'm about to run back up to change, I notice that a man has gotten up from his seat at the bar to approach us. He's probably closer to my mother's age than mine.

"May I say that you look lovely tonight? May I buy either of you a drink?"

Eva's inner mama bear takes over and she thrusts me behind her. "Thank you for the compliment. However, we have a prior engagement."

She grabs my arm and hisses into my ear, "See, total strangers hitting on you? That's a good sign. Now, stop fiddling with your dress and smile like you mean it."

I give her a ridiculous jack-o-lantern smile, and she slaps my arm.

"Behave." Still, she can't hide her grin. I glance back, once more, to creepy grandpa, who winks at me. I see that his eyes are still following us as we're ushered into a private room, set apart from the rest of the dining room by heavy black curtains.

I take a deep breath and straighten my shoulders. Eva's right. If I really am going to look like a total slut, then I need to own the dress. Especially if I'm going to be face-to-face with Chris Jensen in about two seconds.

"Hallie Caldwell. Who would have imagined us meeting like this?"

The booming voice definitely did not come from the mouth of Chris Jensen. I give Marcus a wicked little grin that matches the one on his face.

"What exactly did you imagine, Marcus?"

"The way I see it, we move towards each other from across a crowded dance floor and then I sweep you into my arms. If I remember correctly, you had moves. But dance floor or not, it's surprisingly good to see you."

His teasing words are filled with unvarnished warmth, and I'm stunned to realize that I'm actually happy to see him, too. I ignore the flabbergasted faces of the men in suits around the table and offer my hand to Marcus, who promptly kisses it.

"Hello, Marcus."

"You look beautiful."

"Thank you." I study him for a minute. "You look the same, I think. Older, but the same."

That elicits some chuckles.

"How do you two know each other?"

The question comes from a perky-looking blond girl, scribbling furiously with a stylus on a tablet in the corner of the private room. She quickly looks down in embarrassment when one of the men scolds her. For a moment, I feel sorry for her. Then I realize I'm going to have to answer the question.

Marcus steps in instead. "Hallie and I are old friends. Golfing buddies, you might say. She used to humiliate me, and you all know that I don't admit that easily, but it's been a long time since she's kicked my ass on the course. I've gotten much better since then."

"It would be hard for you to get much worse. If I remember correctly, you ended up throwing more than a few clubs into the ocean on our last jaunt to Pebble Beach."

"Your memory is clearly damaged."

He gives me a quick grin before pulling out my chair. He's not so chivalrous when he turns his attention to Eva.

"Eva. Of course. I was hoping Hallie would be unaccompanied by her bulldog, but I suppose we must make sacrifices for the honor of the writer's presence."

Eva's not going to like that one at all.

Nope.

For a second, I think she's actually going to crawl across the table to gouge his eyes out, but she merely shakes her head and gives him a menacing glare. I can practically see the fumes coming off her, but she's managing to keep it together. For now.

"At least I managed to show up on time. Where's your client, Marcus?"

He hesitates slightly. "Tied up."

A shiver of disappointment crosses my spine, but then I see the faint concern behind Marcus's eyes. He isn't telling the whole story. Of course not. I remember all too well. How many times had I been the one to say that for Chris? I even used the same words. Tied up.

Marcus settles back into his seat, and as someone starts to make introductions, I dig my nails into his hand. I have to know whether Chris is all right. I can't help thinking that there was something that I should have done. I shouldn't have left him like that, all alone in the room.

"Where's Chris? Tell me," I hiss into his ear.

"He's fine, Hallie. Fine."

I glance at him through narrowed eyes.

"Then why isn't he here?"

"Hallie, it's not your problem."

"What do you mean, it's not my problem? Of course it's not my problem. But that's not the question I asked. Where is he?"

"Still a spitfire, huh? He's at a meeting." There's something that Marcus isn't saying, but before I can ask what it is, his fingers tighten on mine. "He's pretty wound up, Hallie. I know I shouldn't be telling you this, but you need to tread lightly."

Eva looks at me questioningly, but I shake my head in response instead. I need to tread lightly? What the hell, Marcus?

I turn to him to ask my question again, but he's already released my fingers. He turns to the group, and I know that he's quickly morphing back into the dynamic, public version of Marcus. I'm impatiently tapping his hand under the table, but he merely bats it away.

"Let's speed up the introductions, shall we? These two here are Eva and Hallie. They want to make sure that this movie makes as little money as possible. They see it as a thought piece, a reflection of modern society and its imminent downfall. Everyone else around this table is in the movie business, and we're trying to make money. These two purposes are at odds with each other, so we'll bitch and moan, and we're all going to have to make concessions. Ultimately, we're going to make a fucking great film."

A number of people around the table raise their glasses and toast his words, but it's only seconds before people are rapidly firing questions and numbers and names across the table. It's a faintly familiar scene, but it's been a long time since I've played this particular game and I have other things on my mind. My head starts to spin.

"So, what would you say if I said we could make this movie in Vancouver for half the cost of a Chicago shoot?"

"If we make these tweaks…"

"We need a female star with some kind of name, but we don't need to spend a fortune…"

"That's the casting department, and we need someone to head it up…"

"Are you planning to be on set?"

"What exactly is the producer role here?"

Marcus gives me one last annoyed glance before moving to the other side of the table, and while I want to demand the answers I seek from him, I know I can't just scream at him in front of all of these people. So, I try to listen to all the ways in which they're planning to cut up and remix and rewrite Ben's work. I can't muster any more than weak enthusiasm and nonsensical arguments. I think I actually told someone that the movie should be shot in Chicago and not Vancouver because Vancouver doesn't have enough snow. Now, everyone thinks I've totally lost my marbles. Great. Thankfully, Eva is living up to her bulldog nickname, going toe-to-toe with anyone and everyone and taking particular pleasure in making Marcus squirm.

After he concedes a particularly contentious debate about the ending of the movie, I see him give Eva an appreciative stare, which she responds to with a swift kick to his shin under the table. Those two will be fine without me.

Finally, I find a slight break in the action and I reach for my bag and start to stand up. Whether I'm getting information from Marcus or not, I need to find Chris.

"Thank you all for inviting me," I say. "It's been a pleasure. I have to admit that this is all a bit overwhelming for me."

I hear a few surprised murmurs, but I'm already up from the table and in the throes of my best innocent girl act. I'm getting too old for it, but I can't think of another way to make a graceful exit.

"All this talk of numbers and back-end has my head spinning a bit. I promise, I'll be more helpful with the rewrites. I'm definitely better with a computer screen in front of me. But it was so nice to meet you guys. Let's do this again soon."

I leave the room before anyone else can offer their opinions about the screenplay. I'm out the door of the restaurant before Marcus catches me.

"He'll be…"

"On the roof," I finish. We stare at each other.

"Hallie…"

"Yes, Marcus?"

"It really is good to see you. Even if you brought the devil herself along for the ride."

"Eva is good people. And I think you might be good people, too."

That's my little thank you, for telling me about Chris, for protecting him, for being a friend to me a million years ago. The air is thick with things unsaid and unseen, and I try to lighten it.

"You can add that to the list of things I never thought I would say in my life."

"Hallie?"

"What?"

"I'm sorry. About Ben. About Chris. About all of it."

"That's kind of you." I mean it, and I squeeze his arm. "I'll see you soon, okay? You're not going to get the nice Midwest Hallie Caldwell, either. I promise, I'll be in the fighting spirit. We can go a couple of rounds. Eva may be the bulldog, but I remember how to fight with you quite well, and I think I have a few unfair advantages."

"I'm sure you do. I look forward to it." He winks at me. "Be careful. You're sitting at the grown-ups' table now, and so is he. Rewriting history isn't as easy as it sounds. Believe me. I've tried and tried and tried."

I ignore any of the subtext and instead take that at face value, which causes me to place an impromptu kiss on his cheek.

"Eva loves beluga whales. Can't get enough of them. There's even a little stuffed one in the top drawer of her desk. Coincidentally, I hear they have a pretty nice aquarium here. They might even have some beluga whales there."

"Who even said I was interested?"

"You don't fool me. Not one bit."

"Neither do you, Hallie. Make sure he's all right?"

"Yes. I will."

He pulls me into his arms for a long embrace.

"I missed you, kid."

"I missed you too, old man."

He shakes his fist at me and blows me a kiss before disappearing back into the room. I don't want to waste any more time, so I take long strides to the elevator bay. Unfortunately, running is seriously out of the question in these heels.

When I reach the stairwell on the highest floor, I tentatively push on the doors, which are marked by a gigantic, "Do not push. Alarm will sound" sign. It's been a long time since I've done this, but I remember that generally, the signs are all talk and the alarms don't actually sound. I'm hoping that's still the case. Sure enough, I manage to open the door a bit and it looks like I'm not actually going to be the cause of a hotel-wide evacuation.

I'll take the minor miracles wherever I can get them.

Chapter 16
CHRIS

I'm still twisting the bottle in my hand, feeling the cool glass between my fingers, even after listening to all of the war stories of the people who've fought this battle time and again. I push it deeper into the pocket of my coat and remember the Polaroid and the way her smile makes everything around her disappear.

Maybe I can still catch them at dinner. But before I can make it back inside the hotel, I get hit by a barrage of flashbulbs from the paparazzi stalking the front door. I raise my hand to shield my face, but I don't think I'm quick enough to avoid all of them.

I've never been one of those guys who boohooed his bad luck to be so rich and famous that people actually wanted to buy the grainy photographs of me doing exciting things like getting a cup of coffee. I even like some of the paparazzi.

That doesn't stop me from wishing that just once, they would leave me alone.

I step into the elevator. My fingers curl again around the little glass bottle in my jacket pocket. I'm not going to have a drink. I'm not going to have a drink.

I think about going to dinner, but I don't think I'm strong enough to see her, especially if she's just going to keep saying goodbye.

Instead, I make my way up the stairs at the end of the hallway. I push on the door, knowing that the alarm will not, in fact, sound.

Flakes of snow fall on me the second I open it, but I don't feel the cold.

She's there.

Chapter 17
HALLIE

I'm not even sure that he'll even be on the roof, but I want to believe that he hasn't changed that much, that he still does his best thinking in the open air. The cold whips through my body and I shiver in the wind as I glance around.

He's not here.

My heart drops.

I make my way to the edge and peer out over the city, the flakes of snow melting as they fall into my hair.

Where could he be?

Just as I'm about to give up and spend the rest of the night worrying in my room, I hear a slight thud and I stiffen. It's either him or security. At this point, I'm not sure what I would prefer.

There's impatience and anger in his face when I turn around to meet his eyes.

"What are you doing on the roof, Hallie? I would have expected Marcus to come up here. Not you."

I shrug my shoulders in response and cross to him, staying just out of his reach.

"Sorry to disappoint. I'm sure you had a great, indignant speech prepared, too. You'll just have to save it for the next time Marcus pisses you off."

His shoulders slump. "I repeat. What are you doing here, Hallie?"

"Freezing my butt off, Jensen."

"I didn't invite you. Go back inside."

"I wanted to make sure that you were all right."

He takes my shoulders in his hands and turns my body so that we're staring directly into each other's eyes.

"You shouldn't have to ask me if I'm okay. You should never have to ask me that."

He's shaking a little and his skin is cold to the touch.

"Let's go inside, Chris."

"I don't want to go inside."

He sounds so much like Grace that I have to laugh.

"Yes, you do. But more importantly, I need to get back inside before I actually, literally, begin to freeze. I let Eva talk me into the fashionable choice when I should have gone for jeans and a sweater."

He opens his mouth to protest, but he nods when he inspects my shivering form more closely.

"Fine. We'll go in."

He reaches the stairs first, and I follow until he comes to an abrupt halt about halfway down.

"Hallie, I thought you needed time to think. To consider. Just a little time, you said. No alternative meanings."

I can't fathom why he seems so angry. He's practically shaking with it. Then, I look more closely into his face.

"Chris, what's wrong?"

"What isn't wrong?"

"You're shaking. Come on."

"Come on what, Hallie?"

"Talk to me."

"What do you want to know?"

I want to know everything, but I can tell that isn't what he needs to hear right now. When we reach the bottom of the stairs, the floor is empty, but I don't want to have this conversation in the middle of the hallway. I'm not sure what conversation I want to have. But I know that I need to keep him talking, that I can't just let it be. Not when he looks like he just got hit by a freight train.

I open the door to my room and expect him to follow me. Instead, he remains in the hallway, looking pitiful.

"Come inside."

"I can't."

"I'm not going to attack you. Scout's honor. Come inside before I have to scream at you."

He's reluctant. "Only for a minute."

I shut the door behind us, and he sits tentatively on the end of the bed. I hand him a bottle of water from the minibar, and that act manages to elicit a small smile.

"I thought you said minibars were the devil."

"I thought you said they were God's little gift to mankind."

He doesn't respond to that, but I notice that he reaches into his pocket before beginning to play with the edge of the blanket, touching it again and again with his hands and shredding the corners.

"They're going to charge that blanket to my room, you know."

"Bill me."

"Why were you headed up to that roof, Chris?"

He spins his head very slowly to face mine.

"My name is Chris Jensen, and I'm an alcoholic."

Obviously, I know that. I must have known, even back when we were kids and everyone drank too much. I also knew from the second I saw him in New York that he had gotten sober. Sam's observations had only confirmed it. I still feel relieved when I hear him say it aloud, when he admits to me that he knows it, too.

"I haven't had a drink in three years." He turns to me with a fierce expression. "And I didn't have one tonight. I wanted one more than I've ever wanted one in my life, but I didn't have one tonight. You know, in case that was what you were worried about."

"I wasn't worried about that."

It's true. I've seen Chris drunk, and I've seen him tipsy, and I've seen him everywhere in between and beyond, and he isn't any of those things. It doesn't make my worry any less potent.

"I did AA. The twelve steps."

"I hoped for it, and I'm glad to hear it now."

"I may have skipped the most important one. Making amends. I told you I was sorry for New York, but maybe that's not really what I'm sorry for."

"I'm sorry, too."

"What do you have to be sorry for?"

"Oh, a million things. For being young and stupid and for not telling you what I really thought and felt. For not demanding that you get the help that you needed. I was just as complicit in a lot of it as you were." He starts to talk, but I shake my head. "Please don't. Not if you're only going to offer an apology that I don't want to hear."

"Hallie…"

"Why were you on that roof? You still haven't answered the question."

He looks out the window and his words are barely audible. "I had the bottle. From the minibar, funnily enough, God's great gift to mankind. I put it to my lips, and I almost took a drink, even while I was on the goddamn phone with my sponsor. He told me to get my ass to a meeting, so I got my ass to a meeting. Of course, I even took the goddamn bottle with me, which is like bringing gasoline to a fire. I went up to the roof to clear my head and to think. I really fucking needed a drink."

He pulls the bottle from his jacket and hands it to me. "Keep that, please."

I take it from him and tuck it away. "But you didn't have a drink."

He shakes his head in frustration. "That's not the point. And you still haven't answered my question, Hals, and I asked first. Why are you here? What were you doing up on that roof?"

The total subject change. By far the most annoying weapon in his arsenal.

"I did answer your question. I was worried about you."

"Why?"

"Why not?"

"I don't need to be saved."

"I think everyone needs a little saving every once in a while. But I didn't come up there to save you. I came up there to make sure you were all right."

"What do you think? You think I'm all right?"

"I don't know."

He buries his head in his hands and when he lifts his head again, the look in his eyes nearly shatters me.

"I never wanted you to see me like this, Hals."

"Like this? Really?"

I've seen him in far worse states. I try to push those memories from my mind, because thinking about Chris like that makes me remember that last terrible night in London, when everything had fallen apart.

He reaches across the distance I've put between us and takes my hand in his.

"Like this. Sad. In need of saving, no matter how pathetic that might be."

"Last week, I was in need of saving, no matter how pathetic that might be. I owe you one." I cover his hand with mine, feeling his skin vibrate under my fingers. "This is the only way I can think of to thank you. To check to see if you're all right."

"Can you sit with me awhile?"

"Of course."

I've always thought of silence as the enemy, so I usually fill it with nonsensical words and silly observations.

But now, with the weight of life resting heavily on both of our shoulders, we sit for long minutes, letting the silence fill in all of the years stretching between us. There are a thousand things left unsaid, but I'm not ready to dive into that particular wreck.

So, for the first time in my life, I find solace in silence.

And in the warmth of his hand on mine.

The minutes pass in nothing more than a heartbeat. While I should have had time to prepare for it, his next words shock me out of the magic of the moment.

"I have to say it, Hals. I can't be with you, in this room, without saying what I've needed to say for five years."

His face is wracked with pain. I don't want to hear this. I try to cover my ears, but I'm not fast enough.

"I don't know when or if I'm going to see you again, and I can't let you slip out of my life without telling you how sorry I am. I'm sorry for not telling Marcus and the publicity people to fuck off, because I know it bothered you and I just pretended like I didn't notice. I'm sorry for London. I'm sorry for breaking your heart. I'm sorry for being young and stupid and drunk and for not realizing that I was throwing away the love of my life just because I could and because I was a fucking alcoholic who couldn't admit it to himself. I'm sorry that you had to clean up my messes and apologize for me. I'm sorry for all of it and a thousand more things that I probably did and that I can't remember because I was so fucked up that I didn't see you falling away from me."

His face makes me want to weep.

"I'm sorry, too. I gave up on you. I didn't know how to help you, so I just gave up. I shouldn't have done that."

He gives me a sad smile and stands up.

"No. You shouldn't have. But I shouldn't have let you. I'm sorry, and I can't atone."

As he opens the door to leave, I remember one last true thing, something that he told me long ago. I call after him in a soft voice.

"Chris?"

He turns around and I whisper it so that only he can hear.

"It's a hell of a thing to apologize to someone you love. Because it means that you have to admit to that person that you're not perfect, that they're not perfect, that no one will ever be perfect. Because in saying you're sorry, you're really admitting that you're human."

"Someone smart must have told you that."

"You told me that."

He gives me a bittersweet smile. "I forgot to tell you that you look beautiful tonight. But then again, you always do."

With that, he's gone. There's a terrible finality about those words that's magnified as the door shuts between us.

I sink into the bed.

Why do apologies always feel like goodbyes?

Chapter 18
CHRIS

5 Years Earlier
London

"Jesus. What the fuck? They expect people to walk on this shit?"

I glance down at the black and white tiles, which are arranged in geometric lines and shapes. The beats from the club are still pounding out a conflicting pattern in my head. I should have just taken another pill and kept dancing. That movement, unlike walking, was doable.

"It's just some floor tile, Jensen."

Marcus has his arm around me, but I throw it off.

"I can fucking walk, asshat."

He lifts his arms. "I never said you couldn't."

I stumble slightly.

"What kind of an asshole agent are you? The club was open for at least another hour or two. I'm supposed to be celebrating right now. I'm done with the fucking movie, and you made me enough money that I can pay thousands of dollars to stay in your SHIT HOTEL."

I yell the last words at the night clerk. He looks at me like I've just defaced a portrait of the queen before immediately picking up the phone on the desk.

"Chris. Shut. The. Fuck. Up," Marcus hisses, before rushing over to talk to the guy at the desk.

"What are you saying? You better not be apologizing right now. They're the ones who should be apologizing for this fucking ugly ass floor," I yell, the sound of my voice echoing loudly through the lobby.

Marcus gives me a vicious death stare, but I choose to ignore it. Fuck him. Seriously. He talks to the clerk in hushed tones before coming back to my side.

"Get your ass upstairs, Chris, before they call security and kick us both out of here."

I give him a little salute. "Aye, aye, captain. I was just going to do that. I need to see Hallie. Where the fuck is she? Why didn't she come out with us? What's the point of having a girlfriend if she won't even come out dancing? Useless."

Marcus grabs my arm and shoves me into the elevator and pushes the button at least a dozen times.

"She did come with us. Don't you remember?"

I remember dancing. With a girl in a red dress. Who may or may not have been Hallie. Fucking hell. The music is starting to pound its beat again.

"Sure."

"Sure." Marcus takes a long, even breath. "Chris, I think you should stay with me tonight. There's no use in waking Hallie up right now. The two of you are supposed to fly back to the States tomorrow, and I'm sure she would appreciate a little sleep."

"You know what I think Hallie would appreciate?" I try to remember what my next words are supposed to be, but my head is fuzzy and I've lost my thought, so I frown at Marcus instead.

"Chris, it's not a good idea."

"Since when were women ever a good idea?" I lean back against the cool metal of the elevator and let it linger on my skin for a minute. Bile is starting to rise in my throat and I manage to choke it down again. I feel like shit. And I need Hallie.

"Except for Hallie. Hallie is always a good idea."

"Fine. Hallie is always a good idea. Just like it's a good idea to let her see you like this. But what do I know? You're just going to do whatever it is that you want to do anyway. Just like always."

The elevator doors suddenly open to a dizzying array of enormous plants and an endless series of doors with numbers. I look to Marcus for help.

"It's 1235."

"I knew that."

"Of course you did. You know everything, right? You're perfectly aware of your limits."

"Are you trying to say that I can't handle myself? Fuck you, Marcus. And your little dog, too."

Just as the elevator doors start to close on his face, I realize that I have no idea where I'm going.

"Hey! Where's my room?"

"1235. I'll see you tomorrow. Try to actually get your ass to the plane on time. Not like last time."

I shove my middle finger in his direction and try to make myself stand up straighter. Hallie. Where's Hallie?

I tap each of the doors as I pass them. 1234. 1236. What the hell is the number again? And where is my fucking key? I dig through my jeans, and I can't even find where my wallet is supposed to be, so I knock again and again on the door that seems like the right one.

"Hallie. Open the goddamn door."

I hear a click. Hallie is standing in the middle of the door frame, curly puffs of long hair floating all around her face. She looks pissed. Very, very pissed. She moves aside to let me in before shutting the door behind us. With a slightly disgusted look, she takes a step back and then another.

"Hallie. My love."

I cross the distance between us, pick her up and swing her into my arms. I start to cover her face with kisses, but she's wriggles against me. I'm knocked off balance and she sways precariously in my arms.

"Chris. Put me down. Put me down now."

"Nope. Not until I get what I came for."

"Chris. Now."

I lock my arms tighter around her body and push my lips into her hair.

"You smell like honey. Why do you always smell like honey?"

"It's called taking a shower. You should try it." She manages to free herself and the lack of weight in my arms throws off my equilibrium. I stumble backwards and she flicks the light switch on.

"You're drunk."

"Good guess! Twenty points to a Miss Hallie Caldwell for being such as astute judge of drunkenness."

I kick off the shoes I've been wearing and toss them in the trash can. I never want to see those goddamn shoes again.

"I'm glad I get points for being such an astute judge of your particular kind of drunkenness, but it doesn't take a genius to guess that you would come home drunk. You've come home drunk every night we've been in London. And we've been here for almost three months."

"You got to give the people what they want, baby."

"And tell me, how exactly is you being drunk every night giving the people what they want? What exactly is that supposed to accomplish? Enlighten me."

"I'm living the dream. Just living the dream. The people want to see someone who's doing that. And I am."

I flop onto the bed and try to forget that the world is not actually rotating. I mean, it's rotating, but my world isn't. Something like that.

"Is this what the dream is supposed to be? Tell me, Chris. When exactly did this, you drunk in some hotel room, become living the dream? I thought..." She bites her lip and looks away from me. Instead of actually telling me what she wants to say, she picks up the jeans that I threw on the floor and folds them neatly.

"Never mind what I thought."

"No. Tell me what you thought. You're going to say it anyway, so tell me what you really think."

She turns to me with her hands on her hips. Everything is spinning and her face is slightly out of focus.

"I think you've been drinking too much. No. That's an understatement. I think you've been drinking so much that you need to get help before it's too late. I think you've let the James Ross and the *Ecstasy* success go to your head. You used to laugh about being a big movie star. Remember? You told me that you were afraid that this," she motions around the hotel suite, "was going to change you, that playing all of these different characters was going to make you forget yourself. You were afraid that maybe you wouldn't like the person that you were becoming."

"Well, I was fucking wrong. I fucking love this. I fucking love me. Who wouldn't?"

"I don't. I don't love this. This isn't a movie. You're not playing a character right now. It's just you and me."

"This is me. This suite, and this life, those things are all me. I'm sorry if you can't accept that, if this is too much for you to handle. I should have thought about that, really. I mean, with your background, this is all new for you."

"With my background? My little Midwestern, small town, small life, small dreams background? That's what you really want to say, isn't it? That this isn't my world. That this was never going to be my world. Well, maybe you're right."

"Maybe I am. You're jealous. You're totally and completely jealous. What is it? Are you still mad about the fake girlfriend thing? That was all Marcus's idea. And the James Ross people. That's Hollywood bullshit, Hals. I've told you that a million times. We had to make it look real, so I kissed her once for the cameras at the premiere."

"This has nothing to do with some fake date that you took to a premiere. It doesn't even have anything to do with the fact that we can't be seen in public because some producers that you've never even met are afraid that having a girlfriend would make you less desirable to the preteen set. I'm not jealous. You're an asshole, did you know that?"

She's looking at me like she's never seen me before.

Part of me wants to fall at her feet and take back everything I said, and pretend that this hasn't been festering between us for too long. But I can't. I'm too angry with her, and maybe even with myself. I feel myself falling further into the hole, but I can't stop it.

"Oh, who's the asshole? Of course you're jealous. What are you doing in London, Hallie? Besides taking advantage of the free room and board, that is."

"I don't know what I'm doing here. I really have no idea what I'm doing here."

She bites her lip again and turns so that only her back is visible to me. I can see her start to shake. I should want to comfort her, but the fact that she's turning away makes me even angrier.

"You need to get your own dreams, instead of hanging around me like some stupid puppy dog. You need to figure out who you want to be in life, because I can tell you right now that I don't need a nursemaid, or a mother, or another person trying to tell me how to live my life. I mean, really, don't you think it's time that you figured out how to have a life outside of me?"

She spins around suddenly and faces me head-on. "I think you're right about that. I do need to figure out how to have a life that involves something and someone other than you. Because you know what I don't want? I don't want to keep doing this. Because you do need a nursemaid, or a mother. Someone needs to tell you how to live your life, because you sure as hell aren't doing a very good job of that right now. I'll tell you right now, though, I didn't apply for the position of personal assistant to a movie star."

"No. You applied for the position of my girlfriend. I don't see you turning down any of the perks of that, though. That's probably what you wanted all along, to get a taste of what it would be like to be rich and famous. Isn't it? How was it, Hallie? Fucking a movie star?"

She takes a long breath and her eyes narrow into slits.

"You once told me that you were never going to turn into your father. I have to say that I think you're doing a pretty fine imitation right now, except for the fact that your father realized his mistakes and he tried to atone for them. But you're not sorry about anything. And you never will be."

Chapter 19
HALLIE

5 Years Earlier
London

As soon as I say the words, I want to take them back. I'm not sure he's even heard anything I've said, up to that point, but I know the word father caught his attention, because his face fills with rage.

"Chris…I didn't mean to say…"

"Yes, you did."

"I just…I'm scared for you. That's all."

"Scared for me? That's a load of bullshit, Hals. You think…you think that I'm like my father, huh? Like this?"

He picks up the glass tumbler from beside the bed and throws it against the wall. The shreds of glass shatter and spill onto the carpet. I shrink back into a corner and cover my face. This is how the world ends.

At least, this is how my world ends.

"Now you're afraid of me? You're afraid I'm going to hurt you? Like that guy did? Back when you were in high school?"

"What are you talking about?"

"I've heard you talking on the phone. To Ben. I bet there are a lot of things that you shared with Ben. A lot of things."

There's a nasty little undertone in his voice and I shake my head.

"That's unfair."

"Yeah. A lot of things in life are unfair. The fact that my girlfriend of almost two years, the one who supposedly loves me to the ends of the earth and back again, tells some random guy everything about her life—that's unfair. Damn it." He holds the edge of the counter with his hand and I can see the barely concealed rage starting to shake his body. "I'm willing to accept that because you've managed to infiltrate every part of me. You're stuck so far inside my head that it makes me crazy to think about you and Ben, with your hands all over each other. That's it, right? You're leaving me because you've had your fill and you're going to run off and be with him now."

He's acting like a lunatic. I don't even know what he's saying. He takes a step closer to me and takes my chin in his hand. He reeks of whiskey and I can practically see the smoke coming off his jacket, and I don't want him to touch me. For the first time since I met him, all I can think about is how to get his hands off me.

"You're scaring me, Chris."

"If you're so afraid, why don't you just leave?"

He places his sticky lips near mine. I push him away.

"Because this isn't you. The drinking and the late nights and the partying and the movie premieres and taking a Valium every two hours just to get through the day. I know you. The real you…he doesn't scare me. The fact that the real you might be lost forever…that's what scares me."

"I don't even know what you're talking about. This is me. And if you don't like it, then leave." He lets out a vicious little laugh and moves away from me. "Run away, Hallie. It's what you're good at."

"Have another drink, Chris. It's what you're good at."

"I think I will."

He walks over to the minibar and takes a small bottle of whiskey and drains it before picking up another, then another.

"I can't do this anymore."

It's another second before I realize that I've said the words aloud. I grab my purse and the suitcase that I packed earlier that night, which is sitting neatly in the corner of the suite, and move them closer to the door.

"I think it's time for me to get my own life. Isn't that what you said? That I have to find another reason to live outside of you?"

I sound bitter and angry, but I can't keep either of those things out of my voice, because I think that maybe he was right, that maybe I need to be someone besides Chris Jensen's hanger-on.

The inevitable tears are starting to bubble in my throat, but I will not give him the satisfaction of seeing them.

He glances down at the bottle and looks back up at me. "Come on. You know I didn't mean it. I just had one too many drinks, you know, with the movie finishing and going back home and I guess maybe I was a little bit drunker than I thought."

He laughs nervously, and I see a flicker of the Chris that I fell in love with. He's taking steps towards me, his face filled with contrition. It weakens my resolve, but I can't let it, so I take another step towards the door, the suitcase in my hand.

"You did mean it. And I think I did, too."

"I'm sorry. I love you, Hals."

He does still love me. I can see it in his eyes and I can feel it in the tender touch of his fingers in my hair. I'm not sure if it's good enough. I'm not sure if it will ever be good enough.

I have two choices. He still loves me. I still love him. I can stay, and I can try to fix this. I can try to fix him. I can try to fix me.

In an instant, I see our life spread out before me. This scene will play over and over, in another hotel suite in another city, after another night at the club. We'll keep repeating these words until there's nothing left but anger and regret.

But there's another option. I can run away, as he put it. I can leave this hotel room and try to put together some semblance of a life without him.

The bitch of it is that I still love him. I will always be hopelessly, crazy in love with him.

I look deeply into his eyes, which are already starting to haze over with the extra infusion of alcohol. It makes the decision easier, but no less painful.

"Goodbye, Chris. I really hope that you manage to find whatever it is that you're looking for. Because I'm not it."

"Hallie, stop. Stop."

His face crumples and I almost break down right there and then. But I'm already turning away. I can't let this drag out any longer. I can't stay here.

"Hals, you still love me. I know you do. You can't just throw this away. Please. Don't do this. You know you're going to regret this in the morning. I'll even go get those bagels from that place in Notting Hill. We'll call it apology lox. We're going back to the States tomorrow and you can go dancing with Sam and everything will be fine."

I turn back to him and force myself to meet his eyes. I pray that he's drunk enough to believe the lie that I'm about to tell.

"I don't love you."

It costs me more than I can bear to say it.

"What?"

It's easier to say it this time, because he's already turned away from me. I don't have to lie with my face, only my words.

"I don't love you."

His body shakes slightly. It would be imperceptible to almost anyone else, but I've spent the past two years of my life memorizing every movement of his muscles. He's hurting, and every impulse that I have is telling me to throw myself into his arms and try to forget that this whole night even happened. There's a good chance he won't remember anyway. I'm halfway across the room when he turns back to me, his face contorted into a rueful little grin.

"What a sick little game you've been playing, Hallie."

"I didn't mean to…"

"Save it. I never want to see you again. Don't call. Don't write."

"Chris."

"Don't say my name. Because I can promise you that in a few days, I won't remember yours. I'm planning to forget that you ever existed."

I pick up my suitcase and force my legs, which have turned into stone, to move.

"Take care of yourself. Please."

With that, I shut the door between us.

I manage to make it to the elevator before I shatter.

Chapter 20
CHRIS

5 Years Later
Chicago

I've had five years to think about the things that we said to each other in that hotel room. I'm no closer to figuring out what I could have done differently, other than not letting alcohol and fame turn me into a total jackass. But it was already too late for that by the time we got to London.

The old maxim is that time heals all wounds, but this particular wound has stayed fresh. It doesn't help that I pick at the edges every once in a while. I guess some small part of me is still hoping that I can conjure up an alternate version of events, some reality in which she doesn't utter those words: *"I don't love you."*

The sun is starting to dawn over the horizon, but it doesn't feel like a new day. It feels like the same old shit.

I clench my hand into a fist and punch the wall in my hotel suite.

Nothing is resolved. My apology, five years too late, hadn't magically rewritten history.

Pull it together, Jensen.

I bury my head in my hands before standing up and pacing back and forth. I've given her enough time to think. I can't keep doing this again and again. There's only one way to fix this, and it doesn't involve pouting. I grab my jacket, because I fully intend to pound on her door until she answers. There has to be something to say. Anything to say.

I'm halfway to the door when I hear a voice and the click of a lock.

"Jensen!"

The sight of Marcus standing in the middle of the room enrages me. I take the opportunity to use some of the less popular swear words. Even he looks impressed.

"Are you finished, Jensen?"

"How the hell did you get a key?"

"You're not the only one that can be persuasive."

He's smiling a bit too brightly, which means that he's lying. He must be here to see if I had been drinking. I'm some kind of drunk, but it's from the lack of sleep and Hallie's particular brand of intoxicant. Not alcohol.

"Did I pass the test?" I ask sarcastically. "See? No alcohol bottles. I don't smell like the bar. And I promise, there aren't any naked girls hiding under my bed."

"Well, that's a damn shame, because Hallie Caldwell seemed sure as shit bent on finding you."

"Get out of here, Marcus. If you came to haul me off to rehab, I'm afraid that you're probably sorely disappointed right now. Go."

I glare at Marcus and slam the bathroom door shut between us. I place my hands on either side of the sink and stare into the mirror. Great. On top of everything else, I look like shit. The five o'clock shadow has turned into a full-on beard. My eyes are wild, and I look like I haven't slept in days. Which, of course, I haven't.

"I didn't come to drag your ass to rehab. We need to talk," he calls out, his voice drifting out from under the bathroom door. "Jensen. Come out."

There's an uncharacteristic seriousness there. I open the door, but not before glancing at the gold-plated mirror one more time. The mirror and the marble shower look exactly like those in the twelve hotel suites before this one. When did I stop noticing the sameness?

I stare into Marcus's ashen face.

"What is it, Marcus?"

He takes a deep breath and then his phone rings. He glances down at it and then looks apologetically at me.

"I have to take this one, Jensen. Don't do anything stupid right now. Just sit right there and give me a second."

"No fucking way, man. Come on, get out of my way."

He shoves an iPad into my hands. "Sit the fuck down, Chris. Look."

He picks up the phone with a resounding, "Shit" and moves over to the window. There's something about the way he says it that makes me sit down. I slump back into the couch and finger the iPad, but Marcus's conversation catches my ear.

"Did you get the name of the guy who posted it? What? Stop. No, this isn't an opportunity. No. Jeff, you fucking don't know anything about it, so you need to fucking shut your pie hole before I decide to fire your sorry ass. You don't know shit about shit. You're supposed to be on top of these things. It's been floating around the internet for the last fifty-seven minutes. Do you know how long fifty-seven minutes is? I thought we had a PR team who was supposed to take care of this. But the way I see it, you don't seem to be doing a very good job managing the crackpots. I can find someone in five seconds who could do better. There's a desk clerk at this fucking hotel who's never done an iota of PR in her life who could have done better. There is one thing you can do. Get the security here immediately…I know and I don't care. This is going to be a fucking disaster. We're in major damage control mode, Jeff. Call Serafina. She needs to get her ass on this immediately."

Marcus turns back to me, holding the phone to his ear and motioning frantically to the tablet. I pick it up and show him the password screen and he shakes his head.

"I have to go, Jeff. He hasn't even seen it. Yeah, I know. I'll tell him. If it's not down from that fucking website in the next ten minutes, someone is getting fired. You have no idea how much I want that person to be you."

He hangs up the phone and turns to me.

"I told you that I didn't want the security team, Marcus."

"We've got bigger problems, Jensen." He takes the iPad from my hand and enters the code and hands it to me. "Look."

I take a deep breath.

"Oh, God."

"Yeah, man." His phone rings again and he glances once at me before lifting it to his ear. "I have to talk to Serafina. We're going to get it taken down. I promise. Just give us a few minutes."

It's some scandal blog, awash with garish colors and bright headlines, but I'm not looking at the latest photos of whatever celebrity's miraculous weight loss.

Instead, I stare at the hundred pictures arranged haphazardly around a larger image of Hallie and me standing at the elevator the day before. A knit cap is pulled over my face, but there's no doubt that it's me, looking lovingly into Hallie's eyes. Pasted over the picture, in big, red letters, is a single headline: *Caught in the Act: Chris Jensen and Hero Teacher's Wife.*

I've seen most of the other pictures before. They're mostly shots of Hallie after Ben's accident and pictures of the two of them together, in addition to stock photographs from movie premieres and the Thailand movie promos and the James Ross set. There are a few that my eye lingers on a little bit longer—a picture of Hallie and me at a party in Prague, a shot of the two of us on a beach, one of us dancing in a Vegas club. Christ, where did they find those?

I give Marcus a searching look, but he shrugs his shoulders helplessly before barking more orders at Serafina. Just as I'm about to rip the phone from

Marcus's ear to demand answers, I see a link at the bottom of the page that stops my heart.

Oh, She's a Ho: Hallie Caldwell. A Scandalous Affair. A Secret Love Child?

There's a picture of Hallie and Ben holding the outstretched hands of a tiny girl with deep brown curls, but a thick red line is drawn through Ben's face and mine is superimposed over it.

I glance at Marcus, and the stricken look on his face matches my own, even as he continues to talk to the publicist.

"I'll look. I haven't seen that one yet. But I have to go, Serafina. Yeah, get it taken down if you can. Yeah, I think it's probably too late for that. Uh huh. We'll handle the security. He needs to get out of here as soon as possible." After he hangs up, he settles onto the couch next to me.

"I wasn't lying, Jensen. We have to get you out of here as soon as we can. You shouldn't read that shit. It will rot your brain."

He's trying to hide the worst of it, but I already saw the headline. And the picture. Just as he lunges to snatch the iPad from my hands, I take it back, clicking the link and holding it just out of his reach.

Hallie Caldwell Ellison is the widow of Benjamin Ellison III, otherwise known as "Hero Teacher," who authored the best-selling Rage *series before dying in the tragic bus accident that captured the attention of America last year. Hallie hasn't spoken to the media since her press conference she held shortly after leaving the hospital, when she asked for privacy for herself and her family after the devastating events.*

The Ellisons have a daughter, Grace, who is now four years old and has been kept out of the limelight until now. However, sources tell us that she's the inspiration behind "Grace of My Heart," the new single from pop sensation 4Sure. Her parentage has come into question with the recently discovery of photographs of Hallie with mega-movie star Chris Jensen, who is best known for playing James Ross in the remakes of the popular 80s action franchise. FFG Studios, Jensen's production company, recently optioned the first screenplay in Rage *series, which Hallie Ellison completed after her husband's death. It wouldn't be the first time Jensen has mixed business with pleasure. His latest conquest was Lena Fair, the prima ballerina currently tearing up the stage in* Coppelia *for the* ABC Ballet Company *in New York, but Lena was just the latest in a long line of pretty faces to show up on his arm.*

Hallie and Ben Ellison ignited a media firestorm when the press dubbed them America's Couple after pictures of the pair from high school seemed to confirm their Hollywood love story without a happy ending. However, Hallie's been keeping a few secrets of her own. Sources tell us that she and Jensen have been engaged in a long-standing affair that began nearly seven years ago, and that Hallie cheated on Ellison numerous times during their marriage. The two apparently have love

*nests all over the world, including New York and
Chicago, where they're currently sharing a hotel suite.*

*See for yourself. But we think the supposedly grieving
widow looks all too comfortable in the arms of the movie
star. She seems to have a particular taste for fame, which
is ironic given her constant and repeated requests for
privacy. But maybe Hallie Caldwell is a better actress
than we ever could have imagined. Perhaps Chris Jensen
could take a few lessons from her.*

*We're currently interviewing a number of sources
with first-hand knowledge of the Jensen-Ellison coupling
and will report the details as soon as they've available.*

Stay tuned!

I hand the tablet to Marcus wordlessly. He shakes his
head as he takes in the pictures, but I can tell that he's not
surprised.

"How bad is it?" I ask, sinking back into the sofa.

Despite the horrific headline, they haven't managed
to dig up anything much, other than the fact that Hallie
has a four-year-old daughter named Grace who lives with
her in a hideaway somewhere. Apparently, not in one of
our secret love nests. Shit. A child. A four-year-old child.
I do the math in my head with a sinking feeling. It wasn't
possible. She didn't have that kind of deception in her,
unless I had been mistaken.

Damn it. Why hadn't she told me?

"Bad. We can try to get the website to take down the
pictures, but the damage has been done. You come off
looking like the guy who's been fucking hero teacher's

wife. To be frank, it doesn't matter that he's dead. He's too much of a saint, and you're too much of a sinner, for the public to forgive you as easily as all that. She comes off like a slut. There's enough photographic evidence of the two of you from a million years ago that this isn't going to go away quietly or soon. You have to admit that it looks like what they're saying it looks like. And the real story is so fucking convoluted that no one would believe it."

"Great. That's just great."

I slam my fist into the couch. "What they're saying about the daughter? Grace?"

"Jensen. We don't even know if there's really a kid. If it's true, then I don't know how Hallie managed to keep the press away from the kid for so long. We should hire whoever she's got working for her."

"Eva."

"Or maybe not."

I glance again at the curly-headed girl, whose face is a replica of Hallie's, minus twenty years.

"Hallie didn't tell you about the kid? I thought the two of you had made nice again."

"Shut up, Marcus."

"Chris. She might not even have a kid. You know what the paparazzi do. They find some totally unrelated pictures of some random kid from Arkansas. They're trying to sell ads, man. And you know what you do to sell ads? You sell a secret love child."

I give him a stony glare.

"Ok. Not the best choice of words. But still. We don't know."

"Marcus, are you really trying to tell me that that child doesn't belong to Hallie? Just look at her. She's a carbon copy of her."

I shove the iPad in his face. He glances at it carefully before setting it back on the table.

"Okay. So, maybe it's her kid." He takes a long breath. "Hallie Caldwell is a lot of things, and you know we've had our battles, but I don't believe that she would have gone off, married some other guy, and pretended to him and everyone else that the kid wasn't yours. It's not in her, that kind of duplicity."

"I thought that, too…"

Now, I wasn't so sure. My eyes linger on the photograph, seeking some resemblance between the girl and myself. I can't find anything, but it doesn't mean that…

"So, find her. Talk to her. She's probably still here somewhere. There's no way she managed to escape without triggering the attention of the vultures."

I only hear the first part of the sentence, the part about finding her, before I'm out of the seat and across the room. He's right. I need answers, and Hallie's the only one who has them.

His phone beeps before I can reach the door.

"Strike that. She's gone. The press managed to get wind of the fact that a mysterious black car with Wisconsin plates snuck out the back garage." As I turn back to look at him, I don't fail to notice that he looks slightly impressed. "I mean, seriously. If we weren't talking about Eva, I'd have to give them props for the disappearing act."

"Marcus!"

"Sorry. Sorry. You could always use some of the famous Jensen charm to see if the hotel has a contact number for her. I would say that we could ask Eva, but I don't think she's in the mood to share anything with me right now. Sorry, man."

"Were you being your most charming self again, Marcus?"

"You know me."

I certainly do. Okay, so there's absolutely no chance that Eva will help. I search my brain for any hints that Hallie might have given me the night before about where she was off to when Marcus interrupts my thoughts.

"You can't go looking for her looking like that. They'll be all over you before you can even get to the lobby."

He's right. I dig in my part for my hardcore disguise, the horn-rimmed glasses and fake mustache and hat. A few seconds later, I look like a middle-aged creep.

"Good enough?"

"Good enough." He tosses me a set of keys. "I think you need security, but I know that you're not going to be able to wait for that. There's a red Corolla in the garage. I had one of the girls rent it as soon as I heard about this shit, in case you got any bright ideas about leaving the hotel without a bevy of armed guards."

"Thanks."

Without another word, I dart out into the hallway. Unwilling to wait for another goddamn elevator, I sprint to the stairs and take them, two at a time, down to the lobby. I see a sea of photogs waiting across the street, aiming their lenses inside the hotel. So far, the security staff's managing to hold them off, but I know that it can only last for so long. I was going to have to make this quick.

I'm slightly out of breath when I lean over the counter to make eyes at the stout woman in her mid-forties who's manning the front desk.

"Hi. I wonder if you can be of some help to me. I'm looking for one of your guests, Hallie Caldwell. It also might be under Hallie Ellison."

The woman gives me a long look, up and down, and when she finally finishes her inspection, she avoids meeting my eyes. When she speaks, her voice is ice cold. "I'm sorry sir, but we're very protective of our guests' privacy."

"I'm a friend of Ms. Caldwell's. I think she may have checked out earlier this morning. I was hoping she might have left some information about where she was heading. Maybe someone spoke to her?"

I give her my best smile, the one on the latest James Ross poster, the one that had, as Marcus put it, boosted box office by ten percent.

She just looks disgusted.

"Sorry, sir, there's nothing I can do to help you."

I'm losing patience. Quickly. That smile has sold millions of movie tickets. Shit. I must be losing a step. I move my hand to run my fingers through my hair, and as I touch the soft folds of knit wool, I remember. No wonder.

I don't have time for this. I yank the hat off my head, push the glasses up on my face, and take a quick glance outside the glass doors. I lean over the counter.

"Look. Do you know who I am?"

It always works. It will work this time. It will.

The woman's eyes are as big as saucers. "You're...you're..."

"Chris Jensen. Yes, I am him. I need to know where Ms. Caldwell is. Those people outside? They're waiting for me. And Ms. Caldwell. I need to find her before they do."

She gives me a hard glare. "I don't have any information for Ms. Caldwell, no matter who you are."

Curious onlookers are starting to look our way. I pull the glasses down over my face and yank the cap back on. I'm contemplating a frantic dash to scour the airports when I feel a long finger tapping my shoulder.

"Hello, Christopher."

I spin around.

Apparently, it is possible to freeze time.

I know this because Claire Caldwell looks exactly the same as she did when she stood in her living room, glaring at me, seven years before.

Chapter 21
HALLIE

My eyes dart around the hotel's parking garage nervously. What was it my mother had just said? Keep the sunglasses on and the windows up. Drive home and don't stop until you get there. I'm still hanging on to the faint shred of hope that the vultures haven't discovered where I live, but I know that it's just a matter of time. Unfortunately, I don't have anywhere else to go, not with a sleepy four year old.

Just minutes earlier, I had been poised at the door of Chris Jensen's hotel suite. I still wasn't sure of what I was planning to say, but I knew that I couldn't let him think that what I said to him in London, that I didn't love him, was true. Then and now. I was going to tell him about Grace, about me, about my life, and I was going to see if there was any way he was willing to take me on, all my messes and fumbling. Because none of it mattered if he still loved me. And I think he did. Does. Did.

But I didn't have the chance to tell him anything. As I was standing there, ready to lay myself bare in front of him, Eva had called, her voice frantic.

"Get in your room and stay there. You were with Chris yesterday and someone saw. It's bad, Hallie. They know about Grace and there are pictures of you and Chris, the same ones I found and a couple of other ones. They're making it seem like the two of you have been together for the last seven years, all the time while you were married to Ben. I'm not sure what I can do about it now. I'm not sure if there's anything we can do about it now. I'm on the other line with Claire and we need to figure out a plan to get you out of this hotel as soon as possible. Give me five minutes. Get your things packed."

I hadn't seen the stories, but I didn't need to. Most of it was probably true, except for the long-standing affair and the fact that I'm sure the stories were embellished with a series of adjectives that I really didn't need to think about. Slut. Fame whore.

Grace is whining and I lean in to kiss her cheek. She's still strapped in her car seat, wiggling impatiently to free herself.

"Mommy, why can't we go to the zoo? You said we were going to see lions and tigers and bears. Oh my!" She rubs her eyes and her bottom lip wobbles. "I don't want to go in the car. I've been in the car all night. Grandma said she wanted to get here early so we could go to the zoo. But now we're not going to the zoo."

"I promise, baby girl, that we will go to the zoo another day. We just can't go today."

"Why not?"

"Because we can't, Grace."

"Daddy would have taken me to the zoo," she says in a quavering voice.

"He can't take you to the zoo," I say, my own voice shaking slightly. "He can't take you because he isn't here."

I slam my hand into the side of the car and stare into her face, which everyone says is a carbon copy of mine. I've never been able to see it.

The only thing I see when I look into her face is Ben.

* * *

4 Years, 9 Months Earlier
Ohio

"Tell me. How did I turn into an angsty teenager? I'm almost 21. I thought I was too old for this crap."

I toss my mom's afghan to the side impatiently, and turn to face Ben, who's sitting on the couch in his apartment, absorbed in his computer.

He looks up. "What do you mean?"

"You know, angsty. Angst-ridden, full of angst?"

I glance into his eyes and see that he's trying desperately not to laugh. I'm not amused.

"In case you weren't paying attention in high school health class, it means consumed with the weight of the human condition. More specifically, it means I'm obsessed with the relation of the human condition to my own messed-up life. It's practically a stage of human development."

I punctuate the statement with a smirk. Now I'm not the only one who's annoyed.

"In case you forgot, I'm an English major, Hals. My senior thesis is basically a manifesto on the development of the angst-ridden hero in science fiction, so I'm well aware of the definition. But thanks."

"Jerkface." I flip him off, but that only makes him appear more like a jack-o-lantern. "I'm trying to spill my guts here and all you want to talk about man-eating dinosaurs or some crap like that."

"So, spill your guts. It's better than watching you mope in silence. I really hope we're talking figurative gut-spilling here. Although I do have to admit, literal gut spilling would be more in line with this thesis that I need to finish."

"No, no, it's fine. I'll just deal with my angst in silence."

I'm only half-kidding. He had done more than his fair share of listening to me whine about my pathetic self. I had been unable to string a coherent sentence about anything interesting together for months now. I was basically a walking CW show and about two seconds away from referring to myself in the third person.

Ben puts his computer down and opens his arms in an invitation. He leans back on the sofa, his head tilted slightly to the side, and studies me cautiously.

"Come here, Hals."

"I don't want to."

"Stop being petulant. In case you didn't know, that means childishly sulky."

I stick my tongue out at him, and we both laugh. I groan and nestle myself into the crook of his elbow, letting his warmth envelop me.

"I never thought of myself as someone who was all about the drama. And yet, here I am, with twelve million half-eaten pints of ice cream, pouring my heart out to my best friend. It's been three months since I dumped my boyfriend. It's not even like I got dumped. I dumped him. I'm whining like a toddler here."

Ben doesn't say anything.

"But I mean, actually, the real question is why on earth you would even put up with it. You were the one who wanted me to transfer to Ohio State with you. Maybe you weren't aware that you were going to have to put up with months and months and months of listening to me moan and cry and whine. And there are probably more months to come. Because I'm a brat."

"Dear lord, let's hope not." Ben looks heavenward and makes the sign of the cross in an exaggerated gesture. I punch his arm.

"That's the fighting spirit." He winks at me. "I knew if I kept you around long enough, you'd at least take a peek out of the bell jar."

I bury my head in my hands. "I'm sorry, Ben."

He tweaks my nose affectionately. "Yeah. You should be. Brat."

"Nerd."

"I know you are, but what am I?"

We both laugh.

"I'm turning over a new leaf. No more whining."

He's dubious. "Really? But you're so good at it."

"At least that's one thing."

"Hey. Moaning is also a strength. Crying. Sobbing. Laughing when you're not a total mess. Pretty much anything that involves making noises."

"What a great talent. I should take it on the road."

"Don't sell yourself short. There are any number of lucrative careers built around making noises."

"Like what?"

"Train conductor."

"I don't think train conductors actually use their own noises. They have whistles for that."

"Porn star."

I wrinkle my nose. "Maybe. I need a name, though."

"Isn't there a formula already established? Your first pet and the name of the street you grew up on?"

"Ducktales Spruce Street."

"Um, maybe not."

"Okay. You pick the name, I'll make the noises."

He laughs, lightly, and turns back to his computer. "We'll have to work on that. But thesis first. Don't you have a paper to write or something? No papers from student teaching to grade?"

"All done. No more teachers, no more students, no more books. No more sitting in lecture halls. Maybe never again."

"I thought you were going to take what was supposed to be your fourth year of college, but isn't, since you're some kind of genius when you're all lovelorn, which totally disgusts me, by the way, and do the master's in counseling. That was the plan as of last week. New York.

Teacher's College. Sam and you tearing up the dance floor."

I give him a secret little smile. "Decided against it."

"What?"

"I went to the interview at Two Rivers in Ann Arbor for the math teaching job at the school you're going to work at, and guess what? I got the job. So, you're stuck with me for another year, at least."

"What?" He places the computer on the coffee table and fixes his eyes on mine. "Hallie, why didn't you tell me that?"

"Because I just decided. You need someone to keep you in line. I think the classroom will suit me, at least for a little while. It'll be fun. Don't you think? Maybe we can even be roommates."

He looks slightly sick to his stomach. I thought he would be ecstatic that I was going to come with him, but he doesn't exactly look thrilled at the prospect of working with me.

He squeezes his hands together and stares up at me. "Hallie. I wish you had told me."

"I'm telling you now." I search his face, my resolve crumbling. "I can probably still go to New York, though, if you don't want me around. I thought it would be fun. But maybe I was wrong."

"It could be fun." His voice is strained, and it doesn't match his words.

"Ben, come on. What's wrong? If you don't want me interfering with your job, just say so. I can still tell them no. I can take rejection. I'm not going to crumble."

"It's not that."

"What is it, then?"

He takes a deep breath. "I think I need a break from you."

That stings. A lot. "Oh."

I turn my head away and start to put my computer back into its bag.

"Don't do that. You wouldn't…" He looks up at me once, an unreadable expression in his eyes.

"I love you."

My answer is automatic. "I love you, too, Ben."

He merely shakes his head in frustration.

"No, Hallie. I think I might be in love with you. No. I know that I am in love with you. And I have been for a long time." He groans. "Damn it. I think I just said that aloud."

"Ben…"

I stop myself before I can say anything else, because whatever it is that I was planning to say isn't good enough for this incredible person who's picked me up more times than I can even count now, who I love more than almost anything in the whole world, who's been my best friend since we were kids and who saves my life a little more every day.

"You still love Jensen. I get it. I do. Kind of. He's a fucking asshole, but you love him anyways. My being hopelessly in love with you doesn't mean that we have to stop being friends. It doesn't mean that we have to lose each other. It just means that I need a break, that's all. I think I just need a break from having to look into your face every single day and to think that there's nothing I can do to ever make you love me like you love him."

He looks over his shoulder at me and shrugs helplessly. I want so badly to tell him that none of that is true, that I no longer love Chris, but I think we both know that would be a lie.

"Ben…"

"Stop. Don't say it."

I stand up and press my hand against his cheek. He holds it there for a second longer than I can handle before he stands up and wraps me in a hug.

"Go to New York, Hallie. Go and hang out with Sam and dance all night and play cards and maybe go to class every once in a blue moon and most importantly, get over the asshole. I'll be here. I'll wait for you."

I break away from his grasp and hold him an arm's length away from me. "I don't deserve you."

"No, you certainly don't." He manages a quick grin. "Don't forget that, okay?"

He leans in to brush his lips against my cheek, but he lingers a nanosecond too long, enough for me to feel the quick pulsations of his heated skin against mine. I turn my face to his in sudden surprise and just as I start to break free from him, he leans down and touches his lips to mine, just once, enough for me to smell the chlorine from our morning swim that's still sticking to his hair. Hesitantly, I push my lips against his again, needing to derive some comfort from his closeness.

It's nothing like kissing Chris. Ben's lips are less demanding, asking questions instead of answering them, and I'm lost and confused when he finally breaks away, curling long strands of my hair between his fingers.

"We can't do this, kiddo."

"I know." Even as I say it, I knot my hands into his t-shirt, letting them bunch the fabric. He lets out a low groan and slides his hands through my hair, unknotting the curls slowly, one by one, staring into my eyes as I start to run my fingernails up his chest. I lean in for another kiss and let myself forget about everything else in the strength of his arms.

Eventually, he breaks away, panting heavily.

"Hallie, you need to stop this before I can't."

"I don't want to."

It's true. I'm not selfless, or charitable enough, to care about the cost—to him, to me. It feels too good to feel his worshipping hands against my skin, to be secure in the knowledge that he would never hurt me.

As he begins to gently strip away my last pieces of clothing, I know irrevocably that I love him, that I will always love him. I have to believe that it will be enough, because I can't bring myself to hurt someone that I love so much again.

Maybe it's not the passionate fire that I once had, but maybe this is better, the slow, gentle kind of love that washes you in warmth and light. The biggest fires burn everything in their path, and I've had enough of that. Maybe this, a slow-burning flame that rises and falls but never entirely dies down, is exactly what I need.

So, I respond to his touch, arching my back and moving silently against him, letting him possess me, body and soul, letting him take away the endless ache in the place where I think my heart used to be.

It still feels like a betrayal of Chris and me.

As we move together, I try to forget that.

I love Ben. He loves me. Everything will be fine.

His eyes, soulful and sweet, stare into mine and I tell myself one last lie—everything will be fine.

* * *

4 Years, 9 Months Later
Chicago

"Mommy?"

Grace is staring at me with huge eyes, so much like Ben's that I want to scream.

"Yes, baby?"

"I said, if there's no zoo today, I want to go to a zoo sometime really soon, like tomorrow, and if there's no zoo, I want to go to the park when we get home. Can we go to the park, please?"

Frantically, I unbuckle her car seat and gather her up into my arms, clasping her wiggling form close to me.

"Yes, Gracie. We can go to the park."

I think. I do quick calculations in my head, trying to figure out when the press will descend. Eva and my mother left strict instructions for us to go home, to pack, and to be ready in the morning to move to whatever hideout they've managed to find. I'm pretty sure we have at least one night, and I can't begrudge Grace a trip to her favorite park.

"Mommy, that's excellent news."

She sounds exactly like my mother, and I grin and put her back into the seat. After checking to make sure that she's secure, I settle myself behind the wheel and take a moment to adjust the mirrors and another long moment to make sure that I've regained complete control of myself.

"Ready to go?"

When I look back, I realize that she's already dozing against the seat, obviously exhausted from all of the driving. Ben always had that particular talent, too, the ability to sleep wherever, whenever. I, on the other hand, couldn't sleep anywhere, even on the damn planes which always made me a little weepy.

As I start to drive, I check the backseat every few minutes, just to make sure that I hadn't imagined this perfect person that had somehow emerged from my body.

I have a lot of regrets. Given the fact that I rarely stop to think before I speak, it's not really all that surprising. But there are other little thoughts that shame me and they have nothing to do with all of the times when I've stuck my foot inside my mouth. The more serious regrets torture me a little bit every day.

I regret that I wasn't the wife to Ben that I should have been. He deserved a wife who loved him and him alone for all of his existence. That person wasn't me, even though I tried to love him with my whole self. It hurts me, even now, to think that he must have known it, felt it somehow. But I could never regret our marriage or our daughter or the brief time I had with him, filled with jokes and teasing and ice cream sundaes and laughter. I could never regret Grace and our flower house and Two Rivers and the teenagers who he taught in history class and I talked to about jerk boyfriends and high school cliques. I couldn't even regret the fights over who was going to take the garbage out or make dinner.

That's what I didn't understand, all those years ago—perfection never lasts. It's how you manage the imperfections that creates a life. It's how you decide to make it through another day. It's how you decide to take a chance, even if your instincts towards self-preservation tell you not to.

I pick up the phone to call Chris. I need to explain the pictures, because I know Marcus forced him to look, even if Eva demonstrated some uncharacteristic sensitivity. I need to explain everything.

But a phone call isn't enough, this time.

There's a pretty great zoo in New York. I think Grace would like that.

Chapter 22
CHRIS

"Your fan club is waiting for you," Claire says, pointing to the opposite side of the lobby. I can see the start of a smirk on her face.

She's right. I follow her finger and see a small crowd gathering. There's a sea of cell phones raised at the two of us. At least one of the amateur photographers probably captured the visual evidence of the shock I just had. Great. Like I needed another thing to worry about.

"Wave to your public, dear. It's rude not to." She smiles beatifically at the prepubescent teenage girls who are scampering closer to us, before taking my arm in hers to skillfully sidestep the small crowd. "We should get a coffee, I think. And perhaps we can see if your knowledge of anthropology has deteriorated over the years."

"Dr. Caldwell…"

"I think perhaps we've grown past that, Christopher. Claire will do. However, I do think we want to avoid those unscrupulous characters."

I follow her gaze and see the cluster of paparazzi outside, their numbers growing by the second.

"Yes. We should definitely avoid that."

Five minutes, a detour through the kitchens, and a mad dash down the street later, we're sitting in a hole in the wall coffee shop just off Michigan Avenue. I stir my latte until all of the foam has disappeared. The fake mustache makes it hard to drink, anyway. I'm trying not to demand answers, since Claire Caldwell is probably the last person in the world who will give them to me, but the picture of the curly-headed little girl lingers in my mind. I have to wait for her to make the first move.

She rests her chin on her hand and stares up at me.

"I don't remember you as a man of such few words. If I recall correctly, you're prone to make some serious leaps in the use of logical fallacies, and you even throw in a straw man argument or two, but I didn't think silence was a part of your repertoire."

"I think I remember a straw man or two coming from you, too."

She leans her head back and laughs, and the entire room fills with a full, rich, throaty sound that makes me spill the coffee onto the table in shock.

I don't think I've ever heard her laugh before, and while I've never been able to see much of Claire in Hallie—they're too different, in both looks and manner—they share the same laugh. Claire immediately puts her napkin over the spilled drops and smiles at me, a real, genuine smile.

"It's been a long time since I've seen your face, Christopher. Five years?"

"Do you mean to tell me that you're not a regular moviegoer? Or, is it just that you're just not a fan of my work?"

She flicks a packet of sugar into her coffee. "I didn't say that."

"To answer your question, the last time I saw you was in New York."

"I wasn't sure if you remembered."

I cringe, because I do remember, at least most of it. She came to visit us in that summer before London, and I had been somewhat less than my best self. I think I called her a vicious bitch. Another one of my finest moments.

"I'm sorry for that visit, Claire."

"I know you're sorry." Her lips are drawn in a thin line, and all traces of her smile are gone. "I hope those days have passed."

"They have."

"I'm glad to hear it." She wipes the table with a napkin and I can tell that she's decided to drop the subject. I breathe a sigh of relief.

"I've followed your career, you know. You've done well for yourself. I can hardly say I'm surprised at that."

"Thank you, Claire. I assume you're still teaching?"

"No, I gave that up when…" She stops mid-sentence. "I gave it up about a year ago."

"You must miss it."

"I do. Every day." She sighs. "However, I didn't drag you here to talk about the myriad of reasons why I miss the classroom. Besides that, I'm sure that you probably have other engagements. You must be a busy man. So, let's get down to the real reason why we're both here."

"Yes, ma'am."

I haven't called anyone ma'am in a very long time, but there's something about Claire that always makes me feel like a small child. Hallie used to say that in another era, her mother would have been an inquisitor. It certainly feels like I'm on the chopping block.

"I know you saw my daughter when she was in New York. I know that you saw her while she was here."

I lift my eyes upward to meet hers. "Did Hallie say something?"

Her face relaxes into a smile. "No. She didn't. But the photographs of the two of you plastered all over the tabloids gave me a pretty solid hunch that my assumptions were correct."

"Oh."

"I knew before I saw those pictures, though. I know my child, Christopher. She's never been able to keep a secret. When she was seven, she tried to tell me that space aliens had broken the vase in our living room. She didn't get halfway through her very carefully rehearsed story before she broke down into tears. While she may have changed her tactics over the years, she's never learned how to hide her feelings. And when I picked her up from the airport last week, she had that same dreamy look in her eye as she did when the two of you arrived in my home to tell me about some nonsensical plan to run off to Prague."

A dreamy look in her eye? This is definitely not that conversation I thought we would be having. But Claire's not finished.

"Tell me this, Christopher. Why did you come looking for my daughter? Why did you have to pick that particular screenplay? Is there a reason that you couldn't leave well enough alone?"

I check her face to see if it's a trick question, if she wants me to say that it was all part of a grand plan. Her watchful eyes stay steady on mine.

"I don't want you to tell me what you think I want to hear. I want you to tell me the truth."

Even if Claire Caldwell scares the living shit out of me, I have nothing left. I have to lay my cards out on the table.

"I didn't know that it was Hallie's movie. Ben's movie. I read the script, and something about it made me desperate to have it. I guess I should have known that it was hers. Theirs. Whatever. I read it again, a dozen times, over the last week, and I think I figured out why I needed it so badly. The words, they sound like her. The whole thing, it feels like Hallie's. I know that must sound silly, but it's true. And I needed it."

Claire looks puzzled. "You knew nothing about what happened? Ben's accident? The book? I find that extremely hard to believe."

"I didn't know the movie was hers. I didn't know that she and Ben had gotten married. And I didn't know that Ben had…"

She nods. "That explains it, then. I didn't believe that trash they printed, but I had to see for myself."

"Claire, if I had known…"

"That's neither here nor there. You can't do anything about the past but dwell in it. Believe me. I know."

There's regret there, and understanding. She lays her hand on top of mine and I stare up at her.

"What are we doing here, Claire?"

"I needed some new material for my James Ross fanfiction."

It's an impressively deadpan delivery, so much so that I don't even dare to laugh.

"You would at least thought my daughter would have had the sense to pick a man with a sense of humor. You can't have it all, I suppose."

"You know, there really is some decent fanfiction out there. You wouldn't happen to be larvae1961, would you?"

"You got me. I'll admit it. I do love that movie."

"Your daughter had a lot to do with that. The director of that movie, Hallie's biggest fan, by the way, stopped speaking to me the second she left."

It's true. Alan would have had me blacklisted, if that were still possible. He handed off James Ross to some music video director who had ruined the franchise. All because he was angry with me.

"Do you love my daughter, Christopher?"

I don't hesitate.

"I told you this seven years ago, and there hasn't been a time since that it wasn't true—I love your daughter to the ends of the earth and back, Claire. I love her so much that I couldn't bear the thought of trying to apologize to her when I was anything less than my best self. I love her so much that when she told me that she didn't love me, I crawled into a hole and stayed there for almost a year. I love her so much that she's the first and the last thing that I think about every day. I would do anything for her. I would even stay away from her. I'm hoping you're not going to tell me to do that, but I would do it. You know her best. You tell me what to do. You tell me, because I just don't know anymore."

Claire tilts her head to the other side, smiles at me, and then bends her head down to write something on a napkin.

"She left about an hour ago. She's on her way to her house in Lake Geneva. The address is there; it's just off Alla Vista Drive, but you'll probably find her in the neighborhood park if you plan on leaving now. My granddaughter is even more persuasive than her mother was at that age, and I suspect she'll have convinced Hallie to stop at the park, even if it is an ill-advised notion."

I'm in the process of grabbing the napkin from the table, but I stop when I hear the word granddaughter.

"Claire, I have to know whether…"

"It's not my place to meddle in my daughter's affairs, Christopher."

"You just gave me her address."

"I did, didn't I?" Her steely eyes meet mine for an impossibly long moment. "Grace is Ben's child. I know you won't believe that until you've seen her for yourself, but I can promise you that. I can also promise you that if you do anything to hurt that little girl, I will murder you with my bare hands. I'm sure there will be a long line for that particular job, but I will get to the front of that line."

I take a deep breath. Claire wouldn't lie to me about something like that. She couldn't. Still, the tiny seeds of doubt sown into the back of my head remain. It still doesn't explain why Hallie hadn't mentioned her existence to me. What if she hadn't told her mother? What if…

"I thought you were in a great hurry, Christopher. If I had been aware that you planned on gawking at me all day, I would have taken my time to create a more dramatic effect."

I pick up the piece of paper and stare down at the address.

"Thank you, Claire."

"I fully expect that you'll find some way to repay me for this favor."

"I will. But right now, I really have to find your daughter. The park?"

She nods sheepishly. "Don't tell her I told you. She would massacre me."

"I won't. I promise."

Chapter 23
HALLIE

"Mommy, higher. Higher."

I push her again, hearing the ringing bells of her laugh as she gets further and further away from the ground.

"I need a bigger push. Higher!"

She sounds like Eva. That thought fills me with no small measure of amusement. We've apparently been spending too much time with agents and producers. How else would a four-year-old sound like she belonged at the head of a boardroom?

"Baby girl, you're going to fall off the edge of the earth if I push you any higher."

"No, I won't. The earth doesn't end. Everybody knows that."

Of course. Everybody knows that.

"Gracie, it's getting late. We should go."

"One more big push. You haven't even seen me on the swings in forever and ever. You were in New York and Chicago."

Great. Now my daughter is trying to guilt trip me. I glance around at the nearly empty playground and sigh.

"Ok. One more big push."

"You better make it a good one."

It sounds like something Grace would say, but the voice is too deep and it's coming from the wrong direction.

I glance around the nearly deserted playground. I blink twice, because my eyes must be deceiving me. Chris is leaning against the seesaw, staring at the two of us. How long has he been standing there? I slow the momentum of the swing with my hands before taking Grace's hand firmly in my grasp and crossing the playground. She stares up at him with wide eyes before nestling closer to me.

"What are you doing here?"

Grace gasps and turns her face to mine. "You shouldn't talk to strangers, Mommy."

"Can't argue with that logic." His words are teasing as he crosses over to us, but his voice is strangled.

Damn it. Even the sight of him walking, the most mundane of mundane acts, makes me want to fall down. I ruffle Grace's hair and take a long, deep breath.

"Gracie, honey, he's not a stranger. This is an old friend of mine, Mr. Jensen. Chris, this is my daughter, Grace Ellison."

He kneels in the dirt and offers her his hand. "Hello, Grace."

"Hello, Mr. Jensen." She stares at him with wide eyes. "Mommy, he's not a stranger. I've seen him before on the TV."

"Grace, you know you're not supposed to watch the TV. We have very strict rules about that."

"Grandma always lets me watch a little." She covers her mouth. "Oops. I forgot. She said not to tell you."

"You should always tell me things like that. Especially if they involve Grandma. Grandmas don't always know best."

"That's what she says about mommies."

I can't help but laugh, and when I meet Chris's eyes over Grace's head, I see that he's laughing, too, at least in the instant before his face turns into a mess of confusion. There's something else there, too, and it looks an awful lot like fear.

I want to explain why I didn't tell him about Grace, but her watchful eyes are darting back and forth between the two of us. I shake my head almost imperceptibly at him and he nods, once.

"Are you going to come to dinner, Mr. Jensen? We're making pizzas, because it's Friday, and that's pizza day. We were going to the zoo, but I think the zoo was closed or something, because we couldn't go."

"Gracie, Mr. Jensen has other things to do besides having pizzas with us." I look up at Chris with a little grin. "Like being on the TV."

"Actually, I think my calendar's all clear. I would love nothing more than to come to pizza night. You'll have to show me how to make them, though. I'm afraid being on the TV doesn't help much with pizza-making."

"I'm a great pizza-maker," Grace says, just before releasing my hand and skipping over to where her pink backpack is resting against the swings.

"Maybe I'll let you make mine," he calls out after her.

He turns back to me and there are a thousand unanswered questions in his eyes.

"Not now," I hiss, before turning to call out, "Great," so that Grace hears me.

As she busies herself with putting on her sweater, I fix my eyes on Chris.

"What the hell are you doing here?"

"Your mother told me where I could find you." He's smug. "Told you she would come around."

"Unbelievable."

"It is, actually." He motions to Grace. "Why didn't you tell me?"

There's a faint menace underlying his words, and it immediately puts me on defense.

"It's not like we've been having a lot of long heart-to-heart conversations lately. A couple of trysts, platonic or not so much, don't exactly make for good opportunities to talk about other things. Like four-year-olds."

Before Grace can reach us, Chris grabs my arm fiercely. He holds me captive, his eyes boring into my own.

"Damn it, Hallie. You should have told me. You have to tell me."

In an instant, I realize his mistake. I take a step back and shake my head violently.

"No! Chris. No. No."

I release myself from his grip and look him dead in the eye, and the verdant green almost knocks me onto the ground. I manage to stutter out an explanation.

"She's not...she's...she was...Ben's daughter. She's not yours. Ours, I mean. She's Ben's daughter."

I can't read his expression, although I see that the anger in his face has softened.

"I could never do that." I touch his arm softly. "Do you really think I could have had our child and not told you? That I could have raised our child with another man, without telling you? Chris..."

"I wouldn't have blamed you." He releases the breath he's been holding and looks back at me. "But..." He looks back up at me with a kind of wonder. "You have a daughter, Hallie. A little person who's a piece of you. You should have told me."

"I..." I'm searching my brain for an explanation, but I'm saved by Grace's sudden reappearance. She holds her backpack out to me, and I take it from her and try to place my hand over hers.

She apparently has other plans, because she beams up at Chris and puts her small hand in his instead.

"You know, Uncle Sam is on the radio. But it's not exactly Uncle Sam. Uncle Sam has bands and they play on the radio. The best one, 4Sure, called me to wish me a happy birthday and they sang the best song ever and Uncle Sam says it's going to be a big hit, and it's all because of me. I think the radio is better than the TV, don't you? But I never met anyone who was on the TV before, so maybe that's better. Do you want to tell me about being on the TV, Mr. Jensen?"

Chris meets my eyes over my head and whispers, "Oh, she's yours all right."

I can't help it. I start laughing, and I don't stop until tears begin to stream from my eyes.

"You have a pretty laugh, Mommy. You should laugh more."

I stop laughing, and the breath catches in my throat. Chris gives me a comforting look before turning back to Grace and bending his head close to hers.

"Has anyone ever told you that you're a very smart girl, Grace?"

"Sure. Lots of people. But my teacher says that I'm obstinate." She stumbles a little bit over the word before jutting her chin out. "I don't think that means smart."

He's matching her, step for step, as they approach the parking lot. I can't do anything but follow.

"Obstinate is better than smart, even if some people might not think so. You know, people tell me that's I'm obstinate, too. I like to think it means that you're absolutely convinced that you can get what you want and you go after them. You should never give up on the things that you want."

"Then maybe I like being obstinate. See, Mommy? I told you that you should have gotten me that kitten that I want. I won't give up now. I'm obstinate."

"Thanks. Really. I mean it."

"Is that sarcasm I hear, Hallie? Grace, you're more than welcome to be obstinate, but you should stay away from sarcasm. It's a very bad habit and your mom has sarcasm in spades."

"I'm glad I invited you to pizza night, Mr. Jensen."

"Me too, Grace."

"Me, three," I mutter, just under my breath. There's more than a trace of sarcasm.

* * *

I'm putting the last of the pizza dishes into the sink as Chris and Grace discuss the merits of various pizza toppings, which alternately makes me want to laugh and cry. My daughter has completely fallen under Chris Jensen's powerful spell and I can do nothing but watch it happen right in front of my eyes.

Grace giggles. "Veggie pepperoni is better for you than real pepperoni."

"It tastes great, too." He gags, which makes me spin around.

"Oh, wait. Is that sarcasm I hear?"

"Certainly not." He spins Grace's chair so that she's facing him. "We won't let her get away with baseless accusations, will we, Grace?"

"No?"

"No."

Grace tries to laugh again, but it turns into a yawn.

"Okay. Enough of the mockery. Grace, it is already past your bedtime. You need to get to sleep before Mr. Jensen tells you any more of his ridiculous stories."

"Chris's stories, Mommy. He told me to call him Chris."

"We'll talk about that later." I shoot him a death stare and lift Grace into my arms. "Say goodnight, Grace."

"Goodnight, Chris. I want you to come to every pizza night so you can say more stories about the elephants that you saw in the water and the people in the restaurant."

"We'll see about that, Grace. Sleep tight. Don't let the bedbugs bite."

She giggles. "My daddy used to say that, too."

My heart falls into my stomach.

"He sounds like a very smart man. And maybe even an obstinate one." He stands up and does a little bow for her, which takes some of the tension out of the moment. "It was a pleasure to meet you, Miss Grace."

"You too, Chris."

"Come on, ladybug. Let's get to bed."

Grace protests all the way up the stairs.

"Mommy, I want to stay up to play with the grown-ups. I am four. Four."

"There will be plenty of time for you to play with the grown ups. Just not right now. Not yet."

I expect a battle, but the drive from Chicago has worn her out and she's practically sleeping as I ease her into pajamas and pull the covers up to her chin.

"Kisses?"

She kisses both of my cheeks, all over. I cover her with a few of my own and by the time I've gotten enough of staring at how absolutely beautiful she is, she's drifted off into sleep.

I catch the door softly as I exit and make my way down the stairs slowly. Even though I've had a long time to think about what needs to be said, I still don't have any way of saying it. When I get to the kitchen, I see him barefoot, wiping down the table with a sponge from the sink. Even domesticity looks good on him. Damn it. Again.

He gives me a soft smile before taking the last plate from the table and placing it in the dishwasher.

"She's a great kid."

"She is. I think I'll keep her."

"Why didn't you tell me, Hals? There was certainly time, even amidst platonic and not so platonic trysts, for you to tell me about the most important person in your life. I can only assume that you didn't want me to know."

I pick up the sponge and scrub at the nonexistent crumbs on the counter before letting out a long sigh and turning around to stare into his face.

"I couldn't figure out a good way to tell you."

"Bullshit."

"Fine. I couldn't figure out if this, you and me, was real or not."

He crosses to me and places a hand on my arm, a fierce look in his eyes. "Really, Hals? You couldn't figure out if you and I were real? I call bullshit on that one, too."

I hear a soft moan from upstairs and I shake my head and put a finger to my lips. "We can't wake her. Come into the living room."

He promptly shuts his mouth and lets me lead him down the stairs into the living room. He draws in a breath as he takes in the full-length windows that look out over the garden and the warmth of the room. I've never been much of a decorator, but I'm proud of this room, with its cool blues and overstuffed couches.

"This is beautiful."

"Yeah. It's pretty good, isn't it?"

He settles onto one of the couches and leans back with a contented sigh. "I almost forgot that couches were made for people to sit on."

I give him a puzzled look. "What?"

"Never mind. Just something Marcus said once." He fixes his gaze on me again. "Time's up, though. Answer the question. Why didn't you tell me that you had a daughter?"

I consider taking the seat next to him, but I think that would be a very bad idea, indeed, so I decide on one of the armchairs instead.

"I don't know, really. I think I was afraid of mixing my two worlds. Being with you was like being the better version of my old self, before I got all sad and post-traumatic stress-disordery. I was afraid that telling you about Grace would break the spell. I was afraid that letting you infringe on my real life would make me wake up from the dream."

He searches my face. "Because I'm not part of your real world, right?"

"I don't know. Are you?" I stare back at him. "Chris, New York was an aberration. I didn't think I was ever going to see you again. I thought it was just a one-time thing, you know. A way to rewrite history, to forget all of the terrible history between the two of us, a way to end things with something good. I thought that would be it. You would go off to your life and I would go off to mine. And then I saw you in Chicago…"

He cuts me off.

"You cannot be that blind."

"We didn't even know each other anymore. We don't know each other now, Chris."

"Bullshit again. You know me better than anyone ever has, and you always will, whether you want to or not. And whether you want me to or not, I do know you."

"There's too much terrible history here for a future to make any kind of sense."

"I don't believe that, and I don't think you do, either."

A single tear falls from my one of my eyes. He makes a movement to get up from the couch but I hold my hand out to stop him.

"No."

"What happened to us, Hals? What's so terrible that it can't be fixed?"

"I think there's a long answer and a short answer. Which one do you want?"

"Both. Short, then long."

"We had the fight to end all fights. We both said some things that I don't know if it's ever possible to recover from. The kinds of things that make your stomach sick when you think about them, even seven years later. I called you a…"

"I know what you called me. I know what I called you. I didn't mean it, Hals. It was the alcohol talking. You were never a fame-monger."

I wince, because the words still hurt, even after all these years.

"Or a gold-digging prude?"

It's his turn to wince.

"I'm so sorry."

"There were grains of truth there. I lost myself. I lost everything about the person I wanted to be, everything I once wanted for myself. I became so wrapped up in you that I forgot that there were things that existed outside of you. And while I would contend that fame-mongering was never really in my grand plan for myself, and personally, I think the statement was a little unfair, what you said would never have had the power to get to me if there wasn't some truth there."

He stands up and takes a step towards me. There's never been a man who moved so well. I shake my head, because his nearness is too intoxicating and I need a clear head.

"No, we're not done yet, Chris. You said you wanted the long version."

He sighs and takes a step back from me. "As you wish."

"We were eighteen years old."

"So?"

"So, what do you know about life when you're eighteen? The rest of your life is nothing but a bunch of big beautiful tomorrows. There's always time for a vacation in Bali, time to decide that you want to become a rocket scientist. Nothing is out of reach. Hangovers are something that old people get, for chrissakes."

That manages to elicit a small smile. "There are still a bunch of big, beautiful tomorrows."

"You don't know that."

"No, I don't know that. But I can hope for that. It's better than wanting to crawl into a hole and die alone, without ever having to risk your heart again. Smart, Hallie, really smart."

"I'm not afraid of the risk. Not anymore, at least."

I take a deep breath and give him my last secret, the one I've kept locked away.

"I'm afraid that I'm not good enough for you. I wasn't good enough for Ben. Here both of you are, in possession of these incredibly talented, prodigious minds, great minds who are brave enough and bold enough to share themselves with the world, and here I am, just some girl who managed to have enough good fortune to grab some coattails to hang onto. I'm nobody special. I'm not meant for the bright lights and the cameras capturing every move I make. I mean, I fall down. A lot. Do you know how many pictures they would get of me falling down? Instead of Chris Jensen: Lothario, they could have Hallie Caldwell: Klutz. I live in flip flops. Heels are some gigantic mystery that I'll never be able to figure out. But it's more than that."

He's staring at me like I really have lost my mind. I look directly into his eyes and try once more.

"Here's the thing, Chris. I'm never going to be the best painter, or the best screenwriter, or the best candy wrapper sculpture maker. A perfect day for me is sitting in my little cabin and reading books to my daughter as she falls asleep. But that's not enough for you, and it never will be. You happened to be destined for greatness and I came along for a little while and it was fun, but it wasn't me. I'm a pretty simple girl, and your life is too big for me."

Chapter 24
CHRIS

I want to laugh it off, to tell her that the thought that she wouldn't be enough for me is a preposterous notion, but her solemn expression and the fat tears rolling down her face stop me from dismissing her words entirely.

"Hals, you once told me that maybe the world would be a better place if there were more people who wanted to be good and fewer people who wanted to be great. Do you remember that?"

"And you said that it was all nothing but a bunch of foolish talk."

"I was wrong. You were right."

"Oh, come on."

"You were. And that's what I want—a chance to be good, not great. That's only going to happen if I'm with you."

I kneel down next to the chair and take her chin in my hand and force her to look at me.

"Hallie Caldwell Ellison, you're the strongest person I've ever met. You managed to keep yourself together while the rest of the world fell apart around you. It takes more guts to wake up every day and do that than it does to write any stupid book or play a part in any stupid movie."

"Bullshit." She looks up and gives me a small smile. "I call bullshit on that."

"Nope. Besides that, by your definition, all of our lives are small. The fact that people are willing to pay to see me pretend to be someone else for a couple of hours doesn't make the important things any different."

"That's a ridiculous statement. You…you fly around on private jets and take meetings with people who make more money in one second than most people will ever see in their lifetimes. Everyone knows your face and your name. Everything you do is on the front page of some magazine for people to read. You can't tell me that having a dedicated team of paparazzi makes you a normal person."

"I didn't say that that I was a normal person. There are no normal people. What I said was that my life, not my job, not the fact that I happen to make movies for a living, but the life I want to lead, is small. I want to make the people that I love most happy. If you want to call that small, go right ahead, but I don't agree with you. That's the biggest kind of life I can imagine. And I cannot imagine a life without you in it."

"It's too much. I can't even think about…"

She's retreating back into herself again, inching further away from me and sinking into the chair. Shit. It's time to pull out a joke. Hallie likes jokes.

"By the way, I'm not letting you get away with the greatness thing. I mean, did you see *Breakdown*? Anyone who's seen *Breakdown* has to admit that there's no chance that I was ever destined for greatness. Maybe professional bird calling, though. Do you think I need to go to school for that? Is there such a thing as a professional bird calling school?"

There's a subtle loosening of her muscles and a miniscule change in her face that just might be the beginning of a smile.

"No, I don't think there's such a thing as a professional bird calling school. I could be totally wrong, though. You never know."

"I'm sure there has to be at least a certification I can get from the internet."

"I'm sure there is. But I don't think you would make a very good bird caller, Chris. You're a movie star."

"I don't have to be."

"Yes, you do. You have to make *Rage*. There's no one else I would trust with it but you. It's more important than you or me or anything else."

"So, I have to make *Rage*. But that will be it. No more movies. Just as long as you give me one chance. One shot. That's all I want, Hals."

She gives me a beseeching look before moving across the room to stare out into the blackness of the night.

"I've said it before, and I'll say it again. You were born to make movies, Chris. It's so much a part of you that I can't imagine it being any other way. I love the way you tell stories. It's a wonderful gift, and I wouldn't ever want you to give that up. Not for anyone and certainly not for me."

"I would, you know."

"I know that you would."

"I would do anything for you."

She's still not looking at me, but something in the air, between the two of us, changes, and then her voice cuts through the silence and she spins around to face me, her enormous blue eyes filled with questions.

"Are you sure, Chris? I mean, really, really, really sure? I have a four year old daughter, and neither she nor I can just make decisions based on some whim. If you haven't thought about that, if you aren't totally, one thousand percent positive that being with me is what you want, then you need to just walk out that door and go. Now. Because if you want me, if you want to make a life with Grace and me, it's not going to be easy."

She looks so fragile that I resist the urge to run across the room and throw her into my arms.

"I love you, Hals. I've always loved you. I will never stop loving you. And if you're actually saying what I think you're saying, I would love nothing more than to spend the rest of my life making you and Grace absolutely, perfectly happy."

I see the smile start to spread across her face, starting at her lips and reaching her eyes. She's still uncertain, but I open my arms and she flies across the room and into them. I lift her up and draw her in for a long kiss. She manages to free herself after a long moment and she stares at me with huge eyes.

"Hallie, I…"

"Stop." Her smile grows wider and I run my fingers through her tangled curls, not knowing why she wants me to stop but not really caring, either, because every question I ever wanted to ask already has its answer in the way her body fits perfectly against mine. She pulls back and frees herself from my arms and stares deeply into me.

"You always get to talk first. It's my turn. I love you. I love you so much that it makes my head spin and it makes me want to scream and it makes me want to stay with you, like this, forever. Just like this. I think I probably fell in love with you the second I saw you on that goddamn balcony and don't tell me that I'm remembering it all wrong, that it was actually the diner or the park or the apartment, because I think I had to have known the moment that I saw your face for the first time, Chris Jensen. And I will always love you. And I wasn't sure if it was going to be enough, but I've sat in enough hotel rooms trying to figure out how I was going to survive you again to know that my only answer to the question is that I can't survive you again. I love you. I love you."

She says it all in one long breath, and I can't keep the enormous, shit-eating grin off my face.

"Hallie Caldwell, I plan to spend the rest of my life loving you. And making mistakes. And fixing them. I love you and I will keep loving you forever."

I lean down and kiss her soft lips. I still can't quite convince myself that this isn't some kind of incredibly realistic dream. When she eventually pulls away, she looks up at me with a little contented smile.

"So, man with the plan, what do we do now?"

"I may have a few ideas."

"There also may be a curious four year old just waiting to pounce on me any second now, so your ideas might just have to wait."

I groan. "Seriously, Hals?"

"Seriously. Get used to it. Also, if she decides tomorrow that she doesn't like you, I'm kicking you out."

"I think I would be more worried about her deciding that she doesn't like you anymore. Give it a week, and she'll be eating right out of my hand. If you don't believe me, I'll let my nephews do the vouching. According to the pair of them, I'm the coolest uncle ever. You're so not ready for this action."

"Diana! How is she? I can't wait to see her. It's been too long."

"To say that she'll be thrilled to see you is a serious understatement. I stopped calling her every day because she never manages to get off the phone without getting in a little dig about how her idiot brother was a jackass and lost the best thing to ever happen to him. I'm surprised she hasn't disowned me."

"Is she still in New York?"

"Yeah."

She makes a face. "I hate New York. But I love you so much that in my totally mixed-up crazy state, I even had the bright idea of dragging Grace along with me to New York so that I could find you."

"Why not? Come to New York, I mean."

"Um, because the entire celebrity press corps is probably camped out in front of your apartment? Can you even imagine what it would be like if the three of us showed up there, bags in hand?"

"We're going to have to deal with that sooner or later, but it doesn't matter anyways, because I have another apartment. Come on. New York. The big city. I bet Grace would love it."

"I hate New York."

"You do not. You're just saying that. Give me five days, Hals. I'll show you around my New York."

"I've heard that one before."

We both smile. I run my finger down her cheek, wiping away the last remnants of wetness.

"I'm serious. Five days, with you and Grace in New York. I'll pull out all of my creepy disguises and you two can pick the best one for me to wander around the city in."

"I'm still not sure if taking my daughter to one of our infamous rendezvous sites is the best plan right now. That's what they're saying, right? That I'm a giant slut who cheated on my husband with you?"

"I take that to mean that you haven't seen the stories?"

She shakes her head, and I cover her hand with mine.

"Don't read them. Just don't."

"I wasn't planning on it. I know. We could go to Vancouver and check out some of the *Rage* locations. I like Vancouver. Don't you like Vancouver?"

I do happen to like Vancouver, but I am a man with a plan, as she put it, and my plan for what happens next requires her and me, and Grace, in New York.

"Hallie. If we go to New York, you can see Sam, and we can go ice skating and to the Empire State Building and we can go do all of the touristy shit that you love and I love because I'm with you. Come on. You know you want to say yes. You just know you do."

"Can we go to the zoo?"

I spin around to see Grace, wide eyed and wide awake, with a very guilty look on her face.

"Grace Ellison, you know the rules about getting out of bed without permission."

"Mommy, I want to go to the zoo. You promised the zoo."

"I want to go to the zoo, too," I add, crossing my arms and trying to match the pout on Grace's face.

She gives me an exasperated look, but I can tell that she's melting. I wink at Grace and her eyes widen even further and she does a little twirl and runs to her mother, whose last defenses crumble.

"Fine. To the zoo we go. But that doesn't mean that I have to like it."

Chapter 25
HALLIE

"Keep them closed."

"I've been peeking this whole time anyways, so I don't understand the sudden need for great secrecy. We're on the Upper East Side."

"You are such a cheater."

I pull my hands off of my eyes and grin at him.

"Yep. Proud of it, too. Like you really thought I was going to be able to keep my eyes closed for an hour-long car ride? Come on. I hate surprises, and that little factoid shouldn't be a huge shock. I've never liked surprises."

"That's a sentiment that I don't think your daughter shares," he replies, looking mischievous.

"We still need to talk about all of your little surprises."

"We can talk about it after we pick her up from Diana's apartment tomorrow morning. My dear sister only has boys to spoil, so I have a sneaking suspicion that you might need to save the lecture for her, too."

"I have a sneaking suspicion that she isn't going to send her assistant to FAO Schwartz to get one of each toy in every color."

"No, but Diana might take her to every children's boutique in the city to pick out one of each outfit in every color. Lots of pink. Lots of tutus."

"Save us. Please."

"Grace deserves to be spoiled. Every girl deserves to be spoiled. Even you, who hates surprises."

"I wouldn't exactly call myself a girl anymore, Chris."

"Fine. Shriveled-up hag, then?"

I punch his arm lightly and fall back against the leather seats of the limousine. Before we got to New York, I thought I was prepared for his lavish lifestyle. I was completely wrong. His absolutely massive second apartment, complete with six bedrooms and an enormous terrace overlooking Central Park, was grander than anything else I had ever seen, his childhood monstrosity included. Before we arrived in the city (via private airplane, of course), I'm also fairly certain that he instructed his assistant to decorate one of the bedrooms in his apartment with every single toy from all of the stores Manhattan had to offer. The thought that I was the one who was going to need to fret about Grace suddenly deciding that she disliked me had crossed my mind, more than once.

No, bird calling wouldn't have suited him, I think, as I glance through my fingers at the strong line of his jaw. And that's all right. That sense of extravagance is all a part of the person that I fell in love with a very long time ago. It didn't mean that I was going to let all of the spoiling, of both Grace and me, slide.

We were definitely going to need to have a long chat about the toys. And the apartment. And the private jet.

And the limousines. And the puppy with the red collar with the name Buster imprinted on it.

"Okay. We're here. Eyes closed for this part. No peeking this time. Cheater."

I reluctantly cover my eyes as he takes my arm and helps me from the car.

"Okay. Open them."

I laugh when I see the blinking neon sign reading "Late Night ood."

"This is where it all started. I was a fledgling movie star, you were a mysterious girl from a party wearing flip flops, which I think was a very sensible choice given the snow, and we were both party refugees."

"Oh, shush. And this is not where it all started. We met on a balcony. Sorry, wait, what's the fancy word that you New Yorkers use? A terrace."

He shudders. "Yeah, well getting back to that terrace would have required a phone call to Sophia Pearce, who's probably off ruining more lives right now. She's probably halfway through her fourth marriage."

I laugh. "So true. Maybe her fifth."

"So, we'll just pretend, for argument's sake, that this is where we met."

"I cannot believe you dragged me all the way over here to reminisce about old times, Chris. There are a million diners in Brooklyn. We could have stayed there, in case Grace needed me or got homesick or something."

"She will not get homesick. She's probably running circles around my nephews right now. Besides, this diner has the best coffee in the city, if we can ever get someone to deliver it."

"Also true. All right. Let's get some coffee and maybe you'll remember to ask for my name this time."

I toss my head and his laughter follows to the booth where we once sat, where I had once asked a million questions about movies and Hollywood and managed to fall in love with him in the process. I settle back into the booth and grab a menu from the table, and I look around for a waitress, maybe even the same one with yellowed teeth and a faintly annoyed expression, but I don't see anyone.

"Chris. You're such a slowpoke." I look around, but he seems to have disappeared into thin air. "Chris! Where are you?"

He emerges from the back room, carrying an enormous bouquet of roses that obscures his face.

"You are so insane. You can't let me get used to this kind of thing. I think you might even spoil me more than you spoil Grace."

"My intention is exactly that—to get you used to this kind of thing."

He hands the flowers to me and gives me a long, sweet smile. "I love you, Hals."

"I love you, too, Chris. I have to give it to you—the flowers are completely, absolutely beautiful and I will be a girl about that. I love flowers."

"I know you do."

He takes a deep breath and I can see that he's trembling slightly.

"Are you cold?"

"No."

He looks up, his eyes shrouded in a haze of uncertainty.

"I've made a lot of mistakes."

"Oh, God, not that again." I shake my head in exasperation. "I thought we promised to stop apologizing to each other. What was that you said? There's no changing the past, but there's plenty of changing to do for the future. If I hear the words 'I'm sorry' come out of your mouth one more time, and you're not apologizing for buying my daughter a puppy, which you should definitely apologize for, by the way, I will…"

"Stop talking, Hals."

There's something in his face that makes me listen.

"I want to wake up every morning next to you. I want to read stories to Grace and kiss her goodnight. I even want to go to Disneyland, because you wanted to and we never got the chance. We never got the chance to do a lot of things, but we have another chance to do all of that now. We're lucky enough to have the chance to do all of that now. Neither of us is perfect, but we're perfect together and I want to spend the rest of my life basking in that perfection."

Suddenly, he's on one knee, holding out a small box and smiling up at me.

"Marry me, Hallie. Marry me and let me love you forever."

The pressure in my chest spills over and I look into his beautiful face, filled with hope and a tiny bit of fear and I feel myself start to smile.

Fat, happy tears are sliding down my face. I look up at him and, unable to find the right words or any words, I nod. He crushes me to his chest, touching my face and hair and lips and holding me for long minutes that stretch into forever.

He holds out a long silvery chain and offers it to me. "I thought you could wear Ben's ring on this."

The fact that he considered even that small thing fills me with indescribable joy. I glance down at it, the simple diamond that Ben and I had bought together, and gently pull it off my finger and slide it onto the chain. I try to put it on, but my fingers are trembling too much to close the clasp, so Chris takes it from me and fumbles for a minute before sliding it around my neck. The weight is cool against my skin, and comforting.

"I'll give it to Grace when she's older," I say, still touching it. Suddenly, I cover my mouth with my hands. "Grace! I can't say yes without…"

He gives me a quick grin. "Already asked her. In fact, she picked out the ring. I would have gone for simple but elegant. A miniscule diamond, because what was it you said? 'I'm just a simple girl.' I thought, well okay. I'll buy Hallie a small diamond, the most miniscule one that I can find, because she's a simple girl."

"Liar."

"I am not! I fully intended on simple." He stares at me with wide, innocent eyes. "However, your daughter had other ideas."

He opens the box to reveal an enormous diamond ring, which I gape at wordlessly. He slides it onto my finger and I stare down at it before opening my mouth to protest.

"Grace said the only way I could ask you to marry me was if I bought you this ring. And was I really going to argue with the logic of a four year old? Certainly not." He smiles. "However, I do have to admit that I like her taste better than yours. She even had a few redecorating ideas that I might take up. A pool, I think, is in order. Maybe even a water slide."

"There's an idea. The neighbors would love us. A water slide in New York."

"Or Michigan or Lake Geneva or wherever you want to go, Hals. Wherever you want to live. As long as you promise me one thing."

"What's that?"

"You don't throw Buster out into the street. It would break Grace's heart."

Like I would really throw an adorable puppy onto the street. Still, it's a bargaining chip.

"Fine. Buster stays. Under one condition."

"What?"

I look down at the ring and watch as a glint of sunshine hits it, causing light to dance across the room.

"I need to know that this is a forever kind of thing. You and me. And Grace. You don't get to take this one back."

He pulls me in for a long, lingering kiss, the kind that still takes my breath away, even after all of these years, and then pulls back to stare deeply into my eyes.

"Hallie, I promise you that this is definitely a forever kind of thing."

Epilogue
CHRIS

6 Months Later

"So, how does it feel to be a happily married man? I mean, I know you've only been happily married for a grand total of two hours, but that must be long enough for you to make some grand proclamations. But maybe not. It looks like your wife is having a pretty good time on the dance floor. Without you, I might add."

"Watch yourself, Marcus," I say lightly, with a quick glance at Hallie, who's giggling with Sam as they twirl around the tiny dance floor. "As to the marriage question, I would have to say that it feels pretty damn good. Think you're ready to join our ranks?"

We both turn to look at Eva, who's sitting at one of the tables set up in the rooftop garden overlooking the city lights, immersed in a conversation with Claire and Diana. Marcus laughs.

"We just reached the point where we can have a meal without hurling insults at each other. If we manage to make it through a weekend, then we'll talk about marriage. But that will never happen, so I don't need to worry about it."

I grin at Marcus's horrified expression. "We'll see about that."

"Sure. When pigs fucking fly, Jensen. Now, look. I know you and Hallie are off to Bali or Belize or the Canary Islands for the honeymoon…"

"Disneyland."

"Or that." He gives me a sideways look. "Disneyland? Seriously?"

I shrug. "You have to give the womenfolk what they want."

"Fine. So, you're off to Disneyland, but I'm getting heat from the studio about the second screenplay. Now that the first movie's in the can and all the big shots are assured that it's going to be a blockbuster, they're clamoring to get started on the next one, so I can't let you and Hallie slack on that, even for a few days. You also need to make sure that you get all the best lines, because personally, I think she was holding back on that first one. But now that you're married to the screenwriter, you can get in on the action…"

I hold my hand up. "Stop. Just stop. You have got to be kidding me. We're at my goddamn wedding, and you're trying to talk shop right now? Marcus. Get a life."

"I agree with that sentiment," Eva says, putting her hand on Marcus's arm. "Chris, mind if I borrow him? Congratulations, by the way." She places a light kiss on my cheek and I smile back at her.

"Thank you. Please, take him. Take him and never give him back. He's trying to give me grief about the screenplay."

"Marcus!"

"What? It's got to get done. Tell me that you weren't saying the same thing last night."

She gives me an exasperated look. "I'll get him off your back if you tell Hallie that she has two weeks before I'm in the same camp as Marcus."

"Seriously? You, too?"

"Yeah, seriously. Go. Steal your bride back. Sam has a bad habit of monopolizing her, especially when there's dancing involved."

She winks at me.

"One week. Hallie has one week before I start calling every hour on the hour," he calls out over his shoulder, just as Eva drags him onto the dance floor.

Just as I'm about to follow Eva's advice, I feel a light tugging at the corner of my jacket. Grace is staring up at me with huge, sad eyes.

"No one will dance with me."

"Well, let's remedy that immediately. Shall we?"

I swing her into my arms and she lets out a little gleeful shriek. We make our way past a few of the dancing couples, and I set her down on the dance floor and twirl her under my arm.

"Again," she pronounces.

I'm only too happy to oblige, at least until the constant spinning starts to make me dizzy. Grace shows no signs of slowing down. Obviously, she inherited her mother's dancing prowess, shimmying around the floor like an old pro.

"Uncle Sam is a better dancer than you are," Grace says, sticking her chin out and grinning up at me.

"Yeah, yeah, yeah."

"That's my princess," Sam says, as he and Hallie come to a stop near us. "How about a dance, Gracie?"

"Yes. Please. Just one thing first, Uncle Sam."

She reaches out her arms for me and I pull her into them, relishing the way they clasp around my neck.

"I'm really glad that you married Mommy," she whispers. "There's lots and lots of dancing, and I like dancing."

I laugh and kiss her cheek before placing her down again and handing her over to Sam, who promptly swoops her into his arms.

"Are we really going to Disneyland tomorrow?" she calls out hopefully.

"Yes, we really are going to Disneyland tomorrow."

I hear her jabbering away at Sam as they float across the dance floor.

"She's wrong, you know," Hallie says, nestling herself into my open arms. "You're a better dancer than Uncle Sam any day."

"Liar."

"Nope. And besides, I have an obligation to defend my husband's honor," she whispers into my ear, her fingers curling around my hair.

"I like the sound of that."

"Me, too."

She beams up at me and she's incandescent, basking in the glow of the white candles placed all around the edges of the rooftop garden of the apartment that we had bought together, because, as she put it, "We needed a place to make our own, the three of us."

"Want to dance?"

"With you?"

"Yes. With me."

"You kind of have two left feet." She gives me a mischievous smile before settling herself into my arms. "But I suppose I can make the sacrifice."

"What happened to defending the honor of your husband?"

"Eh. Overrated. Teasing is better. Lots of teasing."

I feel the curves of her body relax against me as we start to move slowly to the music. I touch the barely visible swell of her stomach with my fingers, still disbelieving that we had created a new life together, in more ways than one. She gives me a secret little smile as her enormous blue eyes fix on mine.

"I love you, Hals. And Grace. And Buster. And the yet-to-be-named Jensen. I was thinking…maybe Samuel Benjamin? I think that's a good name for a kid."

She touches the side of my face and looks deeply into my eyes. "That is a good name for a kid."

"Then it's decided."

"I love you, Chris."

"You know, I think I could get used to this perfectly happy thing."

"How on earth did you remember that?"

"I remember everything."

Her lips cover mine and we share a long, lingering kiss before she draws back, a soft smile playing across her features.

"I think I could get used to being imperfectly happy with you. As long as it's still a forever kind of thing."

"Imperfectly happy it is, then."

If you enjoyed this book, you'll want to check out
Falling into You, **which details the beginning of Hallie and Chris's story…**

When Hallie Caldwell, normal girl extraordinaire, perpetual wingwoman, and queen of the friend zone, accepts her college roommate's invitation to spend winter break in New York, she figures it's a chance to live out her childhood fantasies of a life in the big city. Instead, thrust into a world of glittering parties and oversized bank accounts, she immediately feels like an outsider.

Chris Jensen's Hollywood agent keeps telling him that he'll be the next big star, just as long as he gets the lead role in the reboot of a classic action franchise. When he returns to New York after a two-year absence, he has other things on his mind—his dying father, an irate sister, and the beautiful, seductive, infuriating, and ruthless Sophia Pearce. He's not exactly thrilled when she asks him to be her roommate's tour guide, but he reluctantly agrees.

When Hallie and Chris meet, they're irresistibly drawn to each other. However, Chris's meteoric rise to stardom and long-suppressed secrets from Hallie's past threaten to destroy their tenuous connection, and each is forced to examine whether happy endings are nothing but a Hollywood fantasy.

About The Author

Lauren Abrams lives in St. Louis, Missouri with her husband and a small menagerie of four-legged children. She spends most of her days trying to convince her high school students that reading is fun, although she's still not sure quite what to say about *The Scarlet Letter*. She is the author of *Falling into Forever* and *Falling into You*.

She's currently writing her third novel, a contemporary romance. It will be released in the late summer or early fall of 2013.

The Thank You List

There are a number of people who contributed to this book, both directly and in a thousand little ways that I'm not sure I could ever acknowledge. First and foremost, I was lucky enough to find my soul mate when I was eighteen years old, and my greatest wish is that I'll have enough time on this planet to grow old and wrinkly and wise right by his side. Every time I think about the fact that I get to wake up every morning next to the most kind-hearted, supportive, loving, wonderful, fantastic man in the world, I get overwhelmed by my really fucking good luck. I love you.

My mother first put a book in my hands when I was three years old. She told me to read every day, because reading takes you to faraway worlds and to new places, but most importantly, reading brings you closer to the person you want to become. I'm sorry for being such an angsty brat for the teenage years, and I hope that you think maybe I've turned out okay.

Also, I really do have the best friends ever. They're always willing to sit and ponder the mysteries of the universe with me over a few glasses (or bottles) of wine. Okay, so maybe we spend more time talking about the various pros and cons of The Real Housewives. It only makes us more fabulous.

I need to send a huge thank you out to everyone who read *Falling into You*. It totally makes my day every time I get a note from a reader who tells me that reading my book let them escape from their everyday reality for a few hours or days. I'm completely overwhelmed by the incredibly kind words and well wishes. Thank you so, so, so, so much.

And last (but never least), I want to thank all of the teachers who know that telling stories is its own kind of art, its own kind of escape, who tell their students that making words appear on paper is nothing short of magic. As Mrs. Bittle used to say at the start of every third-grade day, "You are a writer. All you need to do is find your story."

I never set out to write a book for anyone but myself to read. But I think I've found some stories, and I can't wait to tell more.

Printed in Great Britain
by Amazon.co.uk, Ltd.,
Marston Gate.